CELTIC
Shores

CELTIC STEEL {2}

AUTHOR OF HISTORICAL ROMANCE
AND SENSUAL FANTASY

DELANEY
RHODES

CELTIC *SHORES*

Book 2 in the
Celtic Steel Series
By DELANEY RHODES

Delaney@DelaneyRhodes.com

http://www.DelaneyRhodes.com

http://www.facebook.com/delaneyrhodes

http://www.twitter.com/delaney_rhodes

Celtic Shores

Celtic Steel Series, Book 2

Patrick MacCahan just became the new Laird of the O'Malley clan. His new position is met with many obstacles; including a tempestuous new wife, a two-decade long war with a neighboring village, a missing foster child and a pagan witch who overpowers the clan at every turn.

Parkin MacCahan's life just got a lot more exciting. His older brother Patrick has married the eldest daughter of the O'Malley clan. His father is building a shipping empire off the coast of Northern Ireland. Parkin must oversee the operations and coordinate efforts between the O'Malleys and the MacCahans.

In order to dock at O'Malley port, Parkin and his men must sail past the legendary Island of Women. Will Parkin be able to withstand the temptation to trespass the legendary shore? Or will he be invited?

Kyra O'Connell has resided in O'Malley territory all of her life. As the niece of the late Laird Dallin O'Malley, and daughter of the clan's chieftan, she has been part of the inner circle for as long as she can remember. When a spy is found among the villagers, Kyra is asked to take up residence on the Island of Women and to infiltrate their ranks as a spy herself.

Celtic Shores

Copyright © 2012 by Delaney Rhodes

DR Publishing

eBook ISBN: 9780985332600

Paperback ISBN: 0985332603

Cover Design by Kim Killion

Edited by Bev Harrison

WHAT READERS ARE SAYING
ABOUT THE *CELTIC STEEL* SERIES

"Great read couldn't put it down. Can't wait for the next book in the series. You rank up there with Diana Gabaldon of the Highlander series." ~ B. Breen

"I love the story – I thought it was the right mix of romance, a strong female character, historical setting, and magic/paranormal…" ~ A. Alayna

"What a FUN new author with a fabulous and well written storyline! I wasn't sure what to expect, but found myself so pulled into the story that I HAD to finish it before I could move onto my daily "to-do's"; needless to say I recommend doing any and all chores before starting it. I am very much looking forward to the next … books in the series…!" ~ Karen Memmott

"I thoroughly enjoyed Celtic Storms and am way past anticipating the second in the series. I have read historical romance for over twenty years and the way the author transformed the genre and included paranormal elements (witchcraft, ESP, druidism, shape-shifting, etc.) was impressive." ~ S. Sinclaire

I liked the characters a lot, and they seemed well thought-out. The story flowed fairly well, and even included some surprises I didn't see coming! The cliff-hanger ending left me ready for the next book!" ~ L. Alexander

Dedication

To MawMaw MacManus, who taught me it's better to lead my dreams than to follow them.

TABLE OF CONTENTS

DIALECT DISCLAIMER

The characters represented in this work of fiction come from a time and place unlike our own. In an attempt to create as realistic as possible an atmosphere for the reader; there will be some direct emphasis on accent, dialect and pronunciation in the dialogue. What you will find are not, in fact, misspellings or instances of bad grammar on the part of the author. Rather, you will discover phonetically enriched wordings—to symbolize the language and methods of communication in the period and geographical areas represented.

PROLOGUE

O'Malley Castle — Samhain Celebration

Fall 1457

Patrick MacCahan spent the better part of the afternoon meditating in his chambers; contemplating the turn of events that resulted in his relocation to O'Malley territory on the western seaboard of Ireland, and his upcoming nuptials to Darina O'Malley, the now deceased O'Malley Lord's eldest daughter. It had been a trying few weeks —weeks wrought with peril, storms, bloodshed, kidnapping and deceit.

The fact that his father sent his brother, Payton, and fifty of his best fighting men from the MacCahan territories in Northern Ireland to attend to the stronghold should have been a blessing in disguise; were it not been for Payton's antics at the river. Now he must find a way to dissuade Darina's uncle, Ruarc O'Connell, from unleashing an unholy wrath upon Payton and attempt to find some common ground with the man himself, since Ruarc was the chieftan of the O'Malley militia.

But first, there was the matter of Lucian, the elderly O'Malley clan scribe and druid priest who held the respect of the people, and most certainly of Ruarc. Patrick knew he sensed something kindred in Lucian from the moment they met. When he realized that Lucian was the brother of his dear friend and mentor, Airard, from his own clan, he knew why.

Airard trained Patrick in the blacksmithing arts from the time he could wield a sword. However, it was his instruction in mystical matters that was more valuable. Patrick was groomed specifically to take Airard's mantle as priest for his clan; but that was not to be. He was to be married this night to Darina O'Malley, during the clan's annual Samhain celebrations. He wasn't disappointed at becoming the new leader of the O'Malleys, or even with his betrothed. Darina was a fiery dryad of a woman and she was as beautiful as she was cunning. She would prove a worthy match.

No, Patrick longed for the day when his services as a druid priest would begin. He prepared for it, longed for it and waited for it. As it stood, there was already an invocation ceremony planned for the coming year and Airard was to anoint him to take his place during Beltane celebrations. Who would take Airard's mantle in MacCahan territory when Airard was too feeble? That thought kept Patrick awake for hours late into the night and the fatigue was showing on his face.

"Ye asked for me?" spoke Lucian. Patrick was tying his hair off at the nape of his neck while examining his image in the looking glass brought up by Odhran, the castle bailiff. The wedding ceremony would occur in just a matter of hours; and Patrick was busy readying himself in the fifth floor storage room of the Laird's private banqueting hall.

I did. I've need to speak of Darina with ye.

No response.

I ken ye can hear me druid, pressed Patrick with his mind.

"Well son? What need have ye of me services?" asked Lucian, still standing in the doorway between the banquet room and the storage pantry which adjoined. He clasped his hands in front of him and twiddled the golden rope tied around his white cloak.

Ye don't hear me, or ye are pretending ye don't?

Silence.

"I have a qu-que-question about Da-Darina," he stuttered audibly.

"About Darina?" replied Lucian.

"Aye. I d-do," said Patrick as he turned around to face the O'Malley clan's elderly scribe. He walked slowly towards him and clasped forearms with Lucian, who was adorned in his full priest attire. A gleam caught Patrick's eye and he looked down to see that Lucian wore the same shamrock crested ring as he did.

"Where did ye get that?" asked Lucian hesitantly.

Get what?

No response came from Lucian.

"Well?" Lucian asked again.

"Me r-ring?" asked Patrick aloud.

"Aye, yer ring Patrick. Where did ye get that?" demanded Lucian.

"'Twas given to me by an old fr-friend," he replied, noticing the matching ring on Lucian's right hand. It was an intricate piece of artwork indeed. A signet ring of silver with the image of a dragon laid across the background of a shamrock. Two small rubies made the dragon's eyes and fire thrust from its nostrils.

"Would this old friend have a name?" inquired Lucian further.

"Air-Airard. He is the blacksmith of me cl-clan. The MacCahan cl-clan," he clarified.

"Ye ken Airard well, do ye?" pried Lucian further.

"Aye, he is like me s-s-sec-second fathair. He has tr-trained me as a blacksmith for m-ma-any years."

What else has he trained ye for Patrick? inquired Lucian with his mind, now standing only inches from Patrick.

Tell me, demanded Lucian.

Patrick's eyes shot up in astonishment and gripped Lucian's arms harder. They looked at each other for what seemed hours and dropped their arms to their sides.

Patrick walked back towards the looking glass and straightened the MacCahan plaid about his shoulder, repositioning the brooch holding it together.

Tell me son.

I think ye ken verra well, Lucian. Airard is yer brathair, is he no'?

Aye, he is. You must say it, me son.

Say what?

Ye ken, say it.

Patrick grew uncomfortable with the questioning and fumbled with the ring on his hand, looking down and away from Lucian in what seemed like humiliation or fear — Lucian wasn't sure.

Ye are the last, Patrick. Say it.

Nay—I'll not say it. I have no evidence ye are correct, Lucian.

"Ye wear the ring Patrick. There are only three of the Dragon Crest rings, ye know. I have one, Airard has one and ye wear the other. I can only assume it was Airard who conferred it."

"Ye are wr-wrong a-b-about that," spoke Patrick audibly.

"What do ye mean?" asked Lucian confused. "Ye said it was a gift from an old friend."

"It belonged to m-m-my m-ma-mathair," he replied and turned to sit upon the short three-legged stool in front of Lucian. "'Twas given to me when she p-passed; my f-fa-fathair insisted. Airard had it repaired and cleaned pr-prior to giving it t-to me. Me brathair, P-Parkin, was given her silver torc; and Payton was given her d-dia-diadem. I was given me mathair's hair c-comb and this" he said glancing at the ring on his right hand. "I am the only one who d-did-didn't receive a MacCahan cl-clan crest."

Ye sound defeated lad. Mayhap yer mathair knew ye wouldna always be a MacCahan.

Patrick locked eyes with him again. *How could she have known I'd take the O'Malley name?*

Yer mathair wore that ring for a reason son. Do ye no' ken?

What do ye mean?

Ye know what the rings represent, do ye not?

Aye…I think I do.

"Patrick, yer mathair was a druid priestess. Not just any priestess, mind ye."

"How s-s-ss-so?" he asked standing up to face Lucian.

Yer ma was one of only three. There are only three Dragonian's remaining Patrick; myself, me brathair and now you, Patrick. Patrick, ye are one of us.

And what are ye?

Patrick, I've no doubt Airard has prepared ye. Don't pretend to misunderstand me. Ye know what I am saying.

12

"I've nay such idea," he stated aloud, slowly and audibly. He hadn't stuttered and for that he was thankful. "I s-sum-summoned ye to speak of D-Darina," he stated sternly having twisted his ring wrong side with his left hand so that the crest faced his palm. "I've a question, and I w-wi-wish to k-kn-know the truth of it."

"Aye, Patrick, I always speak the truth. What do ye wish to know?

"I w-wi-wish to kn-know why she blames her-herself for her-her sister's d-death."

Ye've been using yer gift with the lass?

Patrick nodded affirmatively.

She won't like that. She's a might skeptical.

Patrick nodded again and grinned.

"I see ye've spoken with her already - in a manner of speaking," Lucian chuckled and straightened his robe. So you know of the babe's identity?" he asked.

Patrick nodded again. *Why doesn't she know? 'Tis nay fair to keep her in the dark of such things.*

'Tis what her da requested. We could only do what our Laird asked. Even his own wife went to her grave not knowing her youngest child remained alive and well in MacCahan castle, and that she had a son and not a deceased daughter.

'Tis no' right, Lucian. I mean to rectify it immediately. Why does she believe she is responsible for the death of this child who is very much alive?

Patrick rose and grasped arms with Lucian again, searching his face for the answer, demanding a response.

"Because, before the child was born, Darina had fallen into the river and was being swept downstream. Anya went in after her and pulled her out. Saved her life, she did."

"However?" asked Patrick.

"However, Anya took a fever from the cold water and was sick in bed for days. She went into early labor. The healer was terrified. We all were. We thought we had lost her."

"S-so ye l-let D'rina think it was her f-fault th-that the babe died?"

13

"We had nay other choice Patrick…we had to protect the child."

Of course ye had a choice. There is always a choice, he rebuked Lucian with his mind as he stepped around him and into the banquet hall.

ONE

O'Malley Castle

Darina stood on the balcony overlooking the bay and watched the sun dance over a wall of waves in the sea. She was ready. The time was near and now all that was left was the wedding ceremony.

Father MacArtrey was missing…having disappeared, at some point, in the last few days…and he was nowhere to be found. Her cousin Kyra, and Murchadh…one of her uncle Ruarc's soldiers…were dispatched to find him; but they were not successful. Mayhap he had fallen into the sea during a drunken stupor; or worse… mayhap he had been kidnapped and sold at a slave auction.

The thought made her giggle out loud. Father MacArtrey would make a horrible servant. He was barely able to stand upright when he was sober, due to his portly shape, let alone when he was full from the drink; which was quite often for a mon of the cloth. The truth was she wanted him here and the fact that he wasn't made her somewhat uneasy. He had brought her great comfort after the deaths of her mother and father and helped her comfort her four younger sisters.

Lucian had graciously offered to perform the rites; an offering that well pleased her uncle as well as her sister, Dervilla. As his apprentice, Dervilla had been learning the trade of the scribe for several years and was quite adept at map-making as well.

Lucian was well established as the clan's scribe. His religious leanings were what concerned Darina. As a druid priest, he was known in the region, and highly sought after for service and counsel.

The trouble was that Darina wasn't a druid, a pagan or a practicing Christian. Her father had offered Father MacArtrey sanctuary after their rival clan, the Burke's, had pillaged their own monastery and the priest escaped with his life. Her own mother, Anya O'Malley, was a druid, as was her mother, and her mother's mother before her. All the women of her family were druids and worshipped the old gods.

She sighed at the thought of what the joining on Samhain would mean to Lucian and how much irritation her sister Dervilla would cause her because of it. She had never espoused any particular god and wasn't about to start now. Her faith had waxed and waned between worshipping them all—just to hedge her wagers—and none, because the mere idea seemed ludicrous.

Are you ready?

She jumped. The imposing thought snapped her back to her moment in time and sent shivers down her spine. She pulled a long, red tendril of hair out of her eyes and straightened her gown. She was becoming anxious. There were many important matters riding on this alliance being formed by her union with Patrick MacCahan, the eldest son of Breacan MacCahan. Her father apparently arranged the marriage many years before and she was never told until recently, just after his death.

"Darina, the ladies are waiting to finish yer hair," called her Aunt Atilde from the threshold leading from the balcony. "Ye are just stunning. Patrick is indeed a blessed mon to marry such a beautiful woman."

Darina blushed as she followed her aunt down the hallway towards the stairs to her chamber.

***

"Walk with me," gestured Lucian to Patrick as they crossed the banqueting hall where the ceremony was to be performed. Servants were hastily working, making last minute preparations in the hall. Flowers adorned the windows, and several long tables had been brought up and were overflowing with the finest foods imaginable. The O'Malley stronghold's situation along the western seaboard afforded the clan access to various seafoods and delicacies. Darina was especially fond of shrimp, and Odhran saw to it that the feast was overflowing with them.

Lucian led them down the stairways and out of the castle towards the markets on the bay side. The markets were closed for the Samhain celebration and wedding reception; but the grounds were crowded with the elaborate tents of visitors and honored guests who came to celebrate the alliance forged by the joining of Darina and Patrick.

I canna believe he has led us out here dressed like this. He in his cloak and priest attire… and me like… this. Patrick groaned as he dodged a wayward hog covered in fresh mud. *Thank the gods the storm has stopped.*

"Aye, thank the gods indeed," said Lucian acknowledging Patrick's thoughts. "It may turn out to be quite a nice day after all," he ventured, through a tight smile.

When they finally made it past the last row of tent houses, they followed a footpath leading uphill towards the port to the north side of the territory. They hiked past thick brush which surrounded a stream flowing from the river, until they arrived at an isolated crop of buildings which appeared to be a crudely put-together maze of thatched roof round-houses joined as one.

"Wh-where are we?" asked Patrick.

"This is the sick-house. We are here to see Vynae, the healer, and Jordy. He is the young boy ye found in Burke territory; and he has an interesting story I'd like ye to hear."

It canna wait until after me wedding? queried Patrick with his mind.

I'm afraid no' Patrick, responded Lucian. *This is a matter of safety and security for all of our clan.*

"Verra w-well then Lucian— let's g-get this matter behind us," sighed Patrick as Lucian pushed the door to the sick-house open and ushered them inside.

The trip from MacCahan territory had been perilous. They were constantly bombarded by incessant rains and the storms that seemed to come with them on their journey. When the foster child, Braeden, who Patrick's father asked Patrick to bring back to O'Malley lands with him, and his nurse, Mavis, ventured off into the night; they stumbled upon a Burke soldier hovering over the body of a grievously injured young boy.

It was known there was no love lost between the O'Malley's and the Burke's. Ruarc, chieftan of the O'Malley military, sent men to accompany Patrick and his group on their journey through Burke territory— to ensure their safe arrival.

Patrick saved the boy's life with the help of Deasum, an O'Malley soldier. It required the unfortunate beheading of a Burke soldier and Mavis had been injured; but the boy lived.

Lucian pushed open the heavy wooden door to the sick-house and it creaked loudly, as if announcing their arrival. They entered the main room where a fire was burning and saw a young boy sitting nearby; sipping a mug of something presumed to be cider and hastily gnawing at a turkey leg.

"Jordy, I'm glad to see ye about. Are ye feeling much better?" asked Lucian, directing Patrick's attention to the boy he had helped rescue.

"Aye. Aye indeed!" replied Jordy, bouncing up from his crouched position near the fire. "Yer the one!" called Jordy to Patrick, as he strode towards the two men who were moving to sit at the table.

"Aye, he is," replied Lucian. "Jordy, this is Patrick MacCahan, the warrior who took you from yer captor, the Burke soldier. Patrick is to wed Darina O'Malley this eve; and he will be the new Laird of the O'Malley clan."

"What is a lair?" asked Jordy nonchalantly, obviously unfamiliar with the term.

"Aye, a laird is a lord, like we have here in Ireland, Jordy," said Lucian. "In Scotland, they call them lairds. Lord O'Malley's wife, Anya, called him Laird, so it took hold among the O'Malley clanspeople."

Before anyone could stop him, Jordy ran to Patrick and wrapped his arms around his waist hanging on for what seemed like dear life.

"Jordy McClure, ye let go o' that mon this instant!" broke the voice of Vynae, the clan healer, as she barreled down the corridor from out of one of the chambers.

"Lucian, what need have ye o' Jordy *now*?" she bellowed. "'Tis nearly noon day, and a might close to time for Jordy to take his nap," she spewed angrily.

Jordy relinquished his hold on Patrick's waist and slid down his legs back to the floor, still grasping the turkey leg with his right hand.

"Vynae, this is Patrick MacCahan," Lucian shot back, but not quick enough.

"I ken verra well who he is, Lucian. Now—why have ye come and why must ye continue to pester the boy so? He's told ye ever-thing he knows!"

"P-pa-pardon me, me lady," interjected Patrick. He took Vynae's weathered left hand in his own and placed a gentle kiss atop it before she could stop him. The healer blushed, softened instantly and let out a long sigh.

"I pr-promise we won't keep him up much longer. We have only a f-few qu-questions and then he can be off to his sl-slum-slumber," Patrick added, still grasping her hand.

"Aye, alright, I s'pose a few more minutes won't hurt anything," said Vynae dreamy-eyed and now caressing her left hand with her right.

"Jordy, sit right down there at the table and let the men speak with ye; and when ye are done, get yerself back into yer bed, ye hear?" instructed Vynae before returning down the corridor and into another chamber.

"Jordy, Patrick wishes to know what ye told me—about what happened," said Lucian directing Jordy with his eyes to speak to Patrick.

"Aye, I'll tell him."

"G-good," said Patrick as he filled Jordy's mug with more cider from a pitcher sitting on the table.

"Me fathair is a textile merchant from MacTierney lands," huffed Jordy as he continued to chew the turkey leg.

"The McTierney's are our allies to the south," shot Lucian towards Patrick. Patrick nodded his acknowledgement and looked to Jordy to continue.

"We were here for the markets and I was playing on the long pier, when…of a sudden…these two men grabbed me. They put me in their boat and bid me to drink from their mug," Jordy stated through haggard breath, in between bites.

"'Twas awful— the drink that is," he grimaced. "Then, they tied a linen about me mouth, and put a sack over me head before they pushed me down to lay on the bottom of the boat. So no one would see me."

"J-Jordy," said Patrick, "did ye ken who the men were?"

Jordy shook his head back and forth indicating he didn't know.

"Had ye ever seen them a'fore?" asked Lucian.

Jordy shook his head back and forth again between bites on the now nearly barren turkey leg. "Never," he said, "and they wore a strange plaid."

"A st-strange plaid?" asked Patrick.

"Aye," said Jordy. "'Twas not a McTierney plaid, and 'twas not an O'Malley plaid. It didn't look like his plaid either," said Jordy pointing to the MacCahan tartan draped across Patrick's shoulder.

"Wh-what did it look like?" asked Patrick.

"'Twas brown with red and yellow lines in it," replied Jordy, matter-of-factly.

"Burke," sighed Lucian as he pounded his fist against the table top. "I knew it!"

"Wh-what happened next, Jordy? Can ye remember?"

"Aye," replied Jordy. "I woke up with a terrible pounding in me head— chained up to a wall in a dark cave."

Vynae skittered back down the corridor towards the table with a fierce look of impatience on her face. "Lucian, I told ye, Jordy needs to be in his bed—now."

"Mi-might I tuck him in?" asked Patrick sheepishly to Vynae as he rose from the table. *This should buy us a little more time*, said Patrick to Lucian, with his mind.

"Verra well, but be quite quick about it," Vynae responded as she grabbed the ragged turkey leg from Jordy's hands and wiped them with clean linen. "Go on," she demanded, patting Jordy swiftly on the backside and steering him towards his chamber.

"Jordy's da will be here on the morrow to take him home," she said. "He was quite happy to hear he was safe on O'Malley lands. Nay doubt the poor boy will be interrogated again at home."

Lucian and Patrick met Vynae back at the door to the sick-house when they had gotten all the answers they could from Jordy.

"Th-thank you, Vynae, for letting us speak with him. It was most helpful," ventured Patrick at the door.

"We best be off," interjected Lucian, "We've a ceremony to attend."

"Th-that we do!" stammered Patrick through a clenched grin. "Vy-vynae, I wonder if I might di-discuss something with y-you, before I return to the k-keep?" he asked.

"Certainly," she responded. "What can I do for ye, me Lord?"

Patrick gave Lucian a deliberate glance indicating his need for privacy. Lucian caught the gesture and bid his goodbyes as he headed back towards the castle.

"Alright dear, what have ye need of?" questioned the healer.

"I am te-terribly exhausted. Our j-journey here was st-stressful and I f-fear I may f-fall asleep or w-worse. Might you h-have anythi...?" Vynae interrupted before Patrick could continue.

"Say nay more. I know just what ye need."

"Th-thank you," he sighed, beginning to blush.

"Just you have a seat and I'll be back in a bit."

Vynae returned from the furthest chamber in the sick-house and trudged back down the corridor to the table where Patrick now sat. She lay a cup full of some type of elixir on the table in front of him and pointed.

"Now—make quite certain ye intend to stay awake; otherwise ye may not sleep for a while."

"Aye," he replied as he grabbed the cup and drank the contents ravenously. "I d-doubt I'll get m-much sleep tonight, w-with it being S-Samhain and all," he said, as he winked at Vynae.

"Well, I guess not," she shot back, a knowing grin arising on her face. "I guess not."

TWO

O'Malley Territory — the Piers

"Tell me again where we are going?" asked eleven-year-old Braeden. He directed his repetitive inquiry to Mavis, for the third time in as many minutes.

"Just come along Braeden," she said exasperatedly. "We are going to fetch a dog from a boat at the piers and take it up to the Inn to Rory. It is to be a present from Patrick to Darina. It is a fine falconry hound and Patrick thinks she has need of it."

"A dog… he is giving her a dog?" Braeden recanted as if attempting to remember what she said this time.

"Aye, he is giving her a dog; and we are to retrieve it from the piers and take it to *whom*?" she drilled.

"To Rory!" Braeden exclaimed obviously proud of himself for remembering. "We are taking the dog to Rory at the Inn."

"Verra good, Braeden. Ye see that boat there? The one with the yellow sun on the flag?" she pointed. "That is the boat. We are to ask for Nidaj and hand him this coin right here in this purse."

"Can I do it?" asked Braeden. "I want to be the one! Please, please Mavis, can I?" he begged and jumped up and down in front of her, blocking her walking path.

"Alright, but only if ye agree to lead the pup back up this hill. I've nay desire to fight with a mangy dog this day, it might get me dress torn."

22

"I will!" he replied and increased the tempo of his steps towards the boat. The closer they came to the boat, the louder the yelps and barks became. It was clear the fewterer had a grand selection of hounds of all kinds, as there were many kenneled areas atop the boat; and handlers were bustling about busily caring for them and discussing their qualities with interested parties.

When they finally crossed to the end of the pier, Mavis spoke up. "Now Braeden, go on—tell 'em ye have business with Nidaj."

Braeden walked hesitantly up the narrow slat which lay between the pier and the boat itself. After climbing aboard, he turned back around to check for approval from Mavis before continuing.

"Sir," he said, tugging at the truis of an elderly man standing watch over the boat's entry point. "Sir, I have need to speak with Nidaj."

"Go on now son, I haven't the time nor inclination to make merry with anyone t'day," retorted the old guard. "Besides, we have much business transacting and ye are getting in the way, ye are."

"Sir," pressed Braeden further, raising his voice this time, the way Patrick had instructed him to speak up in public. "Good sir, I have business with Nidaj and I will speak to him at once," he countered. "I have coin, and I am to take delivery of a particular hunting hound which has been procured by our new Laird, Patrick MacCahan. I dare say, 'twould be dreadful if I return without his purchase. Patrick would be unpleased with Nidaj should I do so."

At the mention of Patrick's name, the elderly guard's eyes shot up. He peered back down at Braeden between heavily grayed, thick eyebrows, before bidding Braeden to remain. "I'll get Nidaj, but the rest is up to ye lad— ye ken?" he asked and shrugged his hunched shoulders.

Before Braeden knew what happened, a small red-and-white spaniel pup was thrust towards him and was attempting to climb him like a tree. Braeden toppled backwards and caught himself with his hands before they could both plunge head-over-feet over the side of the boat.

"Goodness! Braeden, ye get ahold of that dog right now a 'fore ye both end up in the water!" shouted Mavis, who was now glaring threateningly at the elderly guard. Sensing her irritation, the man took ahold of the dog's lead and settled him while assisting Braeden to his feet.

"Son, this one here is a good falconry hound; but he's still got a might bit 'a pup in him. Ye need to control him or else he'll control you."

"I think ye is right," exclaimed Braeden. "And this is the one the Laird picked?" he asked in disbelief.

"It is," interjected a lanky gentleman from behind the guard. "The very one," he said.

"And who are ye?" quipped Braeden to the man.

"Nidaj. I am the dealer who spoke with Patrick. This is the hound he chose. One of me best, his sire was a champion falconry hound from England. I'm sure the Laird will be pleased with this choice."

Braeden hurriedly thrust the coin purse into Nidaj's hand and stepped back before he grabbed the lead from the guard and turned to leave.

"Wait!" Nidaj said. "Ye forgot the papers. Take these with ye, ye may have need of them in the future."

***

"Aye, Patrick, 'tis nearly time. Are ye ready?" inquired Ruarc O'Connell.

Patrick rose from the bench beside the fire in the great hall and walked forward to greet Ruarc who had just come in from the battlements. "I b-be-believe so," stuttered Patrick, a blush rising in his face.

"H-how are ye, Ruarc?" asked Patrick.

"Verra well, verra well indeed. There is a small matter we should discuss involving yer brathair, Payton. But, I believe it can keep until the morrow."

"M-me brathair? Wh-when did he ar-arrive?" asked Patrick, surprised at the news.

"Earlier this day; Kyra went out to meet the men and there was an incident at the river."

"The men— how m-many came with m-me brathair?" questioned Patrick.

"A garrison of perhaps fifty MacCahan soldiers, I believe," retorted Ruarc. "Why? Did ye not know they were a'coming?"

Patrick shook his head back and forth and adorned an expression of surprise that unsettled Ruarc. "I've some explaining to do I see," he said.

"Patrick, yer fathair made these arrangements long ago with Laird O'Malley. These men are to stay here in O'Malley territory and become a part of our clan. He selected the best unmarried soldiers ye had in yer territory. They are here to support and protect..."

"Pro-tec-tion? I've nay n-need for pp-rotec-tion," interrupted Patrick. "I am m-more than cap-capable of protecting..."

Ruarc interrupted Patrick before he could go any further. "Hold on, Patrick. It appears there are yet matters ye should be aware of— things yer fathair has no' been clear about."

"Wh-what sort of th-things?" sighed Patrick shaking his head. *I am yet again in the dark about matters.* "Do g-go on, Ruarc. Please, l-leave n-nothing out th-this time. 'Tis only f-fair I g-go into this m-marriage with f-full disclosure."

"Ye are right about that son." Ruarc stretched his arms as wide as they could go and then tugged at his long red beard until it looked like he would pull it out. Patrick gestured for a servant to bring them ale before returning his eyes to Ruarc's— pressing him for information.

"Verra well, Patrick. I'll no' beat around the bush. I'll just have it out and then ye can ask me whatever ye wish to know."

Patrick nodded and bade him to continue.

"Patrick have ye had time to meet with the men, the soldiers... our forces that is... our military operations?" he asked hesitantly.

"Nay, we only a-ar-rived l-last night."

"I see. Well, ye need to understand that we have only a small handful of experienced men compared to the size of our territory. And, most of those soldiers are not O'Malley clansmen, they are hired men."

"Why is th-that?" asked Patrick confused. "Aren't yer m-men h-here required to s-serve?"

"Aye, they are indeed. However, we lack for... well Patrick... that is to say that... Oh Shite! Patrick, we haven't many men."

25

"Haven't m-many men? How is th-that?" retorted Patrick obviously confused.

"Patrick," replied Ruarc, "we haven't had a male child born to the O'Malley clan in nigh o'er twenty summers a 'cause of the curse."

"C-curse?" repeated Patrick. "Wh-what c-curse?

"I canna believe yer fathair sent ye all this way w'out telling you the full of it," breathed Ruarc through clenched teeth. "I canna ken what he was thinking," he said, shaking his head.

"T-tell me about this curse," sighed Patrick before taking a long deliberate drink out of his mug of ale.

"Patrick, Odetta Burke placed a curse on our clan many years ago. It was said that the curse would keep an O'Malley heir from being born— but it has also kept *any* male from being born of the O'Malley clan, including our villagers and hired soldiers." Ruarc took a shallow breath and paused before continuing, "We are woefully outnumbered…" he paused for reflection and shook his head, "Women," he smiled in jest.

Patrick choked back a hardy laugh and asked, "And…th-that is a pr-problem…how?"

Ruarc returned the smile and continued, "We have nay men for our women, Patrick; none to marry the Laird's daughters to; none to marry my daughter to either. But, most importantly, we have only a small military force; and our best soldiers are women."

"W-women? You l-let w-women fight?" asked Patrick.

"We have no choice. We have to protect our lands and our port. Our women are highly skilled and trained, but we have need of men; strong, young, and *unmarried* men."

Patrick slammed his mug down on the table in front of him sending liquid splashing about. A maidservant hurried to clean up the mess before Ruarc could waive her off.

"Aye, I see n-now. Me da s-sold me off for some men," Patrick snorted.

"Now hold on Patrick. That is no' so."

"And— h-how is th-that, Ruarc?"

"Yer da knew ye were the best hope for our clan. Because of yer…uh…skills…that is."

"Me sk-skills?" questioned Patrick. "Wh-what are you t-talking about?"

"Odetta Burke, the younger sister of Cynbel Burke, the Lord of Burke territory—she is a pagan witch," Ruarc added matter-of-factly.

"And th-that has wh-what to do with me?"

"Patrick," Ruarc whispered and leaned in to speak with him quietly, "Ye are a druid, are ye not?"

Anger rose visibly in Patrick's face and he shot up and out of his chair and headed towards the hearth before Ruarc knew what happened. *Of all the horrible reasons to send me here to marry the O'Malley lass—this has to be the worst I could imagine.*

Ruarc quickly ushered the servants out of the great hall and joined Patrick at the fire. "Patrick, have I said something to upset ye?" he queried.

Patrick turned an angry glare towards Ruarc and wrung his hands together, searching for the words. If he could only just slow down his thoughts, he may be able to get it out coherently. His breathing was staggered and he could feel his pulse pounding in his ears. Never had he been so gut-wrenchingly mad at his father. Never had he ever felt so taken advantage of as he did just then.

"R-Ruarc," he started. Then he stopped, turned to pace the great hall and returned to Ruarc's side again. "Ru-Ruarc. I am indeed a dr-druid. This much me da knows. What that means...my da...has n-no idea. If I am to b-be used as...if I in an-any w-way was bro-brought here to ...."

"Slow down," interjected Ruarc. "Yer da knew that verra little frightened ye Patrick. He said ye are the bravest of his sons and that ye would make a finer leader than he."

"H-he did?" Patrick swung around in disbelief and stood lock-eyed with Ruarc.

"Aye, Patrick. It was he and Airard who chose ye to be the next ruler of our clan. When ye were just a wee boy; right after Braeden was sent to foster in MacCahan castle. We knew that none of our allies would agree to an alliance through marriage, because of the curse. Airard said that if there was a curse, it would no' deter ye from yer duties. And, yer da believed that being of Scottish descent, ye may be able to reason with Cynbel Burke."

"Aye. Me m-ma-athair is a Scot. Me uncles, Alec and T-To-Torcuil Montgomery came with her from the Isles wh-when she married me da. Wh-what has that to d-do with anything?" queried Patrick.

"The Burke's are Scots, Patrick. They were sent here by the English many years ago and they managed to conquer the land they now hold. Cynbel may look favorably on an alliance when he learns ye are a Scot; he is a reasonable mon. After his fathair died, we had hopes that relations would ease between our clans. He is not easily swayed by his sister, Odetta. Most believe she is addled."

"An,d if my be-being a S-Sc-Scott makes nay difference to the Burke's? Wh-what th-then?" asked Patrick.

"Then Odetta Burke would finally get the enemy she deserves…in ye…Patrick."

"Well, ye h-have th-the right of th-that," retorted Patrick.

"What do ye mean?" asked Ruarc titling his head in confusion.

"If th-this w-witch wants a f-fight—I'll g-give it t-to her," he whispered as he grabbed a mug of ale off a serving tray as it went by on the shoulders of a maidservant. "And Ruarc," he smiled, "th-there is nay such c-curse."

Astonished, Ruarc tilted his head and squinched his eyes shut as if in contemplation. "What do ye mean?"

"If there re-really w-was a curse, explain h-how Br-Braeden c-came to be b-born h-here," replied Patrick triumphantly. "Th-there is something g-going on R-Ruarc; b-but it's no' wh-what y-ye th-think."

THREE

O'Malley Territory

Braeden had managed to stomp in every last puddle of mud and pile of horse dung to be found between the piers and the Inn. If Mavis let out another long aggravated sigh she was sure she would lose her breath altogether and succumb to the breathing frenzies. As it stood, only Braeden's boots were muddy—not that the crazed excuse for a hunting hound hadn't tried to sully his truis. No, Braeden and the hound had engaged in a sort of ritual dance all along the path to the Inn; with the floppy-eared hound running circles around him as Braeden dodged and ducked and pulled and pushed against the lead to avoid being mauled with muddy paws. It was a sight for sure.

The sun was high in the sky and cast orange and yellow hued speckles across the bay. Music and laughter filled the air as guests prepared for the reception and Samhain festival later that evening; and the smell of venison and wild game rose up to greet them as they neared the Inn. Mavis' eyes shot up as she caught a glimpse of Rory exiting the rear of the Inn carrying two large water buckets as he headed for the well.

"Nay Rory, lemme have them buckets," she cried. "Come and get this filth-ridden mutt from Braeden a'fore he spoils his truis."

Rory abruptly stopped and released his hold on the buckets; turning around to watch in astonishment the game that Braeden played with the pup. He had never seen such a thing, in all his years. Braeden gripping a four to five foot lead tied around the neck of a beautiful red-and-white spaniel pup whose only goal seemed to be focusing on climbing Braeden like a tree. And Braeden, intent on not dirtying his dress clothes, danced around and around in an attempt to avoid the muddy dog. Rory broke into a tirade of hysterical laughter, unable to catch his breath.

"Go on now, git yer fill mon," retorted Mavis, "'Tis nay as funny as all that." Mavis rolled her eyes and fisted her hands in her skirts in aggravation. "Think ye can do more than laugh now, seeing as how we have other matters to attend?" she shouted to Rory.

Braeden wiped the sweat from his brow and blew out a long held breath; obviously near to worn out. "Master Rory, couldja please come get this beast?" he asked through staggered breaths. "He is a'wearing me out!"

"Is this the pup Patrick intends to gift to Darina?" asked Rory through uncontained chuckles.

"Aye. I ken it is," replied Mavis. "I've nay good idea what will become of him though, once she gets a look'a him." Mavis could not contain her laughter any longer and broke down in a rattle of cackles that sent her into a coughing fit.

"Help me!" cried Braeden over the laughter and amusement of Rory and Mavis. "I am going to let this dog go if somebody doesn't come get him away from me. I am worn clean out."

Rory straightened and pulled a strip of folded linen from his boot. "I'll take him," he said, walking towards the dog and uttering something Braeden didn't understand. Immediately, the dog's ears shot up at attention and he sat perfectly still on the ground as if awaiting instruction.

Astonished, Braeden let go of the rope and asked Rory, "What did ye say to him?" The dog didn't move. Rory uttered something else indistinguishable and the dog crouched on all fours, lying on his belly on the ground.

"I told him to sit still and then to lie down," replied Rory. "He is a finely trained dog, but just like little lads I know, without proper instruction, his mischievousness will get the better o'him."

Rory wiped the dog's paws and belly and removed as much of the crusted mud as he could. "I'll have him washed and put him in the stables with Moya for now. She will see to him until Patrick is ready for him. He should get along just fine with the horses until the kennel is ready. You two best be tidying up yerselves before the reception," he directed to Mavis.

Mavis nodded and called after Braeden, "Alright, come along now. Let's walk down to the piers again and wash off yer boots."

***

Galen Fleming sighed audibly at the sight of the priest's empty cottage. Even the chapel was abandoned. Although Kyra, Ruarc's daughter, and Murchadh, one of Ruarc's best fighting men, searched the cottage for clues, there was no indication of what had become of the priest. They also searched most of O'Malley territory proper—and gone further into Burke lands than they should, to no avail.

Galen was Father MacArtrey's cleric, going on for close to fourteen winters and he was fond of the man, vices and all. When word reached Rome that the monastery on Burke lands had been usurped by the Burke's, and that the priest was the only survivor; Galen was sent from his home in the highlands of Scotland to serve out his commission with the O'Malley clan.

Galen was a familiar breath of fresh air for many of the Catholic soldiers; who were a mix of Viking, Roman and Scottish warriors, as well as some men from neighboring clans. He was the first to call the senior O'Malley "Laird" and the term stuck, a term of endearment and respect that the Scotsmen understood. Darina's mother, Anya, was a Scottish noble. Her grandsire was a Lord of Parliament in Scotland and the O'Malley's happily integrated Scottish and Irish cultures.

"Still nay sign of the priest?" asked Lucian entering the cottage behind Galen.

"Nay. Nay sign at all. I fear something is amiss," replied Galen stroking his long gray beard and shaking his head. "How are ye me old friend," he asked Lucian and clasped forearms with the elder scribe.

"I fear ye are right," sighed Lucian. "Except for the scrolls and manuscripts we found hidden in his bed frame, we've nay an idea what has become of him or why."

"I sent a message to Rome yestereve about his disappearance. I await instruction on how to maintain the chapel and the services. The coin they found, the church coffers, we have given to Minea for safekeeping."

"Good idea," replied Lucian. "Walk with me Galen, let's discuss the ceremony. Patrick nay doubt wishes my involvement, and Darina, wishes yers. I'm sure we can appease them both. What say ye?"

"Sounds like a fine idea, Lucian. A fine plan, indeed."

FOUR

Burke Territory

Father MacArtrey rubbed the goose egg that rose upon his forehead and prayed for mercy. To whom he prayed—he was no longer sure. He was Odetta Burke's spy in O'Malley lands and had been her puppet for far too long. And, his age was getting the better of him. He felt a small measure of redemption when he was able to save the young boy from certain death. By cutting his own wrist, along with the child's, during the sacrifice to Teutates; he had spared his life, or so he thought. He only prayed the boy still lived. When the soldier came to dispose of the boy's body, he wasn't so sure his plan had worked.

Another tortuous night spent below the monastery in the dungeons left him forlorn and distraught. Sharing what the servants called "food" with the rats soured his stomach, and he knew he would retch again if it weren't for the fact that his stomach was already empty.

"Father," said the voice. "Father, are you there?"

I must be losing me mind—I'm hearing things.

"Father, wake up. Are you there?" it rang again.

"Father!" it exclaimed much louder this time. So loud it made the rats screech.

"Aye, I'm here," replied the priest into the heavy darkness. "Who's that?"

"Cordal, Cordal McTierney. What are ye doing back down here in the dungeons?" he whispered as loudly as he could.

"I spared the child during the sacrifice. I couldn't let em kill him," responded the priest.

"What child?" gasped Cordal, rattling the chains that bound him to the wall.

"The sacrifice," replied the priest. "They took a small boy and used him in some sort of ceremony. They were attempting to drain his blood and made me do the deed. Instead of cutting him deeply; I cut my own wrist and used some of me blood to fill the cisterns so that 'twould look like he was dead when he fainted."

"They caught ye?"

"Aye—and now I'm back down here and am told I am to perform another rite tonight during their great service, for Samhain."

"By the stars, Odetta is more addled than I thought. Don't worry; her brathair Cynbel will put a stop to this as soon as he finds out. He doesn't abide her nonsense. If he knew I was down here, he would release me himself."

"If only that were so," murmured the priest. "If only that were so."

"What do ye mean, Father?" asked Cordal.

"Her brathair is dead, Cordal."

"How do ye know," he gasped.

"I watched her kill him with me own eyes, I did," he replied. "She has married Easal and he is the new chieftain and Lord of Burke lands. And worst of all—he is a bigger puppet than I."

***

"Now Braeden, ye need only go in as far as the top of yer boots, ye hear me?" hollered Mavis over the sounds of crashing waves along the shoreline. "I won't have ye getting soaked through; we've a reception to attend this eve, ye ken?"

Braeden kicked at the sand and picked up shells on the shore beside the piers in his lazy attempt to wash off the mud and grime from his boots; before heading back to the castle. It was unusually hot for the season and the combination of light rain from a leftover storm, and the hot sun, cast a humid mist around the piers and draped them in a cloud of white billows.

"Don't venture out so far Braeden, I canna see ye from here," she yelled. Braeden walked so far into the waves, his truis were getting wet above his knee-high leather boots.

"Braeden. Braeden, do ye hear me?" she screamed. Mavis rose from her sitting position on the beach and ran towards the water, searching for any sign of the boy. "Braeden," she cried loudly again into the hazy mist in front of her, cupping her hands and screaming at the top of her lungs.

Panic engulfed her and her pulse quickened as she began to shake. Frantically she ran up and down the beach searching and calling for him. Sweat drenched the back of her neck as she threw her cloak on the ground and stepped knee deep into the crashing waves searching for any sign of the boy.

"Can we help ye lass?"

Startled, Mavis turned to her right and saw three men near a small boat, tugging at the vessel attempting to set off from the shore.

"Aye...I've lost me charge...that is...the boy I was watching. He was only here just a moment ago, and now he does no' answer me call."

"Ah, Lassie. Git ye here in this boat with us and mayhap we can find him together."

Reluctantly, Mavis let the burliest looking man assist her into the small boat. Now thoroughly soaked and frightened, she broke down in a medley of violent tears.

"Don't ye fear now, lass. I've nay doubt we'll help ye find the boy," he said.

Mavis nodded her understanding, but grew cautious. The boat was not moving along the shoreline. Instead, they were headed towards the Isle of Women; between the mainland and the island, and no doubt out towards the deeper sea. She continued calling for Braeden but the men were not helping her search. They were busy rowing the boat as fast as they could.

She heard a muffled moan from the front port side of the boat, and one of the men struggled over a heap of clothing lying tangled near the bottom. She called for Braeden again, and this time the moan was louder and the heap of clothing thrashed about.

Mavis' eyes grew wide in terror. Before her, not ten feet away, lay Braeden at the bottom of the men's' boat—his hands and mouth bound with rope. Their eyes met briefly and she knew what she had to do. The burly man rose to his feet and lurched towards her, stepping over the wooden bench slats as quickly as his plump body would allow him— tipping and shifting the boat from side to side.

Braeden nodded to her, and in one clumsy instant, Mavis flung herself over the side of the boat and into the frigid sea water. Her breath caught in her throat and the weight of her clothing dragged her down under the waves. A frenzy of rough hands blurred her vision as the men atop the water searched and reached to grab her. Soon paddles poked about her and she wasn't certain if they were trying to save her or kill her.

Mavis, she thought to herself. *Catch yerself lass. Ye've nay wish to drown today.* An eerie calm came about her and she floated lightly under the waves for what seemed a millennium before regaining her composure and full consciousness.

The last eleven years of her life were spent caring for Braeden, the baby that saved her. Literally. If it were not for Braeden, the O'Malley men would not have bought her at the slave auction. She would not have a home, a family, a people to call her own. Since her sister Odetta Burke imprisoned her and her husband Cordal for marrying behind her back, the only focus and purpose she had was caring for the boy.

What became of her own daughter, she had no idea. Odetta took the babe the moment she was born and sent Mavis to the auctions. "Unable to even look at her anymore," Odetta said. This would not be the end, her end, or the end of Braeden. He was her life and she would save his even if it cost her…her very own.

Mavis struggled to stay calm under the water; and reached to remove her boots, her plaid from about her shoulder and finally her overdress. Left only in her thin shift, she contemplated her fate. She knew that swimming would be much easier without the extra burden of the clothing and the boots that were weighting her down.

Braeden tussled with the men in the boat until one of them accidently smacked him over the head with an oar he was using to try to get Mavis. Braeden fell back against the side of the boat and nearly toppled over before one of the men covered him again with the pile of linens and settled him in the bottom of the vessel.

"'Tis just as well," said the leader. "He'll sleep for the journey." They watched as Mavis' clothing and boots floated up from the deep towards their boat.

"She'll ne'er make it back to the mainland," one said. "Aye. She is as good as dead," said another.

FIVE

O'Malley Castle—Master's Chambers

Darina inspected her image in the looking glass. The wedding gown her sister crafted was beautiful and her mother would have been be proud. Anya and Darina had shared a unique bond. As mother and daughter, they looked nearly identical. The eldest of Anya's children; Darina was the one who favored her the most, both in character and appearance. Mistaken for sisters on several occasions, Darina had often impersonated her to get her way and garnered the wrath of her father and Uncle Ruarc because of it.

The thought made her giggle and also sprang fresh tears to her eyes. She hadn't cried much since the recent deaths of her parents, at least not where anyone would notice. Stoic as always; she knew her purpose was for her clan and her sisters which required her reservation to her fate.

Is it really that bad? Really?

Her Aunt Atilde told her that her father made a keen match with the MacCahan's. Patrick was a noble gent and would most certainly be a loyal and steadfast husband and had already earned the respect of her Uncle; which by itself was no small feat. He would be good to her. She would be good to him. It might not turn out to be the heart fluttering love she secretly longed for, but it would do.

"Love is a most honorable pursuit, Darina. Ye may still find it. Ye need only to open yer heart."

A chill ran down her spine and the hairs at the back of her neck stood on end. She rubbed her eyes, careful not ruin the powder her sister's had placed there. Hesitantly, she peered deeply into the looking glass again.

"Darina, ye are beautiful."

She was not dreaming. Floating in an ethereal mist inside her looking glass was the outline of her mother's image; shining as if accompanied by a thousand suns. She could see right through the image but she knew it was her. A blissful smile adorned her mother's lips and her blue eyes twinkled as if made of crystal.

"Mathair?" she questioned, tipping her head to the side in disbelief.

"Aye, Darina. I couldna bare the thought of not catchin' a look atcha' on yer wedding day," the image spoke. "I have looked forward to this day since ye were but a wee babe; 'tis why I asked Lucian and Father MacArtrey to make sure to have the wedding today, luv."

"Today?" asked Darina confused.

"Aye, today is Samhain, Darina. The one day when the barrier between our worlds is the weakest. Father MacArtrey and the church call it All Soul's Day. 'Tis is a day to celebrate the dead. To honor those who have passed on to the next world. 'Tis when those in yer world can reach out to those who are from the next world."

"The next world?" she asked.

"Aye," her mother responded. Darina watched in astonishment as the outline of her mother faded in and out of focus in the looking glass before her. The image floated above the floor as if it were swimming on clouds. Tears now stormed Darina's eyes and threatened to spill over.

"Do no' cry for me Darina. I have only a few moments to be here; and there is nay cause to worry on my account. I am well…and yer father…he is with me," she whispered in an echoing voice.

"But...where is that?" Darina cried and stretched her arms out to grasp each side of the mirror. "I want to be there too."

"'Tis not the time, ye have an important mission to fulfill. Ye canna be with me now, but we will be together again. Remember, I am always watching, I am always near. I love ye lass," she said and raised her hands as if to embrace her in return.

Darina edged her face closer to the looking glass, as if she hoped she would fall in. "Mathair, what do I do?" she cried. "I feel so lost, so confused. What should I do?"

"Follow the path that has been set, Darina. 'Tis one that was chosen long ago, but it is for the best. In time, ye will see. Ye are not alone, and ye are protected. There is a mighty spirit which surrounds ye, my child. Ye were chosen for this journey. Ye have nay need to worry, all will be well."

"But, I'm scared," she sighed.

"I know child. Ye will be scared, ye will encounter many frightening things—but ye will prevail. Take comfort in the counsel of others. Let others help ye carry yer burdens; ye've nay need to carry them alone. Patrick is a fine mon, Darina, trust in him."

***

"Must we really tend to this matter now?" asked Ruarc through halted breath; aggravated that Patrick had insisted on speaking with Lucian and viewing the scrolls that were found in the priest's cottage. They climbed the last four steps of the third flight of stairs in the O'Malley strong house; the former castle of the O'Malley clan. It was now home to Ruarc and his family, Lucian, the scribe, and most of the clan council and high ranking military men; since the new castle had been constructed many years before.

"Aye," Patrick replied sternly. "I w-wish to g-get to the bottom of th-this im-im-immedia...uh...now," he nodded, prodding Ruarc to continue upwards.

"Verra well," huffed Ruarc. Come along then, and watch ye step, some of these stones are wearing loose.

Ruarc knew Lucian wouldn't like being questioned and he knew he liked interruptions even less. Lucian and Galen had been holed up in his chamber for the better part of the day planning the wedding ceremony, for which both of them had a part.

"I really have nay idea why these were hidden in Kurt's cottage," echoed Galen's voice down the hallway. "I must confess he is a most troublesome mon; verra hard to get to know—and I've tried."

"I've nay doubt of that, Galen," replied Lucian. "I think we can all say that. He seems a mon of many secrets, indeed."

"Aye, I ken we all can say that," interjected Ruarc from the doorway.

Lucian peered over the table stacked high with manuscripts and scrolls and motioned for Ruarc and Patrick to come inside. Galen tipped his head and scrambled to pull two three-legged stools towards the other side of the work bench for Ruarc and Patrick.

"Patrick, this is Galen, Father MacArtrey's cleric. I'm no' sure if ye two have made each other's acquaintance yet?" asked Lucian.

"Aye, I have h-heard of ye, G-Galen," replied Patrick, moving to grasp forearms with the robed cleric and nodding in respect. "Wh-who is Kurt?" he inquired.

"Aye," sighed Galen. "Kurt is Father's MacArtrey's given name. Ye may refer to him as Father MacArtrey, Father, priest, or Kurt, he minds none of them," he chuckled.

"Me wife, Atilde, calls him 'that mon' on most occasions," interjected Ruarc, with a deep chuckle. "He manages to irritate her to no end. 'Tis a talent I'm sure," he nodded. "One he's honed well."

Galen shot back, "And— it takes quite a bit to irritate Atilde, she's a saint, she is."

40

Lucian passed two mugs of cider towards Ruarc and Patrick and sat down on the bench on his side of the table. "Patrick, are ye eager to discuss the ceremony?" asked Lucian, surprised to see him.

"Nay, he wishes to discuss the matter of the curse," Ruarc replied, shooting a concerned glance towards Galen.

"Now?" asked Lucian, directing his gaze towards Patrick, and waving his arms above the overloaded work table.

"Aye. I wish to b-be app-apprised of all th-that has b-been hi-hid, of everything that has-hasna b-been dis-disclosed to me. B-before the c-ce-ceromony," he spat.

"I can understand that Lucian. Can't you?" Galen asked the elderly scribe.

"Of course," Lucian nodded. "Ruarc, what does he know?"

"He knows there is a curse on the O'Malley clan that prevents a male heir from being born; and that the curse has evidently extended to all who reside in our territory."

Galen stood from the table and paced the chamber nervously, obviously discomfited. He gently rubbed the crucifix which hung about his neck and took a long deep breath before affixing himself at the window overlooking the bay, away from the others.

"G-Galen, I m-mean no dis-disrespect to ye in di-discussing this m-matter. I hope you b-be-believe me," said Patrick softening his voice.

"Galen is familiar with what we discuss, Patrick. I've held back no information from him since the moment he arrived", said Lucian. Galen nodded in the direction of the table and turned back towards the window. "Galen sent to Rome for help with the Burke Witch many years ago."

"Much to the ire of Kurt," added Galen. "He felt it unnecessary and sent a message back telling them not to come."

"That's when I began to suspect something was amiss with the priest," said Ruarc. "We all did, really."

"Patrick," interrupted Lucian. "What is it ye wish to know?"

"I w-would l-like to review the c-curse w-with ye. H-how do you kk-en th-there is a curse to be-begin with?"

"Good question," piped Ruarc. "I told ye he was a sharp mon, Lucian."

Galen strode back towards the table and sat down. "Odetta Burke is no' secretive regarding her intentions. She said from the verra beginning, since before Dallin O'Malley married Anya O'Connell instead, that she would curse their marriage and the O'Malley name. She made it quite clear both through missives and by word of mouth, that she placed a curse on the clan. Her ailing fathair paid her no mind; her brathair thought her addled and her mathair had long since passed. For a while, her clan simply ignored her. Until...."

"Until w-what?" asked Patrick.

Galen continued, "Until she had managed to raise a garrison of fighting men who are loyal only to her," said Lucian. "It started slowly, a few missing sheep, some burned out cottages. We weren't sure where the attacks were coming from. We *thought* we had an alliance with the Burkes."

"No one really believed she had any magic about her, or that she was capable of evil, until she overtook the monastery and killed all the clerics. She crucified three of the nuns, Patrick," added Ruarc.

Patrick's face grew white then red with anger. "Go-go on," he said.

"Kurt, the priest, escaped to our lands and Anya begged Dallin to give him sanctuary," interjected Galen. "He has been serving here ever since."

"After the birth of the third O'Malley daughter, Dallin began to believe the curse was real. Even our hired soldiers who moved here never bore sons," Ruarc stated.

"I s-see. M-may I speak open-openly of me ch-charge?" questioned Patrick.

"Yer charge?" replied Lucian.

"Aye, Braeden, me f-foster," replied Patrick. "May I sp-speak openly of th-that matter?" Patrick searched Lucian's face for permission.

"Aye, Patrick, ye may. I've only just informed Galen of his identity. He is trustworthy. No need to worry about that," replied Lucian.

"If th-this curse is r-real, how is it th-that Braeden w-was born?" Patrick asked.

"That is just what we were discussing before ye arrived, Patrick. And—we have no good idea why that is."

"Do ye kn-know the curse? The w-words to it? Mayhap I can h-help?"

"We were just reviewing it," said Galen. "Here, let me find that scroll." Galen placed his mug down on the side table and began rummaging for the page in the scrolls that contained what they believed to be Odetta's curse.

"Patrick, here 'tis. Let me read it for ye," said Lucian.

"Nay , I w-will r-read it me-me-meself," he retorted. Lucian gave Ruarc an inquisitive glance and asked, "Patrick, do ye read ancient Celtic languages?"

"Aye, of c-course. 'Twas yer own br-brathair wh-who t-taught me, L-Lucian. H-hand it to m-me," he directed. "L-let me s-see what I c-can make of it."

Patrick flipped through page after page in the scrolls; oftentimes going back to the front sections and tracing his fingers around the knotted symbols. He'd settle on one page for a few moments, then go back to the beginning, then flip through more pages, then return to the original page. Much of the ancient writing didn't appear as language at all…but instead…as detailed paintings and symbols in vibrant colors.

Patrick sighed and rolled up the last of the scrolls and handed them to Lucian. An eerie quiet overtook the chamber and no one uttered a word. He took a long, lingering sip on his mug and let out a long-held breath.

"Well?" asked Lucian impatiently. "What do ye make of all this Patrick?

"Did ye find the curse?" asked Ruarc.

"Aye, I f-found the curse," Patrick nodded.

"Can it be broken?" asked Galen. "Can we fight the curse?"

Patrick raised his hand in an effort to avoid further questions. He stood and paced in front of the hearth before returning his gaze towards the table and the men who were looking for answers.

"The c-curse is r-real, but it is n-not a th-thorough curse. Tell me Ruarc, d-did Darina's p-par-parents ever tr-travel outside of the O'Malley lands?"

"Aye," he replied. "They went to Edinburgh to visit with our family there. We are Scots you ken?"

"Aye, I kk-en, as was m-me ma-mathair."

"What has that to do with anything, Patrick?" asked Lucian.

"T-tell me, Ruarc, how l-long ago w-was th-that?" asked Patrick.

"About twelve summers, I believe. Right before we began construction on the high castle. Dallin met the Roman architect while they were there. Why?" asked Ruarc, now confused.

"B-because the c-curse only ap-ap-applies to o-offspring con-conceived on O'Malley l-lands. Br-Braeden must have b-been c-conceived in Scotland," he added.

"Is there a way to break this curse?" asked Galen, urgency in his voice.

"I th-think there is," replied Patrick. "But we h-have bi-bigger pro-problems than th-that."

"What's that ye say?" Lucian asked, growing concerned.

"The b-boy we found on B-Burke l-lands, he w-was dr-drained of his bl-blood, was he no'?"

"Aye, he was. His wrist was cut, and he said they let it drop into bowls a'neath an altar in the monastery. 'Twas to be mixed with wine and partaken of by Odetta and her followers," stated Lucian.

Galen's eyes grew large and his face grew pale. He steadied himself on the stool and clenched his fists on top of the table. "I canna believe it," he said out loud angrily.

"Believe what?" asked Ruarc. "What are ye talking about Patrick? What is going on?"

"I ken," said Galen who rose to stand by Patrick. "I'll send to Rome, we must have help."

Lucian shouted, "Now just wait a minute. What on earth are ye talking about?"

Patrick chose his words carefully, not willing to cause unnecessary fear or speculation. *How to say this without sounding daft?*

"The B-Burke w-witch, she is a D-D-Dearg-due," said Patrick reluctantly. "A bl-blood s-sucker."

"Dearg-due!" exclaimed Ruarc. "'Tis no' possible! They do not exist, 'tis simply a myth," he whispered, astonished at the theory.

"Hold on," said Lucian. "Ye may be right Ruarc. She is probably not *the* Dearg-due we have heard tale about, but she is most definitely a drinker of blood. Patrick— do you really think she has lost her mind to the point she *thinks* she is *the* red blood sucker?"

Patrick nodded. "She has pr-proven ca-capable of b-banishing her own sister. Sh-she has t-taken male ch-children for th-the p-purpose of dr-draining and dr-drinking th-their blood. She no d-doubt be-believes she h-has an un-un-un-earthly p-power. Sh-she m-may b-believe sh-she is Dearg-due."

"She is possessed of the devil!" interjected Galen. "We must call to Rome, we must have help!"

Lucian cast a wary glance at first Galen and then Patrick. "I see no need to involve the Church in this matter; we are more than capable of addressing this matter ourselves."

"I'm no' so s-sure a-about th-that, Lucian," said Patrick. "I f-fear we m-may n-need all th-the help we c-can get. Galen, call to Rome," he directed.

SIX

O'Malley Territory—Strong House—Kyra's Chamber

Kyra O'Connell, daughter of Ruarc, threw up for the third time in less than an hour. After meeting Payton MacCahan, Patrick's brother, and his fifty fighting men, and taking them to the river; she returned to her chamber feeling ill. She was attempting to dress for the wedding ceremony and reception, as well as the Samhain celebration later that evening, when her stomach got the better of her.

If I retch one more time, I think I may faint. Surely this is from swallowing the river water when the men pushed me in. I can't imagine why I'd be ill otherwise.

"Kyra, I've brought ye some broth, dear," said her mother, Atilde. "Ye look a might peaked, lass. Are ye sure you didna eat something spoiled?"

"I'm sure. It must be that awful river water that's making me ill. I think I swallowed more than a mouthful," replied Kyra.

"I still can't understand why that mon thought to play ye thus. What an inappropriate display of brawn. He must be an eedjit to think he can just treat our people this way. Who does he think he is?" spurted Atilde under her breath.

"He thinks he is a Lord's son and brathair to the new O'Malley Laird," replied Kyra. "Besides, he's not as all bad as that. He mistook me for a young boy, that is all. No doubt he believed Patrick had planned some type of jest at his expense."

"Don't ye go setting yer sights on the likes of him, Kyra. He is no kind of mon'. As far as I ken, Patrick is the only honorable one amongst that group of MacCahan lads. I hear tell his brathair Parkin is worse. At least that's what I've been told," she said tipping her head to the side, gauging Kyra's response. "Ye know he has all manner of loose women after him, he does. And several bairns…born of different lasses …each of em, they say. He is not a mon for you either, my luv."

"Ye needn't worry on my account. I've no intention of getting involved with another man," replied Kyra before gripping her stomach and grimacing in pain.

"Kyra, it's most unfortunate that Aidan was killed; but you can't let the death of yer betrothed keep ye from moving on in life dear," said her mother, for what seemed like the hundredth time.

Kyra hadn't thought to ever marry after that fateful day. Aidan was out hunting and was dragging the fallen doe back to the clearing when what they presumed was a pack of hungry wolves attacked. Aidan did his best to fight them off from what they could tell, but there were obviously too many. He lay on the forest floor for possibly two days, bleeding from nearly twenty wounds and puncture marks. Vynae made his last days as comfortable as she could; but in the end, it was the fever that took him. He never regained consciousness; so they never knew for sure what had happened.

It was why her father made it clear that no one would hunt alone again. The dictate riled Darina to no end. She loved her afternoons with her falcon, Riann, and relished her alone time hunting. But that was not to be anymore.

Kyra had an idea what might be wrong with her, but she pushed the thought to the furthest corner of her mind. *I haven't the time to worry about that now.* She and Aidan were handfasted during the prior Samhain celebration; and were to be formally married by the priest on this very day. Instead, it was Darina having a ceremony. Kyra wouldn't let herself think about how unfair this was. She loved Aidan and the life they shared together. Why had the gods punished her so?

She was quite sure she would never love another as she loved Aidan. Growing up in the same village, they spent most of their time together, as often as possible. He was one of only a handful of young men to come to the clan when the soldiers came to O'Malley territory. His father, Murchadh, was Ruarc's right hand man, and was torn to bits at the news of his son's demise.

Kyra knew if what she thought was making her ill was the truth, that she would love the child. She would love the child with every breath she would take, because it was Aidan's. Her parents would love the child and Murchadh and his wife would love the child. There would be no shame. They were handfasted after all. A pregnancy would not prove a disaster, just a momentary set-back. She wouldn't be able to ride long as soon as her father learned, he would put a stop to that. No doubt, she would have to stop training with the others as well.

It was the idea of raising a child without a father that gave her the most pain. She was extremely fortunate to find a worthy husband. Most of the women of the O'Malley clan would never be as fortunate. They were destined to spend out their days alone or together on the Isle of Women.

Kyra knew that fate smiled on her once and the likelihood of it smiling on her again was small. She knew it. Her mother knew it, but wouldn't say it, and her father gave himself away every time he looked at her. Pity was not what she wanted from her family; and she had had enough of that. She was eager to move on with her life, what was left of it. Aidan's death was the very reason she asked to begin working as a messenger between clans. The traveling got her out of the territory and her mind on other things.

An unexpected child would change her life forever; and she wasn't sure she was ready for that yet. How would she break the news to her father or Murchadh? It would only open fresh wounds and heartache anew to her family.

"Kyra, ye should go see Vynae. I'm worried. Ye know that Darina was poisoned not long ago and almost did no' recover. Murchadh has questioned all of the servants and the kitchen staff; no one seems to have heard or seen anything. I think we should treat this as a threat. Yer father will agree with me, I'm sure," she said.

"I will agree with what?" asked Ruarc from the door.

Kyra bent over the chamberpot and emptied what was left in her stomach, before collapsing onto the bed. Her face was pale and a chilling sweat broke across her forehead. A sudden chill overtook her and she began to shake.

"By the gods, has she been poisoned?" asked Ruarc walking briskly to his daughter's bedside.

"Nay," Kyra replied, waiving him off. "I don't think I've been poisoned. I fear I may have swallowed some river water, and it does no' agree with me constitution."

"I will have that insolent bastard's head!" shouted Ruarc, throwing his hands up in the air. "I will speak to Patrick about this — I will. I canna believe he has treated a member of our clan like this. Atilde, ye should have seen the sight at the river. Nay — I take that back; I wouldna wish for you to see it; 'twas dishonorable, to say the least."

"What happened?" gasped Atilde.

Kyra waived her father off and struggled to speak. "Nothing that needs to be rehashed now. I am fine, they did no' hurt me."

"Kyra, you are not fine luv," exclaimed her mother, bringing the chamberpot to Kyra's side table. "Ye have been retching now for quite some time. All the color is gone from ye face and ye look gravely ill."

"I'm fetching Vynae and don't think to fight me on this, Kyra," Ruarc demanded as he strode out of her chamber and down the stairs.

Odetta Burke slammed her fist down on the table so hard, the rafters shook. Easal had never seen his new wife so angry in all his days, so much so that he feared for his own life. He had witnessed her fits of rage before, but nothing that equaled this. Even after she stabbed her own brother straight through the heart, he hadn't feared her, until now.

"I told you to make sure that no-account priest fulfilled my plan! That's all I asked of you!" she yelled across the room to Naelyn, her cleric. "How hard is it to simply do what you're told? You didn't watch him closely enough to make sure he actually drained all the blood from that boy."

"Me lady," interrupted Naelyn, "I am so very…"

"Save it!" Odetta shot back. "I've had enough of ye. Be gone. Get out of me sight; I've no use for ye any longer. Why don't ye go see to that useless sister of yers again, on the Isle of Women? See if you can bring me back some information, since you are no' capable of performing simple tasks here in ceremony."

Naelyn rose from her perch at the end of the table and turned to leave, head hanging low, aghast at the mood change in Odetta. Naelyn had been with Odetta for a long time. She was at the beginning, when Odetta overthrew the monastery. An ascetic student of the nuns, she managed to garner Odetta's attention when she willingly, and without question, followed her orders during the skirmish. For that, Odetta spared her life and gained a helper.

Easal whispered frantically into Odetta's ear and rose to grab Naelyn by the arm. "Nay, lassie, ye come with me," he spurted and steered them towards the front door.

"I just may have use of ye after all," Odetta screamed towards her as the door closed behind them.

"Where are ye taking me, Easal?" asked Naelyn nervously.

"To the dungeons where ye belong, and where ye should have been many years ago," he replied. "Ye've been nothing but trouble since the day I first laid my eyes on ye. Odetta has no need of ye any longer. Ye are only in the way. She has me now, and I am all she needs."

"The dungeons?" she cried in response. "What good can come of me imprisonment? I have been a loyal servant to Odetta. What reason is there to punish me?"

"What reason?" he retorted. "Ye are sloppy and untrustworthy, Naelyn," he said as he half-pushed, half-pulled her towards the rear entry of the monastery and towards the stairs leading down to the caverns below. "Ye heard Odetta, 'tis yer fault the boy was no' properly drained. Me thinks ye have a soft spot somewhere which prevents ye from fulfilling yer duties to Odetta. Ye haven't the stomach for what is to come. Ye are best served down here, watching over the new sacrifice. Mayhap when the Samhain service is over, Odetta may see fit to release ye," he chuckled. "But — I wouldn't count on it."

Easal opened the hidden door that led to the caverns beneath the monastery. The stench nearly choked her. It was as if a hundred corpses had been discarded and left to rot there. They navigated the stairs slowly and were met by Rufus on the way down.

"Well, well, what have we here?" he asked Easal. "Another prisoner?" he asked.

"Aye, Odetta has had her fill of Naelyn. She is to be chained to the walls with the others and see that she is situated next to the sacrifice. I need her to keep him calm."

"Aye, Easal. I'll see it done," he replied.

SEVEN

Burke Castle

*"*When will me mathair return?" asked eleven-year-old Orla Burke.

"I told you that Odetta will be late this eve, lass. She is preparing for the great service tonight. It is Samhain, ye ken?" responded Reni, her maidservant. "She will return just before the new day to dance with ye between the fires," she added. "Have ye finished yer mask, luv?"

Orla paced back and forth before the hearth in her chamber on the top floor of the Burke castle. "I am *so* bored!" she exclaimed. "I've made four different masks and I won't make another until I see me mam," she screeched, stomping her booted right foot for emphasis.

"Orla, I've been yer nurse since ye were a wee babe brought to me with the colic. I'll not be swayed by yer tantrums, one bit…not one bit…ye ken?" Reni returned to her sewing, determined not to let the spoiled child get to her.

Orla blew out a tortured breath and plopped down on the settee lounger beside the fire. "Tell me again, why I can no' attend the service at the monastery," she begged.

"Ye know verra well child that the service is not something for a lass of yer age. Ye've only a few more summers and ye will be right there, attending beside yer mam."

Orla knew Reni was right. She had begged Odetta and her Uncle Cynbel for years to attend the Samhain celebration. She was tired of feasting and playing with the children, she was ready to take part like an adult. She was after all, the daughter of the Lady of the Castle; and as such, she deserved all the benefit that such a position held.

"Tell me again about me fathair, Reni. I want to hear about me fathair."

"That is a matter to discuss with Odetta, lass. I haven't the whole of the story, and I won't go repeating things I don't know about."

Orla rolled her eyes at Reni and stomped towards the window. "'Tis getting dark outside Reni, the sun is descending. Can I *please* go find Shanleigh? We are to take our baskets and go through the village together to gather the offerings. She is waiting on me."

"Orla, child, if you don't sit down for a bit, I'll make sure ye have no part in Samhain this eve. Ye ken?" Reni retorted. *If ye hadn't been brought to Odetta by the gods themselves, I would surely have suffocated ye myself.* A wicked grin crossed Reni's face and she laughed out loud; unable to contain her amusement at the story Odetta had been telling for years about the sudden appearance of a babe for Odetta.

Not that she believed it. Not that anyone for that matter believed it. Odetta was not a woman one questioned. Cynbel didn't seem to mind the new addition to the castle, somehow hoping against hope that the babe would distract Odetta. Orla had done that. Odetta was so engaged with the new babe, it almost appeared she forgot about her sister running off with Cordal McTierney.

***

Mavis floated on her back for what seemed hours. She was frozen nearly to the bone and had lost all feeling in her toes and fingers. Unable to swim against the waves any longer, she turned over and lay atop the water. It was nearly completely dark, and save for the music and lights that streamed from the Island of Women, she would be lost.

She thought back to a time when her life had been simpler. She fell in love with the middle McTierney son, Cordal, and they were betrothed. Their fathers approved the union and gave their blessings. It should have been easy. At least that was how it was supposed to be until her older sister Odetta set her sights on Cordal.

Odetta made her case, to anyone who would listen. She was the eldest Burke daughter and should be married first. Her father didn't have the fortitude to fight the rebellious and troublesome Odetta. After their mother died, he washed his hands of her and basically ignored her. It wasn't until Raelyn, which was Mavis' given name, and Cordal, escaped together that the Burke Lord truly came to grips with the magnitude of Odetta's sickness.

Odetta sent a garrison of men to find them. It wasn't hard. They had returned to McTierney territory to live with his family. After many months, Easal brought Mavis and Cordal back to Odetta's monastery and held them captive in an upper chamber until the caverns were dug beneath the building and the dungeon was complete.

No one knew that Odetta succeeded in capturing them. Not even the Burke Lord — he died and Cynbel took power. Mavis gave birth to a baby girl in that wretched underground cave, and the child was taken from her. Unable to stomach the cries of Mavis for her child, Odetta sent Rufus to take her to the slave traders. As far as Odetta knew, Mavis was dead, and good riddance.

The sound of splashing nearby startled Mavis out of her daydream. She turned from her back and began to paddle upright in the water, frantic that she was not alone. Something swam by her to the right and circled in front. There was movement under her feet and then in front of her. Terror gripped her lungs and squeezed tightly. She closed her eyes, afraid to see what may be in front of her, behind her, and to the side of her.

Now there was more than one of them. A chorus of splashing resounded in her ears. They swarmed her and she was surrounded on all sides. Four. There had to be four of them, because they were everywhere, all at once, and all around her. *Why did this have to happen now?* She was almost to the island, it wasn't that far away. To be attacked by sharks after spending most of the day on the open sea seemed almost unfair.

She made the sign of the cross and said a silent prayer; asking God to spare her life, or at least minimize the pain. She had no desire to be dinner for a school of sharks. Reaching her hands out into the darkness, she felt around her for anything recognizable. She heard them moving in the water; dipping up and back down again and swimming around her feet and legs.

She saw the shoreline directly in front of her. *If I can just swim fast enough, mayhap they will leave me be.* They didn't seem to be as big as sharks, but she wasn't going to wait around to find out. In haste she tore off her wet shift which was holding her down, and dove just under the top of the water — hoping to confuse them. She resurfaced and gasped for air, swung her arms high above her head and made long kicking strides towards the lights on the shore.

She could just make out the outline of the small pier and could see the ferry boat was gone. "Just a few more minutes and I'll be safe," she whispered.

Then she heard it. A high-pitched chattering sound that echoed above the waves; it was quickly answered by more of the same. They were coming her way! In a manner of seconds she felt them underneath her, swimming beneath the waves in synchronicity to her strokes. A loud cry beside her alerted her that they were closer than she originally thought. Her side was cramping and she wasn't sure she could go on.

Mavis broke down. Unable to contain her fear and anger any longer, she stopped to tread water and began screaming at the top of her lungs. "Leave me be! Stop it! Go Away!"

The splashing subsided and everything grew silent. All that could be heard was the gentle cresting of the waves. She could almost touch bottom and knew she was very close to the shore. She turned to the left, then the right. Splashing and twisting, she flailed about searching for her stalkers.

When calm finally overtook her; Mavis continued her swim towards the island. It wasn't long before her feet touched bottom and she stood still for a moment, allowing her body and spirit a rest. *Had I dreamed that?*

The sounds of music and feasting grew louder and she could see the light of the bonfires coming from the center of the island. The realization that she was completely bare hit her all at once. *At least I'm alive.*

There it was again. That high-pitched chatter. It was getting closer. She could feel their presence and wondered if she could outrun them to the sand. *It couldn't be sharks, they wouldn't come this close to the land.*

Determined to survive, Mavis began paddling as fast as she could through the chest-deep water. Spreading her arms as wide as they would go to maintain balance, she sliced through the waves with all the strength she could muster. There was something at her back, getting closer, and another inching up beside her.

The water was to her waist now, which only made getting through it more difficult. The waves were too tall to jump and too big to run through. She half-swam, half-ran through the waves now; nearly out of breath and thoroughly exhausted. Her legs became tangled with something at her feet and she stumbled forward — pounding harshly into a crashing wave.

She picked herself back up and stumbled over something in front of her; catapulting under a crashing cascade of water. Her hands searched for anything she could catch hold of to stabilize herself. She faltered under the water and time stood still. As if in slow motion, she pictured herself getting up and moving forward but felt paralyzed with fear.

Her right hand grasped something she couldn't make out. *It feels like…wet dog! Oh dear God, what on earth is this?* Unable to maintain her bravery any longer, she began to wail and shake violently.

Instinctively, she stood upright and still, as her right hand clasped shut against the wet furry creature—as if challenging the thing to make the next move.

She refused to open her eyes. Overstimulated by the feel of the creature in her grasp, her senses wreaked havoc on her nerves. "*I will not be afraid, I will not be afraid,*" she repeated to herself and then again out loud.

They were all coming for her now. First, there was one to her left. Then there was another at her back, and then one more in front of her. She tightened her eyes once more, afraid to see what surrounded her. Before she knew what had happened, she was doused with a large amount of water, spat right into her face by one of them. The chattering began again and then more splashing.

She let go of the creature with her right hand and felt the water to her left. Just a few feet beside her was another with the same type fur. *Like a wet dog. Thick course hair and a long backbone. I have to see this before I die.*

Hesitantly, she cracked her eyes open, as if them not knowing if she was looking would somehow save her. She peered straight into the biggest set of deep-brown eyes she had ever seen, and the longest whiskers imaginable. It was looking at her as if *she* was daft. It began to chatter again and the others joined in.

Seals! They are seals!

There surrounding her, were four gray seals; they had no doubt been toying with her for hours. She breathed a long-held sigh of relief and relaxed her stance. The one to her right came up beside her and ran its head under her hand as if asking to be stroked. The others started splashing and chattering again and made for the shoreline. She grabbed ahold of the one to her right, and they swam together for a brief moment before she grasped it about the shoulders and let it guide her swiftly to the shore.

EIGHT

O'Malley High Castle — Master's Banqueting Hall

Samhain Eve

Darina wiped the remaining tears from her eyes and straightened the hairpin that held the small, front section of her flowing red mane intact atop her head; as if it were a crown. Thankful for the few words she shared with her mother, she nodded to her Uncle Ruarc to make ready for the service.

Galen and Lucian stood looking forward into the banquet room from the raised dais at the south end of the chamber; while Patrick and his brother Payton waited just inside, mere feet from the door. A harpist strung a solemn and sacred sounding tune, and the servants exited the room only moments prior. Atilde and Minea stood beside Darina's sisters and waited for her to make her entrance.

"Are ye ready, lass?" asked her Uncle Ruarc. "Ye certainly are a picture. Ye are as lovely as yer mam, dear," he added.

With shaking hands, she reached for her Uncle's arm. "I think I am," she replied.

"There's no need to be scared, Darina," interjected her Aunt Atilde from behind her, having left her perch beside the sisters. "All will be well, Darina. Patrick is a fine mon," she added, fluffing her dress and straightening her plaid.

"Where is Kyra?" shot Darina. "I don't see Kyra, where is she?" she asked looking around the hall frantically. "Why isn't Kyra here?" she insisted, her face becoming white with anxiety. She feared Kyra might be upset; seeing how that she was getting married on the day Kyra was to have wed Aiden.

"Kyra became ill, Darina. She is with Vynae at the sick-house. But she is fine, nothing to worry about. Vynae will have her back and ready to attend the reception soon. Ye'll see," added Ruarc.

"We've only just a few more minutes and the service will start," added her Aunt. "Are ye sure ye are alright child? Ye look ill as well. Have ye eaten anything today?"

Darina let out a breath and deliberately relaxed her shoulders and straightened her backbone. She began counting seconds off in her head to dissuade her anxiety, and pinched her cheeks out of habit to add some color. "I'm fine. I will be fine…that is…I'm okay. We can begin whenever ye are ready, Ruarc."

Darina — I am here. Yer family is here and all yer friends are here as well. Ye have the support of yer sisters and Uncle; there is no need to worry. All is well. I will be here — right here. Always.

It wasn't the first time that Patrick trespassed her mind to speak with her; but it was the first time that it made her feel protected instead of confused.

I know yer nervous lass, but we are in this together. I won't let any harm come to ye. From this day forward, ye are mine to protect and cherish. I take care of what is mine, Darina. Trust that.

"Darina, are you alright?" asked her Uncle, staring at her strangely. "Ye act as if ye've seen a ghost."

"That I have," she replied. "But that story is for another day," she replied. "Atilde, I am ready to go," she announced, and clasped her hand about her Uncle's arm, steadying her stance in the process.

Just breathe. Just breathe. In. Out. In. Out. I can do this, she said to herself. *I can do this.*

Just two steps into the banqueting hall and she felt a blanket of calm overtake her. As if she were being hugged by her da; her nerves were no longer on fire and she was completely stable on her feet. Warmth rose in her face, lighting it with color once more, and she could feel her pulse slowing and her body relaxing.

As if she was just shocked, a jolt of electricity shot from the tip of her right hand and up her arm towards her heart.

Patrick.

"Aye. I am h-here, Darina," he whispered in her ear as he took her hand from Ruarc and guided them both towards the dais. "Ye look l-l-lovely," he added.

Look at me, lass.

Unaware that she hadn't raised her face once since stepping into the room, Darina perked her head up and surveyed her surroundings. It was beautifully decorated; flowers and candles and fine food and drink as far as she could see. It was the distinct smell of spikenard oil that caught her attention.

Patrick.

His left hand drew circles in her palm as she searched the room. Catching the eye of everyone in the hall, she turned to look up at her betrothed. Her heart skipped a beat and she blushed.

He really is a fine-looking mon.

Patrick blushed this time.

He hadn't been sure he would ever marry, let alone win the heart of a woman. When he realized he could read her thoughts and she could hear him when he spoke to her with his mind, it brought feelings to the surface he wasn't prepared to deal with. Airard told him that he was not destined to be alone, but that one day, he would find a woman who would respond to him as no one else could. *Could Darina be that woman?*

The fact that she heard him when he spoke both frightened and excited him. Never one to be forward with a lass, he pushed himself to see just how far their communication would take them. When she replied to his utterings, he was shocked.

Her acknowledgment of his telepathy sent him over the edge. Even her anger at his "trespass", as she called it, overjoyed him. Perhaps his life wasn't destined to be dull and uneventful after all. Perhaps this feisty young woman was just what he needed: a friend, a confidante, a partner in life. He was never able to read thoughts or speak telepathically before with anyone he wasn't physically touching at the time.

Perhaps their ability to communicate in such a way without even touching, was a blessing from the gods and maybe, just maybe, he would find joy with another—like himself. He knew Darina's realization that she could hear him and respond frightened her. But he would earn her trust, he just would.

Darina drank it all in. Every inch of him; warm hands, tall muscular frame, deep green eyes, and long wavy chestnut hair that fell below his shoulders. Beautiful was not the right word. Or was it? Just looking into his eyes sent a fire racing through her blood to the point she thought she would combust.

Her pulse quickened and a familiar ache burned in her stomach. Her legs shook and she thought she might collapse. He smelled absolutely *good enough to eat*. The thought made her giggle out loud and Patrick tightened his grip on her right hand as she covered her mouth with the other.

He smiled at her and placed his arm around her back to steady her gait. He chuckled and whispered to her, "A fine m-mess w-we have h-here is it no'?"

"Aye, fine indeed," she responded, smiling brightly. "A fine mess indeed."

***

Mavis awoke with a start. Unable to catch her breath, she sat straight up from her reclined position on a straw mat in the corner of an unfamiliar cottage. She looked around for something she recognized, but found nothing. The smell of burning peat overtook her nose and she began to cough.

"Ye feeling any better there, lassie?" said a female voice.

Mavis searched the room but saw no one.

"I say, are ye feeling any better?" it repeated.

Mavis quickly grasped the linens about her and rubbed her eyes. "Who's there?" she asked.

"'Tis only me," came the reply.

"Where are ye? Who are ye?" pleaded Mavis. Having noticed she was completely bare, she grabbed the linens about her even tighter and tucked her feet beneath her legs in protection of her modesty.

"No reason to do that now. We brung ye up here. I ken we have seen it all," chuckled the voice, now speaking in unison with the voices of others.

Frightened, Mavis rose from her place on the straw mat and stood upright in the round cottage. The ceiling was barely tall enough for her as the thatched roof grabbed at the top of her hair. Looking around, she took in her shelter. There was a peat moss fire burning in the center of the room. A small table towards the other side of the cottage and a pile of what looked to be pelts stacked beside it. Herbs and flowers of all kinds were hanging from the ceiling and there were four stools interspersed about the abode.

The pile of pelts moved and Mavis froze in her tracks. She stooped down to get a better look. If the peat moss fire hadn't been burning she may have been able to see more clearly. She heard a muffled groan and dropped down to all fours this time, intent on finding the source.

"We're over here love," it said. She crawled on all fours towards the sound. As she got closer to the pile of pelts, she became frightened and stopped in her tracks.

"Are ye under that pile?" she asked hesitantly and moved forward to inspect the pelts.

"We will no' harm ye, lass. We brought ye here," they said in unison.

"Who are ye?" Mavis begged.

"Just ye sit down right there and we will show ye," they said, their voices a melody of angels. "We will show ye," they repeated.

Mavis sat back on her feet and waited. Praying that she wasn't losing her mind, she pinched her leg to make sure she wasn't dreaming, and after confirming the fact that she was indeed awake, she bade them to show themselves.

The peat fire rose abruptly and the cottage lit up from the flames. The pile of pelts jostled and moved and from beneath it, a small woman crawled out. The woman moved forward, slowly, on all fours towards Mavis. Horror gripped her heart, and Mavis moved back and away from the crawling woman as fast as she could until she was butt up against the cottage wall, shaking violently.

"Do no' be afraid," the crawling woman said. She rose from the ground and stood before Mavis, completely naked and covered in some type of gooey substance that stank like day-old fish. She walked towards a pot near the table and began to wash herself.

"Who are ye?" demanded Mavis nervously.

"Britta," she said matter-of-factly, still washing herself.

"And I am Incha."

In her peripheral vision, Mavis saw the pile of pelts move across the floor, towards her. Dizzy from what was transpiring, Mavis steadied herself on the ground around her and placed both hands in front of her on the floor, to break an impending fall.

She ventured a look to her right and was astonished to see a seal waddling towards her.

"I said, I am Incha," it repeated.

Mavis rubbed her eyes again, unable to believe what she was seeing. *A talking seal? I have had too much of the spirits.*

"We've given ye no spirits," another voice said. Joining the seal in front of her was another seal.

"I am Liath," it said.

Britta cleaned herself and donned a shift and over-dress and walked towards Mavis, who was still crouching on the floor in front of Liath and Incha.

"Here ye go," she said. "Put this on, ye will feel much better clothed I am sure."

Mavis reached for the shift and scooted as far back against the cottage wall as she could get. A commotion at the door diverted her attention and another woman stepped into the cottage. When Mavis turned back towards the seals, they were gone. In their place, stood two women covered head to toe in the same goo that Britta washed from her body. Seal pelts lay at their feet.

"By the stars!" exclaimed Mavis, covering her mouth and shaking.

"Hello," said the fourth woman who just entered the cottage. "I am Naeyd," she said. "What is yer name?" she asked as she handed a goblet of elderberry wine to Mavis.

"I am Mavis. Are ye the *seals* that were swimming with me on the shore?" she asked.

"Aye, we are," they said in unison.

"Are ye *selkies*?" asked Mavis in disbelief at what she just said.

"Aye, we are sometimes called selkies," responded Incha, nodding. "Are ye hungry, lass?"

Mavis nodded but didn't make a sound. She knew the tales of the selkies, or the seal women, she had heard them all her life. Never once did she ever imagine the stories to be true. "Silly folklore," her brother Cynbel said. "Just a legend…" But here she was, in a cottage shared by four seal women — and they had saved her life most probably.

That was the only explanation. That had to be it. The only reason she survived her plunge into the sea. They were with her all along, the whole way. They watched out for her and prodded her on when she grew tired. They guided her to shore and brought her to their home on the Island of Women.

The island of women! Are they all selkies?

65

"Mavis, won't ye come sit down a bit and eat?" asked Britta. "Ye must be hungry and exhausted. Tell us what happened. Why were you in the sea without a boat on such a day as this? Ye ken it is Samhain, don't ye?"

"Samhain!" shouted Mavis. "The wedding, Braeden, Patrick! I must get back to the castle. Now!" she screamed.

"Hold on," said Naeyd. "Ye won't be getting anywhere tonight. The ferry is docked and the soldier's won't allow passage until morn."

"Until well after midnight," interjected Britta.

"But I must!" replied Mavis. "A boy's life depends on it," she cried.

"Well, then," added Incha. "I should call for Gemma. She'll know what to do."

NINE

MacCahan Castle — Northern Ireland

Parkin MacCahan, younger brother to Patrick and middle son of Breacan MacCahan, hovered over the lifeless body of Isadore McDougal and wept. Wild tears that left him hollow and spent, poured down his sun-kissed cheeks in crashing waves of passion. In all his twenty-three summers, his father never once witnessed such a display of passion from his impertinent middle son.

"Mayhap he is truly saddened?" whispered Airard into Breacan's ear, disbelievingly.

"I doubt that very seriously," retorted Breacan and walked towards the door to the chamber. "Parkin, meet me in me chambers before the noon meal. There is much to discuss."

Parkin looked up from his position at Isadore's bedside and nodded his acknowledgment, wiping away tears with the back of his hand and turning even more theatrical, evidently for his father's sake.

"I wonder when that boy will ever grow up," snorted Breacan angrily.

"What do you mean, me Lord?" asked Airard. "He appears to be mightily affected by Isadore's demise. Does that no' show promise?"

"Dinna let him fool ye, old mon," snorted Breacan. "He is just worried now that he has a motherless babe to deal with. Isadore had no family and someone must care for Winnie since her mam has passed."

"Aye—Winnie. I hadn't thought of that. When Isadore came down with the fever, I didn't think what would become of the toddler should she no' make it through," replied Airard. "'Tis a most unfortunate situation, most unfortunate indeed. Where is Winnie now?" he asked.

"She's with her elder brathair, Macklin. They are waiting in me chambers. How can I tell a boy of only fourteen summers that his mam has passed and he and his young seesta have no one to care for them?"

Airard shook his head and continued forward down the path from the sick-house to the castle, walking beside his oldest friend and Laird of the MacCahan clan.

The smell of roast venison met them from behind the kitchens, and a school of laundry ladies passed them to the right, bustling about with buckets of splashing water and baskets of soiled linens. It was midday at the keep and everyone was going about their business.

Life was almost back to normal; considering that the floods subsided a few weeks before and the ground was nearly completely dry since the storms let up. Nearly eight new cottages were erected and the pier was complete. It hadn't taken as long as they imagined it would, and with the help of some of the O'Malley men, they finished construction on the second small ship just the day before.

Parkin was leaving for O'Malley port in a few days, and would return with goods and wares to sell in the shops and market area being built near the shore. Business with the O'Malley's would be good, and their shipping enterprise would introduce them to new and exciting merchandises and people from around the world.

Breacan was pleased. He was proud of his son Patrick, who was by now the Lord of O'Malley territory and husband to Dallin's eldest daughter, Darina. Payton, his youngest, was sent with fifty fighting men to establish a strong militia in the region and to protect his brother's new position.

It was Parkin that gave him the most grief. He would never make a reasonable marriage match with Parkin. He knew it, Parkin knew it and everyone else knew it as well. The time for Parkin to grow up had come and gone. The thought of sending Parkin to his mother's family in Scotland crossed Breacan's mind once too often, and today…it was back…and it was stuck there.

Breacan entered his chambers with his head held low and the look of defeat clearly written on his face. Airard followed him with a trencher of venison and two mugs of ale which he set upon the side table in Breacan's solar.

"My Lord, Laird MacCahan, have ye any news of me mathair?" asked Macklin sheepishly, holding his sleeping baby sister in his arms and rocking her back and forth in front of the hearth.

"Come here son," replied Breacan. "Lay yer seesta down there on the mat, we have much to discuss."

***

Odetta gasped, and struggled against the weight which held her head down, and the hands which clenched tightly around her neck cutting off her airway. Terror stopped her heart and sucked the air from her lungs. She knew better than to look up into the cold gray eyes of her captor, but she couldn't help herself.

Nearly three weeks since she last encountered the Visitor and she still couldn't get the stench of sulfur and rotten wood out of her head. She wanted to sit up, to grab something—anything to distract the Visitor, but found nothing. Only when she came fully to the realization that she was at his mercy and she was able to let go with her mind, to submit, did he relent.

Sleep eluded her constantly. Perhaps it was eluding her, perhaps she was unwilling to succumb. That was more like it. Since that first time, as a small child, when the Visitor found her by the lake; she remained in fear for her life and in solitude—unwilling to draw anyone else into her horror.

She even spared her own brother, by taking his very life. Not willing to let the Visitor have him, she did the only thing she could think of. Cynbel would not be his host, not while she still drew breath. Even when she sent her sister away, she was being merciful. The Visitor had plans for her as well and Odetta wouldn't let that happen, not if she had anything to do with it.

The bleak, echoing, melancholic brogue of the Visitor split her head in two. Had she the power, she would have taken her own life, years ago. *Subservient. Controlled. Beneath.* These were the words her unholy Visitor used.

Immortal. That's the one that gave her the greatest sorrow. *Immortal and helpless.* Forever controlled by the Visitor and his dark forces. Cursed to do his bidding, whatever his evil mind could conceive. It was better they all thought her insane than know the truth.

"Rise," he commanded, after letting go of his grasp of her neck and rising from the bed.

She gasped for air when his heavy arms left their place on her head. She only dozed off for a mere moment; and there he was as usual. Tears of rage filled her eyes, and she struggled to see.

Rising from the bed, she caught the stench and knew he was near. Fear overtook her and she began to shake. It was soon replaced with rage and an unholy anger took its place.

"Why are ye here?" she shouted into the blackness. "What do ye want?"

"Ye know what I want. Ye've yet to give it to me. Must I do everything?" he echoed back.

The Visitor blew out a short breath, and the room filled with light as two candle stands in the far corners of the cavernous room lit of their own accord. Odetta stood panic-stricken in the middle of the small chamber, face to face with her evil Lord.

The top of her head barely reached his chest. His long stone-like arms hung nearly to the ground and he waived his razor-sharp, black fingernails in front of her face; before scratching a line down the cavern wall…creating some sort of visual depiction of an ancient battle or ceremonial rite …she wasn't sure.

"Me Lord," she ventured hesitantly.

70

"Silence," returned the Visitor. "I am here to collect what is mine. Have you located the nexus?" he asked, spewing rancid steam from his nostrils.

"Not yet, but I am close," she replied.

"Have ye at least acquired or traversed the territory which surrounds the ruins?" he shouted angrily.

"Eaton. Me Lord," she replied.

With one flick of his giant wrist, the Visitor slashed a line from Odetta's right shoulder, across her chest, down over her ribcage and rested his razor-sharp nails in her left side—fully impaling his hand within her flesh. Her eyes met his and locked on in defiance. Blood trickled from her wounded side and pooled about her ankles. She grew faint and steadied herself so as not to pass out.

"Ye grow pale, me puppet," he bellowed. "It's a good thing I've made ye immortal. Otherwise all this time I've wasted on ye would be in vain." Slowly and painfully, he removed his claws from her body, one at a time.

When the last of his razor-sharp nails were removed, Odetta doubled over in agony and fell to her knees. "Me Lord, tell me what ye desire of me—I am yer most willing servant," she begged through clenched teeth.

"Ye know I need the nexus. Ye've had years to locate the nexus among the ruins. I am growing impatient with ye. Perhaps it is time I take a new tribute," he said, as he drew circular shapes down the length of her arm with one of his nails, drawing blood all along the way.

"No!" she screamed. "Please, I can do this, just give me more time. Please don't take anyone. I am so very close to having access to the ruins; I'm sure I can find yer nexus."

"Ye've had plenty of time, witch," said the Visitor. "Why can ye not simply go to the ruins now and return with the nexus?" he asked, as he grabbed her around the neck and lifted her off the floor in front of him; leaving her legs dangling just feet from the stony ground.

Cold, gray, evil eyes burned behind copper-colored lids. He muttered something under his breath; something otherworldly, something so sinister she didn't need to understand the words to catch his meaning.

"I will have the nexus, and I *will* leave this place!" he roared, as the stones shook and the earth quaked at the force of his command. He dropped her to the ground, leaving her a quivering mess of blood and pure exhaustion.

"Ye need more blood," he said matter-of-factly. "Tend to yerself, and find my nexus. I will be back."

A shearing pain gripped her heart and electric-like currents surged through her body. She began to vomit, and a seizure overtook her to the point she was forced to lay flat out on the cold, stone floor writhing in agony. She felt her flesh heating up like it was on fire, and the droplets of blood on her skin began to boil. Her flesh seared back together where it was torn, leaving tattoo-like scars in its wake.

A reminder of his power over me, she thought to herself. *But -not for long.*

CHAPTEN TEN

O'Malley Territory — Sick-House

"Please Vynae, I need to keep this just between us for now," Kyra said to the healer. "I need time to prepare meself before I inform my parents, and Murchadh."

"What manner of secret are ye hiding from us now, dear cousin?" interjected Darina's sister, Dervilla, from the doorway to the sick-house. Smiling as usual, she interrupted her cousin's train of thought and caught Vynae off guard.

"Dervilla, dear, how are ye?" asked the aged healer, wringing her hands and wiping Kyra's forehead with a cool linen.

"I am fine, Vynae. What is this secret Kyra wishes to hide from her parents?" she added as she walked across the table area towards the bench where Kyra reclined. "'Tis no' a big one I hope?"

"Never mind now, Dervilla. What do ye need?" Vynae shot back. aggravation in her voice.

"I'm here for the potion," she responded in a whisper.

Vynae shook her head indicating she wasn't clear what Dervilla was after; and continued wiping Kyra's forehead. "Here lass, drink the last of this, it should help."

"The elixir, ye ken? The potion, for Darina to drink?" Dervilla pressed. "She needs the drink, Vynae. So…ye know…she will no' end up with…"

"Aye, I know what ye are after!" said Vynae. "Give me just one second, I'll be back in a jif," she added as she gathered a basket and walked down the corridor and in to one of the chambers.

"Kyra, are ye feeling poorly?" asked Dervilla, now concerned after seeing the pallor of Kyra's face. She kicked at the chamberpot at her feet and knew she most likely had been throwing up all afternoon. Dervilla sat down on the bench beside Kyra and took her hand in her own, wiping Kyra's sweat-drenched brow with the sleeve of her tunic.

"I ken I have a stomach ache, that is all," Kyra said and lowered herself back down to the pillow on the bench. When she crawled into the fetal position, Dervilla grew wary.

"Kyra, what troubles ye? What can I do?" Dervilla asked.

"Ye can start with keeping yer mouth shut," growled Kyra between dry heaves towards the pot on the floor in front of her. Now on all fours, Kyra looked up at Dervilla with a stern warning glance.

"Kyra, eat ye some of that bread on the table there," yelled Vynae from down the hall. "It should soak up the worst of the vapors."

"What's going on?" whispered Dervilla. "Have ye been poisoned?" she gasped and clasped her hand over her mouth.

"Dervilla, ye can no' tell anyone about this, ye ken?" demanded Kyra. Dervilla nodded and placed a hand on Kyra's back.

"Dervilla, I am with child."

***

"Parkin, come in here son," called Breacan MacCahan from his solar. "We have much to discuss and Macklin here has some things he wishes to say."

Airard pulled a stool from the corner and motioned for Parkin to sit beside Macklin and himself. they being positioned on the bench in front of the MacCahan clan leader's large, table desk. Light snoring rose from the small straw mat where Winnie slept under the window, a purring kitten curled up near her right shoulder.

"Parkin, I have informed Macklin that his mathair has expired," said the elder MacCahan. Macklin let loose with another flow of sorrowful tears and continued to pull at the hole in the top of his truis. Parkin feigned sympathy, and laid a hand on the boy's shoulder and squeezed as if to comfort him. Macklin rebuffed his gesture and edged further down the bench to avoid him.

"Parkin, Winnie is yer daughter, and ye've admitted as much. She is nearly two summers old, and has no other family, save for Macklin," continued Breacan. "When Macklin's da passed, ye wasted no time making the acquaintance of Isadore…"

"And filling her belly with yer seed," snorted Macklin. "And ye hadn't the decency to make an honest woman of me mam," he added, glaring at Parkin with disdain. "She was good to ye, she was…and ye scorned her …and put her out…and refused her hand, and…"

Airard interrupted this time, "Hold on now, me boy, let's no' dishonor yer mam thus. She has just passed. We have to plan a future for ye sister, ye ken? We can no' do that if we are bickering about the past."

"Macklin, ye are but a lad still and yer not ready to, nor are ye able, to care for a babe like Winnie," said Breacan. "No' by yerself anyway. And ye haven't any family local, now do ye?"

Macklin shook his head back and forth indicating he was, in fact, alone in the world after the death of his mother.

75

"Parkin, pray tell what ye plan to do about this…situation?" Breacan asked his middle son.

Parkin shot up off of the stool and folded his arms across his chest in defiance. "What am I going to do about this? What does that mean?"

"It means ye have a child with no one to raise her now Parkin, that's what that means. And it means, I mean to hear what ye intend to do about caring for her."

"Well, I've no good idea what is to become of her, she has no mammy," replied Parkin, matter-of-factly, with a dumbfounded look on his face that dared his father to push him further.

"Parkin, ye've left me no other choice here son."

"What is that supposed to mean?" Parkin responded.

"I'll take care of me seesta," spat Macklin. "Parkin is no kind of mon and has no honor about him. He is no' capable of caring for himself, let alone another person. Will ye no' honor me mam's rents on her cottage and land?" asked Macklin to the Laird earnestly.

"Of course I will honor the rents; ye needn't worry about that Macklin. But Macklin, ye can no' care for a babe and work for the rents too, ye need someone to help ye raise Winnie. Ye need to continue yer schooling as well, son."

"I can raise Winnie just fine. Tara watched Winnie while me mam worked; she will do it for me too, I'm sure. And Parkin can pay her wages for keeping Winnie."

"I will no'!" shouted Parkin. "I will no' pay to have some servant girl set with Winnie while ye pretend to work, Macklin. Ye are just a boy!"

"Well then, Parkin. What is yer plan?" asked his father.

"I've an idea. I think we should send Winnie to Skye. She can be there with mam's family, and they will raise her up right," said Parkin. "I can send coin for her keep and make sure she is educated."

"Ye will not send me seesta to Skye! She is my seesta and I will have yer useless head before ye send her off like some unwanted piece of livestock. She stays with me," commanded Macklin, now standing face to face with Parkin, challenging him to make a move.

Breacan let out a long-held breath and took a drink from his ale. "I was afraid it might come to this," he said out loud to no one in particular.

Airard stood and went to the now waking Winnie. He pulled her into his arms, picked up her kitten and excused himself from the chamber, knowing his presence would only distract Laird MacCahan.

"Ye've done it now," Parkin quipped to Macklin under his breath.

Macklin turned and addressed the Laird. "Me Lord, Winnie is the only living relative I have. Please do not think to separate us. I will work day and night to see her raised and to pay yer rents and to take care of whatever debts me mam may have left, I swear I will."

Breacan shook his head in despair and trepidation. "Macklin, ye are a noble lad. I would be proud if I were yer da. I hate to do this to ye, I truly do. But Parkin has left me no other choice."

"Ye see, Macklin, I was right all…" began Parkin. Until his Father placed a heavy hand on his shoulder and bade him to sit down.

"Parkin, I have coddled ye all yer life. Mayhap it is time ye act like an honorable mon. I want no discussion from ye after I make my decision. There will be no questions, there will be no negotiating, and there will be nothing but doing what ye are told. Ye ken?" he asked. "If ye don't like me dictate, ye are welcome to join yer mam's people on the Island of Skye, ye ken?"

Parkin nodded.

"Parkin, ye are to leave for yer brathair's territory on the morrow. Ye are taking the first small vessel ye completed. Ye will be taking goods back with ye, two ship hands and ye will be taking Winnie *and* Macklin with ye."

Parkin gasped and stood up, ready to rebut his father's dictate before he thought better of it. Breacan raised a warning hand to his son and motioned for him to sit back down.

"Parkin, Winnie is yer daughter, yer own flesh and blood. It's time ye became a worthy father to her. Macklin is yer son as well; mayhap not by blood, but yers anyway, on account of Winnie. Ye owe it to him to provide a home for them. Macklin will make a good stevedore and he will learn a trade on account of yer new enterprise. Train him well."

"I canna raise a child on me own, da. I'm no' married."

"Parkin, ye should have thought of that before. Mayhap ye can fix that, if ye think any lass will have ye now."

"Da, I can't take care of them if I am away and sailing between ports all the time," Parkin said, waiving his hand towards Macklin.

"Parkin, 'tis time ye figured out a plan and made it work. Ye can hire a nurse in O'Malley lands just like ye can here. Find ye a good nanny for Winnie for when ye are away. Macklin will travel with ye… always…between ports. And, if I were ye, I'd be nice to me brathair. He can help ye find a cottage of yer own, and make yer acquaintance with some nice lasses, I hope."

Parkin cried real tears this time, for the first time in a long time.

"And Parkin, don't ye be thinking ye can treat my new grandson like chattel. Ye will be paying him a fair wage for his labors. And, I will be hearing from him every time he comes to port." Breacan smiled and wrapped his arm around Macklin's shoulder and hugged him. "A fine mon ye will make Macklin, a fine mon indeed."

ELEVEN

O'Malley High Castle — Wedding Ceremony

Darina entered the master's banqueting hall on the arm of her betrothed, keenly aware that all eyes were on them. They breathed deeply in unison, as if they had planned it that way from the beginning. The harpist played a somber melody and the wedding guests bowed and nodded as they passed between them on their way to the dais.

"Galen?" asked Darina to Patrick, realizing Lucian stood with Galen at the platform, and not alone as she presumed he would.

Aye, he whispered back to her with his mind. *I knew ye would prefer a wedding in the chapel, but since the priest is missing, I asked Lucian to have Galen assist him. They will both preside over the ceremony, if that is to yer liking, me lady?*

"I like that verra much," she said, as she followed his lead to stand beside him on the platform before Lucian and Galen. The harpist tamped down her playing until only a soft strumming was heard; and Lucian and Galen lit a candelabra spaced between them on the dais.

Lucian raised his robed arms high above his head and bade the wedding guests gather near to hear. "What a fine evening it is to join these two together in the sacred rite of marriage." He continued,

"We beseech the spirits of the north, the south, the east and the west, to breathe over our gathering a breath of anointing, and to witness the covenant these two make with each other. We bid the spirits bind and seal the vows they take in duty to this clan, their clan, our clan."

The guests replied with a hallowed, "Aye," in response, and formed a line to the right of Patrick. Then, one at a time, they stepped forward onto the dais and lay bouquets of lavender-colored minscoth in a spherical pattern around the two, until a perfect circle was formed about them, with only Patrick and Darina inside.

Lucian continued,

> "We pray to the powers of the earth, the sea and the sky—our beacons of life. The earth, which feeds us and shelters us—may it continue to bring bountiful harvest upon not just these two, but also to our lands and all of O'Malley territory. The sea, which washes us new every morning and upon whom the sun rises and descends; may every mortal blessing ride upon yer waves until they have made their home, here with us. The sky, whose sun lights our way during the day and whose stars brighten our path at night—continue to reign over us and guide us with yer all-knowing presence. As our ancestors honor the three beacons of life; so we shall do the same."

Galen passed two goblets of elderberry wine to Patrick and took Lucian's place at the altar.

"Patrick and Darina; may these two goblets of wine represent each of yer souls; full, fresh and alive." He gestured for Patrick to mix them and continued as Patrick poured part of his into her goblet and then poured part of hers into his goblet. Galen continued,

"May yer marriage be filled with every miracle and blessing that Father God will endow to ye. May yer light be like the wine ye held— perfect alone, but complete when together. These guests are witnesses to the sacred oath ye two make to one another and to yer people. Drink now, and taste that the union is good," he said as he raised his goblet in a toast, as did the other guests in the hall.

80

Patrick and Darina drank their fill from the goblets and turned to stand facing one another, hands clasped together, their eyes meeting.

"Let us pray," Galen instructed and clasped his hand with Lucian's. All the guests in the hall formed a circle around the ring of lavender-colored minscoth that set the two apart from the rest of the hall.

"We c-call upon the sp-spirits of l-love, hum-hum-humility and hon-honor to guide our hear-hearts to do wh-what is ri-right in all th-things."

Darina's heart leapt in her chest. *Patrick is praying?*

Aye luv, he responded with his mind, as he clasped her hand tighter, reassuring her of his sincerity before he raised his right hand to the sky in petition.

"We invoke the bl-blessings of the sp-spirits of the north, the south, the east and the w-we-west; and the beacons of our l-liv-lives—the earth, the sea and the sk-sky—and we c-ca-call upon the Chr-Christ-Christian G-God to consecr-crate our union f-for the s-service of all that is n-no-noble and j-just. May our j-joining br-bring with it, p-peace to our l-land, pr-prosperity to our p-people and passion for our p-pur-purpose."

"So be it," said Galen. "So be it," replied the guests. When every head was once again raised and turned towards the couple on the dais, Lucian spoke again.

"Darina O'Malley, be it yer wish to join with Patrick MacCahan this day? To be his wife, companion and champion all the days of yer life? Do ye heretofore take him to wed and pledge to him yer heart, yer hand and yer spirit in the name of the god that resides with ye?"

"It is me wish," Darina said with a bright smile and happy tears pooling in her eyes.

Galen spoke, "Patrick MacCahan, is it yer wish to join with Darina O'Malley this day? To be her husband, companion and champion all the days of yer life? Do ye heretofore take her to wed and pledge to her yer heart, yer hand and yer spirit in the name of the god that resides with ye? And do ye further, Patrick, take the name of O'Malley as yer own, and pledge to carry the noble line of the O'Malley clan for generations to come?"

"It. Is. My. Wish," he stated slowly, loudly, and deliberately with pride on his face. Darina turned and removed the MacCahan tartan from his shoulder, replaced it with her own O'Malley plaid, and secured it with the brooch her father left her.

Patrick let his left hand cup her chin and cheek and leaned down to kiss his new bride. Not an innocent brotherly kiss; that just wouldn't do. He meant to claim her, in front of the gods and every guest in the room. She was his and she would know it, and they would too.

***

"Where are ye taking me?" Braeden demanded of the burly man carrying him over his shoulders like a bag of wool. "I demand ye take me to yer leader at once!" he shouted, now banging the man's backside as fiercely as he could with his childlike fists.

"Culver, I swear mon, lest ye get a grip o' that boy he will fall, and Odetta won't like that ye've marred her sacrifice—she won't," said another man Braeden presumed was not far from them. But he couldn't be sure because they had covered his face with some type of sack so he couldn't see.

"Hush child," the first man demanded, as he straightened Braeden's position over his shoulder after applying a swift pat on his bottom meant to threaten him.

Braeden giggled under his breath. *This will be all too easy,* he said to himself, remembering the training in self-defense that both Airard and Patrick insisted upon. *Just give me time,* he thought.

After leaving the boat on the shore, the men forced Braeden to walk beside them, head covered and holding a rope for balance for what seemed hours. Then it began to storm and they agreed, reluctantly at first, to allow him to remove the cover; permitting him to count off steps and make notations in his mind as to where they were going and where they came from. Little did they know that his observations began hours before when they first left the safety of the watercraft.

Braeden was no fool. He was drilled his entire life about what to do if he were to be captured, kidnapped, or come upon a hazardous situation. For a boy his age, he was well-educated in hand-to-hand combat, and was even able to wield a small sword without much problem—provided it was light weight, of course.

Patrick and Parkin took him hunting and fishing regularly; and sleeping out under the stars was a favorite activity for which Braeden looked forward with much anticipation. He knew how to select a slumber spot, start a fire, hunt for game, clean and dress the food, find the right herbs to season, and how to set up a campsite to avoid predatory animals. He was skilled in tracking as well, and won two contests in a row the prior year during the annual huntsman games.

No fool indeed. These men have no idea who they are dealing with, he thought to himself as he feigned submission. *No idea.*

TWELVE

Burke Territory — Samhain Celebration

"Do ye have all yer masks Orla?" questioned Reni. "And yer cloak, and the extra cloak to cover ye, cause it looks like it might rain. Child? Did ye hear me?"

"Aye, Reni, I have all me masks here in me basket and I have both of these infernal cloaks as well. Now, let me be off, Shanleigh is a' waiting on me she is," replied Orla indignantly, stomping her foot for emphasis.

"Do ye have yer dagger, Orla?"

"Aye. I have me dagger right here in me basket."

"Alrighty then, off ye go, but ye best be getting back a'fore the bonfire lights go out. Yer mam will be awaiting ye in the kitchens—to see what goodies ye collect. Ye ken?" Reni asked.

"Aye," Orla retorted, before hastily draping herself with a cloak, and covering her head and basket with the other.

The rain began to fall in short, shallow bursts just as Orla stepped from the covering of the castle doors into the unusually warm night air. Thankfully her leather boots would carry her through the paths and village byways without problems. No doubt her friend Shanleigh would be at a disadvantage, having only slippers for shoes. At least she was smart enough to bring an extra cloak and a pair of boots for Shanleigh. Nothing would hold up their good time this eve, especially not the rain.

Orla traversed the castle grounds proper as fast as her young feet would carry her. Shanleigh was waiting, and she wasn't the most patient individual. Just two summers her senior, Shanleigh was thirteen, and already her father was searching for suitable matches for his only daughter. Orla had made up her mind already that she was not the kind to marry; and knowing her mam, it seemed unlikely that Odetta would force her into any such match.

Shanleigh's father, Dirk, was the armory overseer for the Burke forces and was highly praised among the Burke clan. Although he and Odetta shared words on several occasions, Dirk believing her addled, it was his relationship with Easal that smoothed things a bit. At least it hadn't affected Orla's ability to maintain her friendship with Shanleigh yet.

Orla rapped at the thick wooden door to Dirk's cottage and called for Shanleigh. The door opened and the smell of fresh mutton stew caught her nostrils. Shanleigh's mam was one of the best cooks in Burke territory, and Orla took every opportunity she could to have her evening meal with the family. It was nice to just sit in a cottage with the feel of family about her; with her not having a father, and her mother, Odetta, being gone so much. Eating with Reni was more like a chore and wasn't pleasant at all. Besides, Shanleigh's two elder brothers always had something entertaining to speak of, and vied for her affection to the extent she never had to lift a finger when visiting.

"Orla, dear, do come in won't ye?" spoke Orla's mam. "Shanleigh is almost ready. I made her change her overdress twice now. She doesn't seem to understand the weather is turning and it will be coming down in sheets soon. She insists on heading outdoors anyway."

Shanleigh barreled from the back of the cottage, hesitantly grasping a handful of masks in her arms and juggling two baskets on her other elbow. Always one to make an entrance, she caught Orla's eye and bid her to watch as she agitated her mam. "Mam, just where do ye s'pose that lanthorn is that Da set out for me?" she asked, dropping the contents of her arms on the long trestle table where her mother was setting out a late evening meal.

"Shanleigh, ye know verra well yer da set the lanthorn near the hearth. Now git yer things off me table a'fore I refuse ye to go t'nite."

Shanleigh ran her hand down the length of her golden-blonde mane and motioned for Orla to help her with the baskets and masks. "Aye, I see it now mam. Won't ye help me light it?" she asked slyly. Shanleigh was accustomed to getting her way and getting help with every menial task she could push off on somebody else. Trouble was, her mother wasn't one of those kinds of people to humor such feigned helplessness.

"Light it yerself ye lazy lass," she replied. "I've work to do," she said as she winked at Orla. "Mayhap Orla can assist ye, if ye be half-witted, methinks Orla might make up for the other half," she cackled as she smacked Orla on the back of her shoulder in jest.

"Here, I brought me extra boots," Orla said and motioned for Shanleigh to change her slippers, "and me other cloak." Orla selected a mask for herself and Shanleigh and placed the others in the baskets, neatly tucked between the oatcakes and apples.

"Now then Shanleigh, ye can share the oatcakes and apples with yer friends, but the other baskets are for gathering offerings for the poor," scolded Shanleigh's mam, "Ye ken, dear one? I will be taking them to the market on the morrow."

"Aye, mammy, we ken," replied Shanleigh as she motioned for Orla to grab the lanthorn and open the cottage door.

"And be back a'fore the midnight rites. Before we run through the bonfires; I need ye back here to watch yer younger brathair," she added, bouncing a curly-headed toddler on her hip.

"Aye, we will," replied Orla, "But we best be leaving now if we are to make it all the way to the north side of the villages to fill our baskets."

"Off ye go then," she replied, "Off ye go."

***

Braeden was enjoying his role-play. He was quite an experienced actor, to say the least. His ability to maintain a straight face while jesting, propelled him into the most curious of situations. Patrick often remarked that his ability to fool somebody might just save his life one day.

Today was that day. Braeden became a compliant and submissive prisoner in dealing with his captives. He gave them no reason to believe that he was anything less than obedient and wouldn't render himself to any trouble. They even believed him to be asleep when the sky grew dark and the rain started coming down harder. When he sensed he was being led down stairs, underground, he peeked through his eyelids. His captors had long since removed the head covering and now he employed a birds-eye view of all the goings-on.

It was the smell that greeted him first, the dreadful stench of rancid food and fetid flesh. Just the thought made his stomach heave. The rattling of metal broke his attention and he realized he was not alone in this underground prison. He struggled a bit to sit up—draped over the shoulder of one of his captors.

"Let me up!" he demanded as if he were the captor. "I mean to get up!" he repeated in as high-a-pitched voice as he could muster, intending to emphasize his youth.

"Hold still ye rascally bastard," his captor exclaimed, grasping Braeden about the waist and setting him down on the bottom stair rung which lead to the caverns beneath the monastery. "There, am I ever glad to have ye off me back!"

"What is the meaning of this? Why have ye brought me here?" Braeden demanded again into the silence.

"Just ye hush now! This once, else we will see to it ye don't live long enough to become Odetta's sacrifice this eve. Ye should count yer blessings we haven't the stomach to do her dirty work for her, else we would have already bled ye dry."

"Bleed me dry! What on earth are ye talking about? Do ye ken who I am? Ye will regret the day ye ever met me! Ye have no idea how much trouble ye are going to be in once P…."

A loud clanging arose from the far, left corner of the cavernous underground dungeon, and a shadow appeared before them. "What is all this fuss about?" demanded the shadow.

"Sit yerself back down now Cordal, we've no need for yer assistance," said the man known as Culver. "Ye," he continued, grabbing Braeden about the shoulders and hurling him down the last of the stairs to the far wall of the dungeon, "will do as ye are told, or else ye will meet yer end with two fewer little fingers."

Braeden gasped and complied, watching in horror as the man chained him to the wall beside a weeping woman and another boy who lay unconscious against the cold wet stones. "Now, drink this here boy, it will make things less painful for ye, trust me," said Culver as he thrust a small cup containing some type of elixir into Braeden's hands. "We'll be back soon enough, ye best make yer peace son, rest and prepare for what is to come."

The very minute the door to the dungeons closed behind the men, Braeden's senses heightened. He may have the lost advantage of sight, but his sense of smell, hearing and feeling took over in an almost wraithlike fashion. From where he was sitting, he could tell he was not alone with the other boy or the crying woman. Even the man who spoke earlier from the back of the cavern wasn't the only other person sharing the dank prison.

When his mouth caught up with his mind, Braeden spewed the contents of the elixir straight out in front of him several feet, the majority of which struck an unintended target. The now drenched prisoner roused a bit and sat up from its slovenly crumple on the barren rock floor.

THIRTEEN

O'Malley Territory

Patrick tightened his grip about Darina's waist and pulled her closer against him as they continued their ride up the steep terrain. Moya prepared the best climbing steed she had, at his request; and Minea packed a basket of wine and fruit to enjoy on their "adventure" as she called it. It wasn't so much that Darina didn't enjoy a surprise every now and then—it was more that riding with her eyes covered was beginning to make her feel dizzy. As if she spoke it out loud, Patrick removed the sash tied across her eyes and softly pulled her cheek towards his shoulder, an indication she should relax against him, safe in his arms.

"Where are ye taking me?" she asked him again, for about the third time since they set out from the Castle after the reception.

I have a surprise for ye, and there is a friend I wish ye to meet. A dear old friend of me mam's; and I ken he wishes to meet me lovely new bride as well.

Darina blushed and a peculiar warmth filled her from the top of her head to the middle of her chest where her heart beat in tandem with Patrick's. She nuzzled closer in to him and he wrapped the edges of his cloak about her, fully encompassing her with his arms. When she sensed their climb was slowing she asked, "Can I look now, Patrick?"

"Aye," he responded as he untangled his cloak from around her shoulders, permitting her to gaze forward across the rocky pinnacle they had spent so long climbing towards. The night air was warm and moist, and the moon was high and full over the summit. She watched in amazement as the stars seemed to twinkle overhead in welcome and noticed the sound of pipes and celebration had all but disappeared. They had traveled a good way from the Castle and they were alone; save for the two sentries that Patrick bade follow two forrach's back on either side of them.

When they finally met with level ground, Patrick slowed. Darina could barely make out the shadows of a stone formation in the moonlight. Almost spherical in shape, the stone pillars were nearly as tall as Patrick and twice as wide. Seven flat stones for stepping lead to a break in the circle, and a flat table-like stone sat in the midst of the coil.

Patrick brought the horse to a halt and jumped down to secure him to a nearby yew tree before assisting Darina in dismounting. She was now wearing creamy-colored silken riding truis with a long plum colored velveteen tunic, a gift from Sanjay and his sister.

"Ye l-loo-look st-stunning D'rina," he said aloud as he held his hands out to her. It was difficult for him to keep his hands off the velveteen fabric for very long. The contrast between the downy tunic and the billowy truis nearly drove him mad. Fully aware that no longer riding with her body pressed against his left a palpable vacancy…he darted to grasp her hand and wrap his arm about her waist…anything just to be close to her again.

Thank ye, she said, unintentionally, with her mind.

"I mean, thank ye," she repeated, out loud this time.

Ye have no need to apologize, luv. Ye may speak with me in any fashion ye wish. I am delighted that ye are more comfortable with me now…it appears, he pressed hesitantly.

"Somewhat," she nodded in agreement and moved closer to his side, enjoying the warmth that emanated from him. *Can ye explain to me what is happening here, or why this is happening at all? I don't ken how this works.*

"M-me n-neith-neither," he shot back to her. *I ken that me mam and I could speak this way, and that me friend Airard, Lucian's brathair, I could speak to him but he could no' speak to me. Why, I don't ken. I would imagine that this is no' the first time this has happened to ye?*

"Nay, it is not," she replied. "My sister Dervilla could read my mind since we were wee ones. However, I suspect a lot of it is simply her skill at reading people as opposed to reading their minds. I have never been able to converse with someone, or speak to someone, who understands me…like I can with…ye."

Patrick swung the basket of fruit and wine with his right hand and held Darina's hand with his other. *Let's stop here.* He spread his cloak over a small patch of level ground upon which a thick batch of fresh green clover grew. Inviting her to sit, he opened the basket Minea sent with them and brought out a wine jug, fresh bread and cheese and dried fruit.

Darina, he said with his mind, *I want ye to know that I understand ye do not know me and ye have no reason to trust or respect me, yet.* He broke off a piece of fresh bread and handed it to her along with a full mug of elderberry wine. *I intend that ye will do both, trust and respect me, in time. And, I ken that I must earn that…as I have come to realize that ye are verra cautious with yer…affections.*

Darina smiled a knowing smile. "Ye have heard of me, now have ye?" she chuckled. *I will kill my Uncle Ruarc, I will,* she thought to herself, only a bit too late.

Patrick tipped his head to the side in confusion. "I'm s-so-sorry?" he asked.

"Oh, never ye mind," she replied out loud. "My Uncle Ruarc likes to think he knows me better than anyone else. He is seldom accurate Patrick, trust me on this. I may be stubborn and bull-headed, but only because I've had to be."

Patrick laughed this time. *He said nothing of the kind. He did tell me that perhaps I had met my match, however. And Lucian seems to think the same.*

"Lucian? What has Lucian to do with anything?" she retorted as she removed her hand from Patrick's and grew cold to his touch.

"D'rina? What gripe have ye with Lucian?" he asked sensing there was more to the story.

"Patrick, I know that ye have a special bond with Lucian, considering yer, uh, similarities," she ventured. "But, Lucian has brought me people and me clan more trouble than we can abide. Things were fine until Lucian arrived, along with his pagan ways, and curses and spells and other such nonsense."

"G-go on," he implored her.

"I know me sister Dervilla trains under him, and for more than just map-making. I am well aware that the hours he spent with me mathair were not just council meetings on clan business. There is witchcraft and sorcery wherever Lucian roams and it has brought destruction and calamity in its wake."

Tell me, what has Lucian caused or cost yer people, Darina?

"Well, if ye don't ken by now, I may as well tell ye," she huffed. Darina stood and straightened her tunic and truis, and paced back in forth in front of the small fire Patrick lit for them. "Ye may want to seek an annulment after this, but here goes."

Darina, there is nothing that would keep me from fulfilling my oath to our marriage, to yer people, to me people. There is nothing, trust me.

Darina composed herself and sat back down, directly across from Patrick, looking him square in the eye as if in direct challenge. Daring him to brave the change in the course of his life she was about to burden him with. Instead of resistance, instead of defiance, her gaze was met with understanding. Understanding she did not understand. A quiet peace she never knew existed. A resilience and courage unmatched by anything she ever experienced.

"G-go on," he said again and placed her hand in his. *I am listening.*

"Well, it's a long story, so I'll tell it fast. Lucian is a druid. When he showed up here, our clan starting warring with the Burke clan to our north. They cast a spell on our people so that we can no longer have male children. There hasn't been a male born to our clan in twenty years."

Patrick nodded and stroked her hand in a silent appeal that she continue her story.

"Well, when I was young, I got pulled into the river and me mam came in after me. Only she was pregnant, and she took fever and she lost the babe. Even Lucian couldn't help her, or save the babe. Mighty fine sorcerer he is, he couldn't save the babe," she cried and clasped her head in her hands.

And ye believe it is Lucian's fault the bairn died?

"Well, aye and nay; I suppose I don't ken," she replied tears now running down her cheeks. Patrick drew Darina close to comfort her, seating her between his legs and wrapping his arms about her, resting his chin on the back of her shoulder.

Darina, tis' no' Lucian's fault yer mathair caught the fever. 'Tis no' Lucian's fault if the babe died. Lucian is no' a god.

Darina shook with the tears that she had held back for years. Unable to share her grief with her clan, her guilt and shame overwhelmed her and created a dark chasm of separation between her and her own family.

Darina, I ken about the curse of the male child. I have spoken about it with Lucian, and I think there is something else going on here. There is more to it than we know. Darina, yer mam was also a druid, ye knew that, right?

"I'm no' so sure about that. I ken she favored the old ways, but I don't believe she was a...witch."

"I'm s-sure sh-she was'na a witch," replied Patrick.

"How do you ken?" asked Darina.

We druids do not believe ourselves sorcerers or witches, Darina. There is nothing sinister or malicious about our ways. Any gifts we may have we use for good. We will not willingly cause harm to others, it is not our way.

"Then why did all these bad things happen after the druids came here?" she asked.

Darina, ye are not an evil person; yet ye have certain gifts, do you no'?

"Aye, I do I guess, but doesn't that just mean I am cursed?" she asked.

Patrick tightened his grip around her and stroked her hand with his own. *No love, it does not mean ye are cursed. It means ye have been chosen by the gods, or by God, for some greater purpose, and ye have been given implements to help ye meet that purpose. Even Christians believe their God bestows gifts upon them to assist in their quest. 'Tis not evil to believe some may have unusual or unique capacities that not everybody else may have.*

Darina collapsed into Patrick's arm, mentally and emotionally spent from the weight of her buried turmoil. Tears formed pools in her eyes and spilled over when Patrick turned her to face him.

"D'rina," he said, "L-lis-listen to me c-carefully."

He cupped her face in his hands and gently pushed back an unruly tendril of long red hair. He met her eyes and locked on, refusing to allow her to look away. Comforting warmth enveloped her, heating her bones, and pulsating through her blood stream until it filled her heart with liquid heat. The ground they sat on began to vibrate and she could feel his heart beat in his hands as they sheltered her face. Still staring into his deep green eyes, Darina reached to trace the outline of his stubble on his cheek.

Listen, he commanded with his mind.

She let her hands drop back down to her lap and attempted to look away from him, before realizing she could not. A spasm erupted at the base of her spine and sent shock waves up her back, to her shoulders, to her neck then to her eyes. A resonant whirring sound grew louder and engulfed her ears. Completely fixated on Patrick, fresh tears sprang to her eyes, threatening to spill over.

Nay. Do not weep, Darina.

Another shock wave hit her square in the heart and nearly knocked her backward. Had he not been cupping her face, she would have surely toppled over.

Look at me, he commanded. *Look at me.*

For a moment, Darina felt she was floating on air. Time stood still, all that remained were she and Patrick. And—there were no words. No words at all. A magnetic attraction danced between their eyes, now merely inches from the other. The ground continued to vibrate, only louder this time and the whirring sound threatened to burst her eardrum. She could not detach herself from his gaze.

Enchanted, she thought. *I have been enchanted.*

No, he replied. *Look at me,* he demanded as he tightened his grip on her face.

As if meditating, she deliberately slowed her breath until it was a simple short drum beat at her temple. She loosened her hold on her muscles, one at a time, until there was no tension left in her body. Patrick removed his hands from her face and placed them on her shoulders, laying one on each side of her neck, and began to lightly caress her.

Still locked in each other's gaze, Patrick asked, "Wh-what do y-you see?"

Darina peered into his eyes, looking, hoping for something, but what? What did he expect her to see except his eyes? Surely he didn't expect her to see into his soul, she was not a soothsayer. She fought the distraction, she fought the doubt and the embarrassment of the situation, she pushed her pride down as far as it would go. She fought with everything in her to see…something…but what?

She blinked and felt as if a hundred-pound wind blew past her face but left her in the same place she had been moments before. Her heart leapt in her chest and a cold chill rose up her neck. There in his eyes, a light, an ethereal figure against the contrast of his deep green eyes. She was no longer staring into his eyes, she was seeing something else. But what was it? It was the outline of a woman's face surrounded by a mist of emanating light, a golden orb of light!

Amazing! Just like the paintings in the chapel, the saint's faces' surrounded by the same golden light. Patrick, ye have to see this…

"D'rina, l-look again," he commanded.

The whirring sound turned into a deep hum, matching her pulse. Her ears pounded in time with the pressure and her fingers felt as if they were on fire. Deeper again she peered into his eyes this time. There in front of her, in the midst of the inexplicable connection between her and Patrick, she saw—herself.

Shocked by the vision of her own reflection in his eyes, she reluctantly moved to break their bond, to look away.

"Nay!" he demanded. *Darina, stay with me.*

Darina, don't ye see it? Ye are divine. Ye are beautiful. Ye are whole. Ye are perfect. Ye are angelic. Ye are "mine."

Unable to tear her gaze from his, she deliberately moved her head and shoulders back, relinquishing her claim to the few small inches that previously separated them until they were at least a foot apart. He dropped his hands from her shoulders and clasped them in his lap in front of him, unyielding in his refusal to look away.

Her image in his eyes grew smaller as she moved further away from him. Her silhouette still draped in golden light; her perspective changed and now she could see all of him, not just his eyes, but his forehead, his face, his shoulders, and chest even. A spasm of warmth shot through her again, a testament that he had grasped her hands in his own.

"D'rina, come b-back t-to me," he said softly, lightly stroking the top of her hand with his own.

Mesmerized by his voice, she smiled and searched his eyes again. She squinted lightly and tightened her grip on his hands. *It hurts me eyes.* Suddenly realizing that Patrick was engulfed in the same cascading golden light, she gasped and broke free of his hands to touch his face. Static electricity shot through the tip of her hand and landed on his cheek.

"I'm so sorry," she said out loud, caressing the pink spot on his face where her finger was meant to land, still unable to unlock their gaze.

"I'm n-not," he replied as he guided her hand to the side of his cheek, rubbing his face in her palm. "I'm n-not," he repeated, unlocking their gaze as he guided them to lay down into the soft shelter of the pallet he made from his cloak.

FOURTEEN

Burke Territory

"What did ye see, Orla?" asked Shanleigh from behind the bushes, mere steps from the monastery entrance. Soaked to the bone from the rains, her voice shook and her hands followed suit. At least a dozen people passed by the sanctuary of their brush in the past few minutes, and thank the gods no one saw them.

"Hush, be quiet else Easal or Rufus hear us," Orla replied as she released the small opening in the brush held apart by her hands. She sat back down on the cold ground beside her friend and stared out into the night.

"Well, are ye gonna tell me what is going on or shall I go knock on the door and see if Naelyn is inside?" threatened Shanleigh. A thunder clap rolled overhead and both girls jumped, startled at the sound.

"Well, they took a young boy downstairs," whispered Orla, who was obviously discomfited at the events that played out in front of her. Pushing her wet hair behind her ear, Orla's hand shook as she spoke.

"Downstairs?" asked Shanleigh. "What downstairs? There is no downstairs."

"Aye. 'Tis what I thought too but I was wrong. They dragged him around back past the gardens, opened a door in the ground and disappeared. There was some yelling and then they came back up without him."

Orla scooted a few paces over and took to her feet again, crouching down to avoid detection. Having extinguished the lanthorn before coming near to the monastery, she felt her way in the dark until they reached a small path that led to the front entrance.

"And just where do ye think ye are going now?" whispered Shanleigh. "Yer mam will have yer hide if she finds out we are here, and I know me da won't take kindly to Odetta's wrath if I'm caught with ye."

"I intend to find out what is going on. Stay close and follow me, there is a window on the east side of the chapel that looks into the altar room; mayhap we can see what all this fuss is about."

"Oh no, I'm not budging. I will stay right here, thank ye verra much," she said as she grabbed ahold of a mask and covered her head with her cloak. "If I'm caught, they will think I'm just another worshipper. Ye best put on a mask as well," she said as she handed another to Orla.

"Verra well," Orla replied as she tip-toed towards the window opening. "I'll be right back. Now, don't ye move."

The moon was high in the sky and it was near to midnight. Almost time for the sacred rites to be performed and the monastery was already bustling with activity. There were people going in and out, bringing in wine; and baskets of food and fish were stacking up against the far table in the back of the hall.

Knowing there wasn't much to see except a room full of masked partygoers, Orla decided to venture around to the back side of the monastery. There she heard her mother's voice and stopped to position herself for a look-see.

"Call him," said a voice that Orla did not recognize. "Call him now, or I will take *ye* as my tribute."

"Please Eaton," responded Odetta. "There is no need to do this, I promise ye I can have what ye seek within a fortnight."

"Nonsense," replied the sinister male voice, "It is apparent I must do this meself and I have need of a host. Call him now, or I will show myself to everyone in the hall. Is that what you wish?"

Just then, a piece of thatched roof broke away above Orla and landed squarely on the top of her head. She froze in terror. She did not know who was speaking with her mother, but she could tell her mother was scared, and nothing frightened Odetta Burke.

From behind the linen window dressing she could see the shadowy outlines of two people. One was her mam, of that she was sure. The other, she wasn't sure was a person at all. It spoke, but its voice was like the echo of the wind in a cave, deep, loud and foreboding. It was so tall its head touched the rafters and it was twice the size of any normal man she had ever seen. And…it scared the hell out of Odetta.

"Please Eaton, not Easal. Let me call for Rufus, surely he will do."

"He willno'!" shouted the shadow, so loudly it shook the building. "Easal is the captain of the guards, I need him to accomplish what I will. Now get him!"

"What on earth is going on?" whispered Shanleigh into Orla's ear from behind her. Frightened by Shanleigh's sudden appearance, Orla lost her footing on the cornerstone she was standing on and toppled head-first into the stony wall, cutting her forehead in the process.

"By the saints Shanleigh, ye scared the skin off me," Orla cried, grabbing Shanleigh by the shoulder with one hand and covering her mouth with her other hand, as she dragged her backwards around the corner to the other side of the monastery wall.

"What was that?" the sinister voice echoed out the window into the night. "Someone was out there," it demanded.

"Of course someone was out there," Odetta replied. "We are gathering for our service this eve, there are people everywhere. My coven awaits me in the altar room. We have a service to attend to. There are far too many people and too much activity for ye to go unnoticed, me Lord."

"Bring me Easal—have him here, in this chamber, when ye are finished with yer rituals this evening," it shouted. "I'll have my host then."

"What was that?" asked Shanleigh through chattered teeth. Visibly shaken, Shanleigh broke into uncontrollable tears behind Orla and made to pass out.

"Oh no ye don't," said Orla as she shook her friend to revive her. "Now, listen to me," she said, placing her hands on either side of Shanleigh's horror-filled face. "Are ye listening?"

Shanleigh nodded.

"Go back to the brush and find the lanthorn. Take it to our cave near the docks, ye know the one?" she asked.

Shanleigh nodded again.

"Get to the cave, light a fire and wait for me there. Make sure no one follows ye, ye ken?" she asked.

Shanleigh nodded a third time.

"Leave me the baskets and the masks, except for yers. No matter what happens, don't take off yer mask. Now go!" Orla commanded.

***

Kyra ate the last bit of bread from her bowl and rose from the table in the great hall to greet her father. Vynae's potion worked its magic and her stomach was no longer tied up in knots, waiting to explode.

She still felt a might squeamish, but a hearty meal was serving its purpose, and she felt the color coming back in her face.

"Are ye feeling better, luv?" asked Ruarc as he reached to hug his only daughter.

"Aye, Father, I am much better indeed," she replied as she wiped the crumbs from the corner of her mouth. "A good meal and I am good as new."

"Ye think it was that swim ye took in the river that gave ye the vapors?" he asked tugging at his beard and mentally castrating Payton MacCahan at the same time, for pushing her into the water.

"Nay, and don't ye go bothering that poor boy, Da. He had no idea who I was and I'm sure he feels a wee bit senseless after that stunt he pulled. Ye yerself didn't recognize me the first time ye saw me in my chainmail. Besides, he is family now, ye need to let it rest."

"Ye sound more like yer mam every day, Kyra," said Ruarc.

"Now don't say that Da. I'll never hear the end of it if ye say that to mam," Kyra chuckled as she rose to leave.

"Now where do ye think ye are going lass?" asked her Uncle Rory, just as he was sitting down across from her to eat.

"I have me rounds now," she replied. "It's me turn on the battlements, to watch the north-facing gates."

"Nay. It isn't."

"It isn't?" she asked in surprise. "I'm fairly certain it is," she countered.

"I spoke with Murchadh," said Ruarc. "And, we agreed that you are to rest, for at least the next fortnight. There will be no more chainmail for ye for a while. And, I want ye to stay off the horses, Kyra. No riding for now."

"Why am I being punished?" she growled.

"I knew she would say that. I told you she would say that, Ruarc," Rory admonished, shaking his head in disbelief between bites. "She is the most bull-headed female I have ever come to know."

Ruarc smiled and replied, "She gets that from her Uncle Rory."

FIFTEEN

O'Malley Territory

Darina lay comfortably on the soft ground beside Patrick, searching the stars for answers, but none came. There was nothing to explain the deep connection she had with Patrick, a man she had known only a few days; or the near spiritual moment they shared together under the canopy of the night sky. Nothing logical anyway.

Darina, what troubles ye?

"I'm not sure if it is this bond we seem to have that bothers me, or the possibility that it will no' last," she replied, and rolled over to lay her head atop his chest, to listen to his heartbeat. She lazily draped a leg over his and rooted her head into the crevice under his arm.

He caught his breath and reached for her, grasping her hand in his. "There is n-no re-reason to f-fear we will l-lose our connection, D'rina," he spoke calmly to her. *Nothing will break our bond, except our own free will.*

She sat up to look him in the eye. "What do ye mean, Patrick?"

Well, I mean that ye can choose to disconnect from me; and I can choose to disconnect from ye.

"Why would I do that?" she asked.

Well, I would hope that ye would'na, but I'm sure there could be reasons ye might want to. And there may be reasons for me to do the same as well.

Give me an example, she demanded, clearly irritated.

Patrick chuckled and sat up beside her. *Suppose I have a secret I want to keep from ye?*

A secret ye want to keep from me, she pushed back, her ire clearly rising.

Aye, a secret, he countered. *Suppose I have purchased a gift as a surprise for ye. Then mayhap, I would need to close up that part of me memory from ye, just until it's no longer a secret, ye ken?*

"I get yer point," she replied. "So ye can choose what to reveal to me when ye want?"

Aye. I can.

And what about me? she asked. *Am I just supposed to be an open well of information for ye? Can I no' have any secrets of me own?*

Of course ye can, Darina. In time, ye will grow more comfortable with yer gift. It will come to ye, with practice. I will na always search yer mind. I respect ye lass. I know ye have need of private thoughts.

"And just what am I thinking right now?" she asked aloud.

Patrick drew her closer to him in a tight hug, wrapping his arms around her and placing his cheek on hers as if to whisper in her ear. *I'm having trouble hearing ye, let me try harder,* he pressed, before placing his forehead on hers and looking her in the eyes.

"Well?" she whispered coyly. "Have ye guessed?" she ventured.

"N-not quite," he whispered back as he stroked the side of her face with the palm of his hand. *I've one more trick though,* he said.

"Really, and what would that be?" she asked breathlessly.

"T-this," he said, before bringing his mouth down upon hers so gently she almost didn't realize they had touched. He grasped the nape of her neck with his right hand and touched her temple with his left, holding her as if she would break.

"Patrick," she whispered into his mouth.

Shhhhhhh, he replied with his mind. *I'm working here. I almost have it.*

"Patrick," she whispered again, tapping him on the shoulder this time. He continued to ignore her and tightened his grip on her bringing her closer to him, tipping her head to the side. "D'rina," he groaned before parting her lips with his tongue, seeking entry. She responded in kind and suckled his bottom lip before pushing him away from her.

What's wrong, he asked.

"Patrick, we are not alone," she replied.

Patrick grew wide-eyed and alert before immediately jumping to his feet. Never, had he ever, been snuck up on in his entire life. Where were the sentries he posted on either side of the ridge? Was it they that interrupted them?

Darina smiled and pointed behind him as she stood to take her place at his side, grabbing his hand for support.

Patrick, who is that, she asked unafraid.

"I am Covar." The ridge echoed and Darina raised her hands to cover her ears. Not twenty paces in front of them, stood the most magnificent being she had ever seen or could ever imagine. Nearly eight feet tall with long blond hair the color of golden wheat, Covar was a specimen indeed.

"Patrick, so good to see ye again my friend," said the being. Covered only at the waist, his well-defined form rivaled that of any Greek god she ever read about. Light shone from his crystal-blue eyes and tiny orbs of light swarmed around him like bees to honey.

Covar, it's been too long, Patrick replied with his mind, but Darina heard him as well. *This is Darina O'Malley, me bride.*

Darina, can ye hear me? asked the being to her mind. Darina turned for instruction from Patrick, who nodded.

"Aye, I can hear ye fine, me Lord," she stated audibly as she bowed before him, unsure how one behaves in front of a god.

Covar roared with laughter and doubled over clutching his side. "I am not a god," he said out loud, continuing his chuckles and sending the tiny orbs of light spinning away from his upper body. Patrick joined the laughter and wrapped his arms around Darina's waist to hold her tight against him.

The orbs came closer to her and she could hear the faint sound of chatter, like an insect passing her ears. She swatted them as they passed by, sending Covar into more fits of laughter.

"Is this who ye wanted me to meet?" she asked Patrick hesitantly, still swatting at the now swarming orbs.

Aye, me luv. Covar and I have been friends for many years now.

"How did he get here?" she asked.

I came here a long time ago. I have walked yer lands for many years, Covar replied.

"No," she said. "How did ye get *here*? This instance, how did ye know where to come?" she asked.

Smart one there, Covar said and motioned for them to join him sitting in the grass.

"What is that?" shouted Darina as she swatted an orb away for the second time. But it kept coming back like a reticent fly.

Darina, look closely. Do you see it? asked Patrick.

Darina sat still for what seemed like minutes, closely examining the still moving orb of light. "By the stars!" she gasped. "Am I dreaming?"

Nay. Ye are not dreaming Darina.

I can't believe it, Patrick. He smiled and gripped her hand lightly. *It's daoine sidhe. I didn't believe they were real.*

***

Mavis finished off a third goblet of wine and handed the empty vessel back to Britta. Certain it would take more than three goblets to see her fully ripe, she reached forward to indicate her desire for more. Britta, however, would have none of it.

"Ye might wish to slow down there, lass. I've need for ye to explain to Gemma just exactly what happened that caused us to find ye floating belly up in the sea," said Britta.

"Aye. Won't ye have some of this fish as well as some bread?" added Liath, the tallest of the seal women who welcomed Mavis into their modest cottage on the island. "'Twill settle yer stomach a bit."

Mavis accepted the trencher of fish and bread that Naeyd handed her, and straightened her posture as she sat on the bench at the table prepared for their late evening meal. Liath finished braiding Mavis' long black hair and wrapped a cloak about her shoulders to make sure she didn't catch a chill. The cooking fire was stoked and the smell of burning peat moss permeated their small abode from the center of the chamber.

"How long do ye suppose before Incha is back with Gemma?" Mavis ventured. "'Tis extremely important I speak with Patrick, I mean Laird MacCahan, I mean Lord O'Malley, the new Laird…Lord, or whatever you call him…Patrick! I must speak to Patrick at once!" she grumbled.

A skirmish overhead alerted Mavis that something was happening on the roof. Before she could contemplate further, Naeyd excused herself and walked outside, before returning with Incha and a beautiful older woman whom Mavis could only assume was Gemma.

"Mavis," said Incha calmly, "this is Gemma, Ruire of our Isle."

The regal looking woman strode forward from the door and took Mavis by the hand, lightly stroking her palm. "Mavis, I've been advised that ye came upon some calamity of late? Is that correct?" she asked.

"Aye," replied Mavis. "These, uh, lasses here assisted me after I was left to the sea by me captors." Mavis hesitated in offering any further information than necessary, not wishing to disclose the true identity of her saviors.

"I see," said Gemma, nodding to Liath. "Please tell me everything ye can."

Mavis rose from her perch at the bench and walked toward the hearth clenching her hands in her skirts. "I mean no disrespect, Gemma, but who are ye and why should I trust ye to get word to Patrick? Why can I no' simply speak with the Lord myself?"

Gemma remained steadfast in her position just inside the cottage entry way. "And who are ye that I should make ye an audience with our new Laird?" she retorted, clearly offended.

Incha stood between them and laid a calm hand on each of their shoulders. "Listen, something terrible has happened and Mavis, as far as I can tell, ye need our help. Gemma, Mavis bares no ill will towards our new Lord, I'm sure of it. Do you ken?"

"And just how would I know that?" asked Gemma.

"Because I came here with Patrick," said Mavis. "I'm from MacCahan territory. I came with Patrick and his charge, the boy, Braeden. He is the one that has been taken."

Gemma's face showed obvious surprise and she bid the women to sit at the table. Naeyd filled six goblets of wine and set them before each of them before Mavis broke down in tears.

"What is the nature of yer relationship with our Lord...Patrick?" questioned Gemma.

"What is the nature of yer relationship with the O'Malley's?" Mavis spat back.

"'Tis a fair question," said Incha, placing a hand on Gemma's forearm, hoping to fend off a disagreement between two obviously bull-headed women.

"I am the Ruire of O'Malley Isle. The Island of Women," stated Gemma, matter-of-factly. "That simply means that I am responsible for overseeing the day-to-day affairs of the women and children who reside here. I take care of their needs. They come to me for counsel and guidance; and I represent their interests with the O'Malley clan as a member of the O'Malley High Council. I answer to no one save the Lord of O'Malley clan himself. That person now is Patrick MacCahan-O'Malley."

"I see," replied Mavis skeptically.

"No one from this island will take an audience with the Lord, before going through me. It is how it is done here," explained Gemma.

Mavis looked at all the women about the table but uttered not a word. She took a long drink of her wine, set the goblet back down upon the wooden trestle table, and stared into the room as if she had lost all her faculties.

Incha spoke, "Naeyd, how much wine have ye given her?"

Naeyd shrugged her shoulders and shook her head as if she didn't know how to answer. She mentally counted the empty wine bottles sitting atop the meat counter near the hearth and winced.

Mavis stood up, "My relationship with Patrick…I mean…Lord O'Malley," she said tipping her head in the direction of Gemma, "is that of a servant."

Gemma nodded her understanding and bade her to continue with a wave of her hand.

"I was purchased at the slave auctions in Burke territory many years ago."

Liath gasped and interjected, "I thought all the slave auctions were closed years ago," she whispered to Gemma.

"Go on," said Incha.

"I recently lost me babe, and was needed to nurse an orphaned infant child. The group of mon had need of a nurse to care for the boy who was going to foster in MacCahan territory. I have been a dutiful and loyal household servant to the MacCahan's for many years. I am not a slave."

"But ye said ye were purchased?" asked Liath.

"Aye, I was," said Mavis. "They gave me me freedom from the first moment they took me from the slave auctions. I am fairly compensated for me work as a nurse and tutor to the boy, Braeden. Patrick is…well…he is like me brathair. That would be the best way to describe our *relationship*," she added, visibly staring at Gemma, a challenge to her earlier insinuation. "There is no impropriety, if that is what ye were hinting at, me lady."

SIXTEEN

Burke Monastery — The Dungeon

Unable to temper her curiosity any longer; Orla snuck around to the back of the monastery, intent on breaching the entrance that led below the main structure. Had it not been for the conversation she overhead between her mam, and some unknown soul, she may have gone on about her own business. But that was not her way. The fear she saw in Shanleigh's eyes did little to dissuade her. Her mam was scared, and she intended to find out exactly what was behind that most unusual development.

Certain she had not been followed, Orla peered around the garden trellis and tiptoed through the muddy pathway, until she caught sight of the iron handle peaking just beneath a lavender bush. Thankfully, the storm drowned out the sound of screeching metal hinges as she pulled the small wooden access upwards. Remorseful she hadn't thought to keep the lanthorn with her, she crouched to enter the dank stairway and let the makeshift door slam shut behind her.

She sensed she was not alone. Obviously, this was some type of baleful penitentiary, meant to terrify as well as punish unfortunate or unrepentant perpetrators. Startled laments sounded below and she wasn't sure whether to be frightened, outraged or sympathetic. Convinced there was no other choice, she embarked on her downward journey to the belly of the caverns by scooting on her backside, one stair at a time, feeling her way with muddy hands. She was convinced mostly because her attempt to reopen the access door was met with solid opposition. Getting into the dungeon was not hard, getting out would most likely prove impossible.

"Who's there?" shouted a young voice from below. "I demand to know who's there."

"Shhhh," whispered a man from the far side of the darkness. "Hush, boy!" he demanded.

Orla sat rigid at the bottom of the stone staircase, unable to move for fear. *Well, I've done it now*, she thought to herself. She wasn't sure if she wanted to climb back up the grimy stone stairs and wait for the overhead door to open…to what she wasn't sure…or if she should continue her descent into the threshold of hell. A hacking cough to her right interrupted her train of thought and she stood to survey her plight with her hands.

Standing at the bottom of the stairs, she could feel a jagged stone wall to her left and also to her right. In front of her was an opening into what she assumed was a hollowed out cave. *A dungeon.*

"Who's down here?" she spoke into the abyss. The cavern grew eerily silent against the external backdrop of storms, and she stepped down further until she stood on the cavern floor. "I said, who's down here?" The sound of metal chains scraping against the rocky walls pierced her ears and she became brave with her demands.

"I demand to know who is down here, this instance!" she cried into the darkness.

"Orla?" said a female voice directly in front of her. "Orla, what are ye doing here? Ye must leave child. Ye are in danger."

"Naelyn?" cried Orla, unable to believe what she heard. "Naelyn, what is this place? What are ye doing here?" asked Orla through relieved tears.

"Orla, don't move. I don't wish ye to fall. I was brought her at the command of yer mathair. I am a—prisoner," replied Naelyn.

Orla reached into the darkness until she found Naelyn resting on her knees, secured by her right wrist, to a chain attached to the stone chamber. She reached to hug her long-time friend and knelt beside her in the darkness. "Naelyn, what is going on? I overheard me mam talking to someone, to something, rather, and she was terrified. I watched some men bring a boy down here."

"Orla, ye must leave at once. The guards, they don't ken who ye are. I'm afraid they will abuse ye if they find ye down here."

"Who is she?" shouted a young male voice. "I'll cause a ruckus if ye don't tell me what ye want, right now!" shouted Braeden from his position just feet from where Naelyn was chained. Huge hands reached across the darkness and gripped Braeden by the shoulders. Placing one finger over Braeden's lips, Father MacArtrey tightened his grip on his shoulders and shook him in a silent plea. Braeden complied, for the moment.

"Naelyn," started the priest. "Naelyn, how can I help ye? I believe I hear the voice of a child?"

"I am no child!" retorted Orla indignantly. "I am the daughter of O..." Naelyn clasped her hand tightly over Orla's mouth and pulled her down against her. "Shh... Ye'll keep yer mouth closed if ye wish to live, Orla. I am not playing with ye now," Naelyn whispered into her ear.

"I've had more than enough of this," exclaimed Braeden as he wiggled out of the clutches of the priest, who was chained mere feet in front of him in the dungeon. "Who's down here? I intend to escape and if ye want to go with me, ye better be identifying yerself now."

A muffled chuckle from the back of the caverns caught Orla's ears by surprise. "How many of ye are there?" she whispered.

Braeden piped up, "I am Braeden. I am sitting just to the left of ye, and next to me is a sleeping boy I am about to wake up. In front of him is a large mon. To my right sits the lassie ye call Naelyn and in the back corner, there is another mon; the one that frightens the guards."

"I wouldn't say I frighten the guards, exactly," said Cordal.

"Well, ye are the only one here with chains on his feet, are you no'?" asked Braeden sarcastically. "There must be some reason they don't want to wrestle with ye."

"Very observant little lad," replied Cordal. "And ye got all that from just listening in the dark?"

"Never mind that," replied Braeden. "Who's going with me when I leave? Ye best be telling me now, a'fore I make my break for it."

"Just how do you think ye are getting free of these chains and outta this prison, son?" asked the priest. "I see no way out."

"That would be yer first mistake," he retorted. "Relying on what ye see instead of what ye feel. Have ye no faith?" he asked the priest. "Who are ye?" repeated Braeden into the darkness. "Who is here with me?"

"I am Father MacArtrey of the O'Malley clan."

"I am Naelyn, and this is Orla."

"I am Malcus MacDugal," spoke the boy chained beside Braeden. "I was taken off me father's boat a few days back."

"And who are ye, son?" asked Cordal.

"I am Braeden Cordal McTierney."

"What kind of game are ye playing here lad? I am Cordal McTierney."

"Well—I *am Braeden* Cordal McTierney."

Orla stood to stretch her legs and noticed that her eyes had adjusted to the lack of light. She bent down to get a better look at Braeden and the other boy. "Why are *ye* down here? What have ye done to warrant this…place?" she asked. "Ye are but children."

116

"We are as old as ye are, ye ken?" Braeden retorted. "And why are ye here?" he asked angrily. "Why would anyone come down here of their own accord; unless they were sent here to spy or for some other menacing reason? I trust ye not," he said, as he attempted to peer into her eyes in the dark; holding his chin high in belligerence and standing to compare his height with her own.

"I hear someone coming!" exclaimed Malcus. "Hush, someone's coming, can't ye hear the handle rattling?" Malcus inched his back as far against the stony wall as he could, subconsciously believing it would somehow shield him.

"How can ye hear anything over the sound of this infernal rain?" asked the priest. "Just relax boy and pretend ye are a'sleeping again."

"I hear it too!" added Braeden. "Listen, can't ye hear it?"

"By the gods, Orla, we need to hide ye; ye shouldn't be found down here!" exclaimed Naelyn into the darkness.

"Come back here lass," instructed Cordal. "Come back here with me, and hide behind me, I'll cover ye so they won't see."

The familiar creek of iron hinges on the hidden door sounded and a stream of light from a lanthorn showed halfway down the chamber stairs. Keys rattled and a rotund guard grunted and cursed as he attempted to traverse the muddy stairs without losing his footing. Naelyn gave Orla a reassuring nudge and directed her through an unlit path in the dungeon towards Cordal who was chained in the back left corner.

"Here now, I won't hurt ye lass," just sit right here behind me, I'll cover ye best I can," he said.

Orla shook violently, unclear if it was because she was completely soaked through, or because she was terrified of who or what had entered the dungeon behind her. Cordal placed a reassuring hand on her shoulder and bade her to remain as still as possible.

The light from the lanthorn grew brighter and soon the cavern was filled with the misty haze of yellow fog.

"Who's there?" questioned Father MacArtrey. "Who's there?" he asked again to the light, unable to make out the form of the person behind the light source.

"Get up," demanded Rufus to the priest. "Yer time has come, Father. The service will begin soon, and ye will get yer chance to make it right this time ye will." Rufus set the lanthorn on the bottom stair and turned back around to face the priest who was now standing. After unchaining the priest, Rufus commanded, "Hold the lamp for me," and turned to face the two young boys. "Which one of ye should go first?" he asked mockingly as he stroked his matted beard in contemplation. "I ken me lady will be wanting a worthy sacrifice this eve," he added.

Orla gasped in shock from the back of the caverns and Cordal coughed to cover the sound. The sound of his chains rattling sent Rufus into chuckles and he picked both boys up by nape of their necks to examine them. "Pity neither of ye are a fine specimen," he spat before slamming them back down to the ground.

"Take me," said Malcus. "I've been here longer than he and I ken he doesn't fully know what is about to happen. Give him time to prepare," he begged Rufus.

"Alright then, I'm in no mood to argue about it," he replied as he bent down to unlock the chain holding Malcus' wrist to the wall.

Naelyn began to weep loudly and Orla dug her fingernails into Cordal's back in terror. "What are they going to do with him?" she whispered.

"They are going to take him to the chapel and drain him of all his blood."

"What, why?" asked Orla. "I don't believe you."

Braeden coughed and the priest blew out the lanthorn light. The wind caught the still open dungeon door and slammed it shut against the ground. Rufus grabbed the now unlocked boy by the forearm and screamed at the priest. "Just what do ye think ye are doing?"

"'Twas the wind, sir," replied Father MacArtrey. "The wind caught the door and blew out the light."

"Nobody move!" shouted Rufus. "Don't even breathe in my direction, else ye will all catch the sharp side of me sword!"

"Ye mean this one?" asked Naelyn pressing the sharp tip of Rufus' sword into his throat. How she managed to come upon his sword was anyone's guess but for now, Braeden saw it as his chance.

Rufus shoved Malcus onto the ground into the darkness in front of Naelyn. She lost her footing and fell forward, losing the sword in the process.

"Ye all fancy yer very smart now, don't ye," he asked. "Easal will be looking for me and when he finds out what ye've done, it won't bode well for ye," he continued backing his way towards the stairway in the darkness.

Rufus made a choking sound and gurgled before collapsing onto the cold, stone floor. The sound of keys rattling startled Orla and she loosened her grip on Cordal. "What's happening?" she asked.

"I say, who is going with me?" interrupted Braeden's voice.

"What happened?" asked the priest.

Malcus spoke up solemnly, "Rufus is dead," he said, before proceeding to feel his way in the darkness to the chains that secured them to the dungeon walls. Naelyn lay passed out on the floor but was quickly revived by Father MacArtrey. The door to the dungeon swung open and moonlight shone down the stairway.

"It's just me," said Malcus, "I opened the door. We must leave at once."

119

Orla followed Cordal from the back of the cavern towards the stairway where Rufus lay with a dagger protruding from his neck, a pool of blood now mixing with the rain and mud.

Braeden hesitated before reaching the first stair and crouched down to remove the dagger from the dead man's neck. "This is mine," he said out loud, before wiping it with Rufus's cloak and returning it to its place in his knee-high boots. "I told ye I was getting out of here," he remarked snidely to the priest and mockingly patted him on the fattest part of his belly as he walked past him up the steps. "I told ye."

SEVENTEEN

O'Malley Territory

Patrick and Darina walked hand-in-hand as they traversed the rocky terrain leading down from the ridge back towards the village and castle. Patrick held tight to his steed and guided them along the gravelly landscape. He whistled a command to the sentries that had accompanied them on their ascent, and they walked in silence, from their locations on either side of the new Laird. Darina took in the breathtaking view of O'Malley lands. The castle and village lay before them to the left near the winding river; and to their right, the full moon kissed the sea.

"Patrick," she said, "tell me how Covar knew where to find us. I sense that he is not one of us. Mayhap he is not from this world at all? Do ye ken…can ye tell me…how did he come to meet us on the ridge?"

Patrick squeezed her hand tenderly and steadied her to avoid a rock in their path. *Covar is indeed not from our world. Yet, he has been a part of the MacCahan clan for as long as I can remember. He was a dear friend and confidante to me mathair.*

"Patrick, where is he from?" she asked.

I'm not really sure, another place, not of our soil. From beyond the stars he said—beyond the stars.

"How did he find us, Patrick?" she asked again. "How did he ken where ye would be?"

"D'rina, ye ca-can-canna ever tell an-any-anyone what I am ab-about to sh-share," he said to her audibly, tipping his head to the side and locking eyes with her.

I understand, she said with her mind.

Darina, ye see this ring, on me right hand? It bears the image of a dragon against a shamrock. This ring is made of some type of precious metal I have never been able to identify. I am a blacksmith, and believe me, I've tried to identify it.

"What does that ring have to do with anything, Patrick?

This ring was left to me by me mam. She wore it around her neck on a chain. It is used to locate the person who wears the ring. Covar can find me or anyone else who wears the ring, anywhere, at any time. Unfortunately, me mam was not wearing it the day she was killed.

"Who else has worn the ring? she asked him.

Well as far as I ken, there are only three of these rings. I have one. Airard from my village has another; and the last is worn by Lucian. The ring bearers are called Dragonians, because of the dragon crest inlaid into the metal.

Darina slowed her walking and paused before Patrick, clasping his hand in her own and carefully studying the mysterious ring which adorned his finger. "I've never seen anything like it," she exclaimed. For a moment, it appeared that the dragon's ruby-red eyes lit up and danced in the darkness. She rubbed her eyes to clear her focus and placed a small kiss atop Patrick's hand.

Darina, I've a question for ye as well.

For me?

Aye. I wish to know what ye meant back there, when ye said ye were pulled into the river?

What do ye mean, Patrick?

Well, ye didn't say ye fell, or lost yer footing, or ye were pushed. Ye said that ye were pulled into the
river and yer mam came in after ye—didya no'?

I suppose I did. Patrick, I swear a hand reached out and pulled me into the water. I've told me mam,
but she swore me to keep it secret. I was watching the minnows at the edge of the river. It was almost dusk
and near time to return to the castle and I saw him.

Him? asked Patrick.

Aye. I saw two large gray eyes behind blazing copper-colored eyelids staring back at me from the
water; and before I knew it, I was pulled into the water. I still bear the scars from the deep scratch marks.
See, look here on my right hand, those lines here, they were deep cuts and I had to be sewn up.

"Yer mathair b-bade ye to k-keep silent ab-about it?" he asked.

"Aye, she did."

"N-not even L-Lu-Lucian?" he asked.

"Not even Lucian."

***

Odetta sat terrified on the three-legged stool awaiting the arrival of her husband, Easal. If there were
any possible way she could have appeased the Visitor's unfathomable wrath and blood-thirsty appetite, she
couldn't think of it. As it stood, she would lose her husband this day. She already lost her brother, as well as
her sister, and her very soul, in the process.

She twisted her hands in her lap and fought back tears, yearning to remember the spell she was
taught so many years ago. She must do *something* to dissuade Easal's fear and pain; she must.

If it weren't for her weakness as a child, she may have avoided this…all of this. Better to have killed
herself than to subject her family to the unknown horrors still awaiting them. At least she left Orla in the

responsible care of Reni, that she could feel good about. Reni would ensure her safety and security and their plan to take Orla to McTierney territory the next week would ensure her safety forever. She would have to finally tell Orla and Cordal's family that Orla belonged to them, that she was Cordal and her sister's child; not her own.

Eaton intended to take a host. She knew what that meant, although she didn't have any desire, or the stomach, to witness the shocking process of a fragile human body transfigured into the host of an inhuman beast. *Easal*. He was good to her: always loyal, unquestioning and non-judgmental. The only true ally she had in the world, and he was about to become a true-to-life puppet for an other-worldly villain.

I must see Naelyn. She will ken what to do, she can always calm me. That's it. I'll go get Naelyn from the dungeons, and together, we will find a way to be rid of Eaton forever.

EIGHTEEN

O'Malley Territory

The ride back to the castle was breathtaking. The descent from the rocky pinnacle, although fraught with instability, offered a view of the sea and port unlike any other. Bonfire lights were still ablaze on the Isle; and even though the celebrations and revelry in the village were winding down, you could still hear the faint bellows of the pipes and the merriment of the remaining guests. The sentries met Patrick and Darina and accompanied them to the stables where Moya tended to the horse.

Walking hand-in-hand toward the castle, Patrick stopped to gaze into the eyes of his new wife under the warm autumn moon. "T-tis a b-be-beautiful eve, luv," he said.

"Aye, it is," Darina replied.

"I've a c-confession to m-make."

"What? Do ye hide a secret in that head of yers, Patrick?" she laughed.

"In-indeed I do," he stated slowly. "And…it awaits y-ye on our b-bed."

"Are ye tempting me Patrick, with yer brawny charms?"

Nay, Darina, 'tis nothing like that. I really do have a gift for ye, it awaits ye on our bed.

"Well, I guess we best be on our way," she exclaimed, eager to find out what surprise he had waiting for her. Jumping with excitement; she clapped her hands together before grabbing his in a feigned attempt to drag him along behind her as she half skipped, half ran, towards the castle.

Wait now luv. We've only just been wed. How do ye suppose it will look if ye go running into that castle dragging me behind? He tightened his grip on her hand before swinging her around to meet him face to face. Their eyes locked, and before she knew what happened, he swept her up into his arms.

"I mean to carry ye to our chamber," he said slowly, and deliberately, never taking his eyes from hers. *As is the custom,* he added with his mind.

"I mean to fight ye then," she said aloud, teasingly. *As is the custom.*

"Ye d-d-do?" he asked verbally, before planting an innocent kiss on her cheek and returning his mossy green eyes to hers; eyes so full of life and childlike wonderment. Darina could almost see the years of his life pass before her as she drowned in their molten depths. If she weren't careful, she might fall victim to his charms. He might be her husband, but she would be damned before he would own her heart. That belonged to her. They might share their bodies…but her heart…that belonged to her alone. *Alone.* Of that she was sure. He was a good man, aye; but her father was a good man, and he was dead. Everyone she ever loved was gone and she wasn't going to be Patrick's undoing, not if she could help it. Tears welled in her eyes.

Darina, are ye alright luv? Patrick interrupted.

"Aye, I do." *I intend to fight ye,* she said, as she began banging her fists against his chest in a mock assault. He responded by tickling her and sending her into a wriggling fit, which made her even more difficult to hold as he walked towards the castle, still carrying her.

"Help me!" she exclaimed in jest to the guests and villagers still awake and celebrating in the castle grounds. "Put me down ye brute!" she added with emphasis, still pushing and pulling at him as if she were a victim of kidnap. Patrick's smile grew wider the harder she fought against him and he continued his tickling

126

assault. Against his chest, she could feel the rumble of his inaudible laughter, growing stronger and less reticent as he climbed the hill. Like a purring lion, his soft chuckles vibrated her entire body shooting warmth down her spine. Soon, he broke into such a deep roaring laughter, she couldn't help but laugh as well.

She needed no further encouragement. His laughter was the most amusing sound she had ever heard. Determined for more, she returned his tickles with her own. Brazenly, she reached her petite hands inside the front of his tunic and grasped him about the ribcage on both sides, before squeezing and prickling the circumference of his well-defined chest.. Patrick sucked in a gulp of air and lost his footing sending them tumbling down the hill together; one atop the other, laughing all the way down, with small burst of 'help, someone help' interspersed in between by Darina.

"Should we intervene, Murchadh?" asked Payton from high atop the battlements. Murchadh shot him a knowing glance and laughed himself. "Nay, I ken they are negotiating their fate together," he responded. "It appears that Darina has the upper-hand," he added.

"I fear she always will," said Payton before leaving his post. "She always will," he laughed.

Darina came to a crashing halt at the bottom of the hill, stopped in place by an immovable obstacle against her back. Out of breath from laughter, it took a moment for the world to stop spinning. Gentle pressure on her back and hot breaths at the nape of her neck, reminded her she rested against the most handsome man in all of her clan. She could make out the faint rhythm of his heart against the rise and fall of his chest. The lion's purr confirmed it. He was still chuckling.

A tangled mess of clover and leaves, they lay still at the bottom of the hill soaking up the moonlight.

Do ye still intend to fight me?

Aye. indeed I do.

Well, I shall have no other choice then.

127

Choice for what?

I see that I must needs carry ye to our chamber, luv. That is if I can get a worthy hold on ye. Ye squirm like a tot. A formidable foe ye are.

Darina smiled and rolled onto her back before turning to face him. Her chest still heaving from their roll down the hill, she placed a hand on her heart and tried to relax before sitting up on one elbow. There were leaves and grass intertwined in his loose chestnut hair because it had become unbound from their tumble down the hill. She reached to remove a twig, and he caught her hand with his own. Turning it, palm up, he placed a lingering kiss on the inside of her wrist, locking eyes with her.

Ye are more beautiful now that I have ever seen ye, Darina.

She blushed and looked down, afraid to get caught in his eyes again.

Why must ye turn away?

She raised her face and met his eyes again.

Ye should laugh, all day long, Darina. Ye are so alive and full of mystery. I canna believe the gods favored me with ye, but I am so thankful they did.

And ye should laugh more often, memy Lord, she added. "It makes the earth quake," she said as she jumped to her feet to get a head start on him, "and me heart leap," she added from her place ten paces ahead of him, trudging resolutely up the hill.

It took mere seconds for Patrick to secure her over his shoulder and top the hill facing the castle. Darina blushed at the sound of cheers and applause from the soldiers stationed on the battlements. "Patrick, Patrick," they cried in unison. She continued her feigned dismay, and kicked and slapped at him as best she could, in between the tickles she got in that sent him swaying around like a drunken man. He came close to losing his footing several more times, nearly sending them back down the hill, but somehow he managed to rest on one knee long enough to balance and move forward.

He gave a swift pat to her backside which roused her humor and she began screaming, "Help me," the closer they came to the castle doors. Odhran, the bailiff, met them at the doors.

"I see ye've been hunting, me Lord," he said as he tipped his head towards Patrick.

"Aye, I h-have in-indeed," replied Patrick.

"Looks a might bit…tough…that one does," added Odhran behind a friendly smile.

"That it d-does," replied Patrick before biting the air in jest. "Th-that it d-does me fr-friend," he said, stepping through the doorway with Darina still slung over his shoulder. She shot Odhran a snarky glance and raised both her hands in admitted defeat, as she was near effortlessly carried up the castle stairs towards the master's chambers.

NINEETEEN

O'Malley Territory

Gemma knew it was imperative that word reach the new Lord of O'Malley clan as soon as possible. Patrick was especially bound to his charge, Braeden, and the fact that he was not only missing, but was deliberately taken, would send shock waves through the clan. The soldiers were given strict orders that none were to leave the island, and none were to leave the mainland to venture to sea either. The wedding brought many guests to the territory and their comings and goings were strictly controlled; at least until morning.

Knowing there was no alternative, Gemma stood on the shore of the Isle and contemplated her next move. She could shift into the image of Riann, Darina's falcon, and fly to hidden caves, which marked the underground entry to the castle, in but a few moments. The tunnels would provide cover as she found her way past the dungeons and then to the council chamber, where she should find Lucian, most likely praying,on this Samhain eve. The problem was, she would be completely bare when she arrived. *Shifting is not without its delicacies,* she thought before reaching her arms into the sky as high as she could and emerging airborne, leaving her clothes in a heaping pile on the sandy beach.

Taking to flight, she hovered just above the trees, surveying the island from a birds-eye view. The bonfires were beginning to die down and by now, most of the island's inhabitants and guests were settling in for the night. A melancholy chorus from the mainland reminded her of her task, and she turned southwest in the direction of the piers. A gentle wind from her right lifted her higher and gave her unusual speed.

With one big thrust, she propelled herself deliberately downward. Spiraling towards the rocky shoreline just to the north of the castle, several ships' lengths past the last pier, she folded her wings beside her and nose-dived into a hidden opening in the rocky formation. She hopped and scooted a few feet inside the tunnel before deciding not to shift back just yet. It was unbearably dark now, and without benefit of a torch or lanthorn, she was sure she'd never find her way.

***

Dervilla and Kyra sat solemnly at the council table, watching the servants as they scurried out of the chambers. Galen and Lucian sat on the other side and appeared speechless. Galen offered the ladies wine, but only Dervilla accepted.

"I brought her here, Lucian," said Dervilla, looking at Galen, "because I thought of all people, ye might be the one with an idea of how to help."

Galen stood and placed a comforting hand on Kyra's shoulder. "I believe I may be able to help too," he added.

"Aye, I ken that Galen may be able to help us see our way through this… uh… situation," added Lucian.

Kyra brushed Galen's hand off her shoulder, shot her cousin Dervilla a look of disdain, and rose from the table to stand before the great hearth. "I'm not sure who the '*us*' is in this '*situation*' ye speak of Lucian. I'm more than certain that neither of ye can carry this child in me belly."

"Kyra, the child is a blessing," replied Galen. "I ken it may be hard to look at it that way, but God has seen fit to bless yer union with Aidan; and ye will bear his child. With or without him, the child is a'coming, Kyra. And the Good Lord must have a greater purpose that we canna' imagine."

"Don't ye ken that I know that? But what am I to do? Aidan's child will have no fathair. Me own fathair has forbidden me to ride, and when he finds I am with child, he will force me to leave me post as an O'Malley soldier. What will I do then?" Kyra asked.

"Kyra, ye've no need to work. Ye needn't the coin. I am yer family as well. We willna' let ye starve, if that is yer concern," said Dervilla.

"Dervilla, don't ye ken I know that?" she shot back. "What am I to do with a child? I've no idea how to care for a bairn. I've been guarding and fighting and training and riding all me life…I've never once cared for a babe."

"Perhaps I can help?" said a voice from outside the chamber door. "Lucian, if ye are in there, can ye come out here for a moment to assist me?"

"Gemma?" asked Lucian.

"Aye. Lucian, I've found meself in need of assistance. Will ye help me now?" she asked.

"Excuse me," he said as he rose from the table and exited the great hall.

***

Odetta didn't believe it possible to continue vomiting after her stomach was empty. She was wrong. By now, her esophagus and throat were spasming involuntarily. Unable to abide the trauma inflicted on her precious Easal, the sight and stench got the better of her, and she retched violently. Already her servant had emptied the chamberpot four times.

"Let that be enough," said the voice of Easal. But she was not fooled. She knew she was staring at Eaton, behind Easal's eyes. He had done his worst. Easal's soul was forever gone from her, but his body would remain—as the host of the Visitor. She only dared to dream he didn't also intend to act as her husband in her chambers. If that were to be so, she would ensure she was beheaded —at once. Better to lose her life than her sense of dignity.

It was all Eaton now. Every square inch of Easal's body, overtaken by the diabolical creature. All that remained was the flesh of a man who looked as if he'd been run through a slaughterhouse. The torn flesh, the rancid stench of sweat and bodily fluids, mingled with a crimson gore that pooled about the feet and ankles of the remnants of her only friend.

Easal. My dear, dear Easal. What have I done?

TWENTY

Burke Lands

"I must stop, I canna keep up any longer. Please won't ye tell me where we are a'going?" said the priest through haggard breaths. He stopped to rest against a tree and watched in horror as the group continued on without him through the dark, wet forest. "Please—wait!" said Father MacArtrey, to anyone at all that would listen. "I beg ye!"

"Follow or stay, it matters not to me," replied Orla through the rain. "Ye, boy, make sure ye are covering our tracks. We don't want to be followed."

"Where *are* ye taking us?" asked Braeden, nodding his head to Malcus to continue his work with the palm branches, dragging them through the mud to disguise their tracks behind them.

Orla stared straight at the priest, "If ye are no' a'coming with us, I must bid ye leave in another direction."

"I said, where are ye taking us?" repeated Braeden, now pointing the tip of Rufus's broadsword in her direction.

"Hold on a second," interrupted Cordal. "Braeden, where did ye get that?"

"I got it off the no count bastard who chained us in the caves. An,dI've no qualm in using it either." He crouched in a soldier's stance...head held high...lifted both arms up and held the broadsword as best as his eleven-year-old body could manage. Shaking violently from fear and the cold rain, he challenged Orla with his eyes.

"Ye don't frighten me, boy," she said, looking directly at Braeden and rolling her eyes as she crossed her arms in front of her chest. "I'm taking us *all* to a hiding place where no one can find us. We need to figure out what to do about... about... about that *thing* back there in the monastery."

"What *thing*?" asked Naelyn, inching her way towards Braeden.

Without moving his eyes from Orla's, Braeden shifted his sword to his right, directly in front of Naelyn. "Just what do ye think ye are about, me lady?" he asked.

Naelyn stopped in her tracks and Cordal interrupted. "What say ye give me that sword there, Braeden? Seeing as how we are both McTierney's, it would appear I am the senior McTierney, and as by right, I should bear the responsibility of protection."

Braeden grunted, acknowledging Cordal's reasoning, and turned the sword handle-up with his left wrist. Stepping back two paces, he swung it to his left in the direction of Cordal and relinquished control.

"Left-handed are ye Braeden?" asked Cordal, intercepting the weapon.

"Nay," replied Braeden. "But I am just as good with me left as I am with me right."

"How is that?" Orla asked.

"Me foster brathair, he is... he uses his left hand, more than his right. He taught me both."

"Smart mon," said the priest.

Orla snorted and made to continue on before turning around to the priest, "If ye canna keep up this time, I will be forced to leave ye behind. Do ye ken?" she asked.

Father MacArtrey bowed hesitantly and said, "Aye, me lady," before catching his stride beside Cordal.

***

The look of shock on Lucian's face was palpable. Finding Gemma standing behind a post in the underground tunnels stark naked wasn't what he expected. "Gemma, by the gods!" he whispered.

"Lucian, may I have yer cloak, please?" she asked coyly. "I had to come at once and the ferries were all docked and ordered to stay thus."

"I see," he replied. "Whatever is so important that ye must come at this late hour? And, under *these* circumstances?" he chuckled.

"I bring word of a kidnapping. I must see the new Laird—at once."

"The new Lord is otherwise occupied, Gemma. 'Tis his wedding night, ye know?"

"Of course, but it was his charge, Braeden, that was taken. I fear we should call for him at once."

TWENTY-ONE

O'Malley Castle — Master's Chambers

Nearly completely exhausted after climbing five sets of stairs carrying Darina, Patrick was about to set her down when a chambermaid met them at the door to their chambers. "Everything is as ye requested, me Lord," she said as she curtsied towards them, casting a wary glance at Darina who peeked up at her from her perch high atop Patrick's shoulder.

"Verra g-good, verra good," he replied. He twisted to reposition her, so that now she was cradled gently in his arms rather than thrown over him staring at his backside.

Shall I have me surprise now? she asked with her mind.

Ye shall indeed. It awaits ye atop the bed.

Atop the bed? Is it a coverlet?

Nay, luv. It is much more than that.

Patrick kissed the top of her forehead and gently sat her down at the end of the gigantic master's bed. She could feel the velveteen touch of rose petals and smell the distinct fragrance of lavender which permeated the room.

I hope ye like it. I bid they prepare ye a relaxing bath after our jaunt up the peak. She heard water being poured and watched as a cloud of steam rose from behind a privacy screen placed in the corner.

A bath sounds just wonderful.

"May I help ye prepare?" asked the chambermaid, venturing towards Darina. Patrick nodded, indicating she should ready herself to bathe, and excused himself into the antechamber.

A commotion amidst the pillows startled her. Before she knew what happened, she was assaulted head-on, by a scrappy excuse for a dog intent on licking every square inch of her face. Startled, she pushed the eager pup off her and stood bolt upright next to the bed, glaring at the animal. With white rose petals sticking out of its mouth, it charged her once more, leaping straight off the bed and into her arms.

"Patrick! Why? What on earth? Patrick... there is a... why, there is a *dog* in here!" she exclaimed. Patrick turned the corner from the antechamber and walked towards them. "Darina, th-this is yer su-surprise," he stated matter-of-factly.

The chambermaid's face grew white in sympathy and she gave Patrick a hesitant, questioning glance. As if to say, '*What on earth were ye thinking*', before she turned and continued preparing Darina's bath.

"A dog? Ye got me a dog?" she repeated, staring disbelievingly into the air.

Aye. But not just any dog, Darina. This is a champion falconry hound. The best of his breed, the best me coin can procure. Lucian told me ye were something of a huntress. I thought ye may want a champion bird-hound.

Darina finally managed to get the overexcited pup to calm down long enough to sit still upon the bed, and out of her arms.

"D'rina, ye do no' l-li-like him?" Patrick asked walking towards her, his disappointment showing.

"Don't be silly," she said, "he's lovely and he'll make a fine hunter." She continued petting the attention-starved animal as she sized him up. He was a fine specimen. Obviously well bred, and with more personality than she was sure she knew what to do with. Indeed, it was the most thoughtful, horrible gift she had ever received. She couldn't help but smile. No one had ever bought her anything so personal… so… just like her. It was touching, indeed.

"Where will he, uh, sleep?" she ventured to Patrick.

"Ah," he replied. Moya has f-fashioned a p-pen for him in the st-stables." *All that is left to do is provide him a fitting name, me lady.*

"A name… that's right… ye need a name," she spoke to the dog. "What shall we call ye?" she asked as he began licking her arms up and down. "I see I shall require that bath now," she laughed. "I shall call ye, Fanai."

"A most fitting name, me lady," said Odhran from the doorway. "May I take Fanai to bed down for the eve, me lady?" he asked. Patrick nodded and Darina threw her arms around his neck and kissed him on the cheek.

"Thank you ever so much for such a thoughtful gift. I love him!" she exclaimed.

***

Completely out of breath and drenched in sweat, Orla sat to rest upon a rock near the shoreline. "How much further?" questioned Naelyn, "I fear the mon they call Cordal can't go on much longer. He is verra weak and has need of sustenance."

"Where is the priest?" asked Orla. "Did we finally lose him?"

"We have no' lost him," said Braeden, slumping down in the shallow tidewater just feet from where Orla was perched. "He is back there, I can just make out the glint from his neck chain in the moonlight."

Malcus followed suit after assisting Cordal to lean upon a nearby rock. "Can we finally take off these masks? It is making me so hot!" he added.

"I think we can now," said Orla. "We've only just a little ways to go, we may be closer than I think. I sent me friend Shanleigh on ahead to the cave; to prepare a fire and wait for me. She willna' be expecting all of ye others, but she knows I was coming."

"What are ye looking for?" asked Braeden. "What kind of place are ye taking us too?"

"'Tis a cave, here on the rocky shore. 'Tis hidden from plain view. I've been coming here with Shanleigh since we were wee ones. We've played here for years. 'Tis big enough to shield us all and will provide good cover during the day. At night though, it may be hard to find. I sent Shanleigh on ahead with the lanthorn to build a fire and wait for me. Without light, we may not be able to find it; and I've no desire to yell about to her, lest we give away the location to some errant guard."

"Ye said she was to build a fire, did ye?" asked Braeden.

"Aye, I sent her on with the lanthorn; she should have had a flame to start with. We always kept dry wood handy in the back of the cave, just in case we wanted to stay the night or bring…uh…visitors with us."

Braeden got up from the shallow waters of the shoreline and topped the nearest high rock, looking out over the beach and rocky coast. The moonlight shone down around them and showed no seagoing vessels in sight. "Well, me lady," he said, "I would bet that the billow of smoke over yonder belongs to yer friend Shanleigh's cave fire. Would you no'?"

Braeden pointed just north of the group and to the right, closer to the shore. From seemingly out of nowhere, a white fog of steam or smoke rose from the rock formations. A narrow white fog, but a fog nonetheless.

"That's got to be it!" said Orla. "Wait here," she said before taking off in the direction of the sighting.

"Here, take this, me lady," said Braeden handing her his dagger with his left hand and squeezing the top of her shoulder with the other. "Just in case ye need it."

"Just in case," she nodded. "Just in case."

TWENTY-TWO

O'Malley Lands — Council Chambers, Beneath the High Castle

"Ruarc, I'm sorry to have interrupted yer slumber," said Lucian, waiving off the sentry that escorted Ruarc below the main tower. Galen had long since retired; as had Dervilla and Kyra, and only Lucian, Gemma, and Ruarc now sat at the council table. The fire had died out and a sparse candelabrum adorned the tabletop, its candles nearly burned down to the wick.

Ruarc filled a mug with ale and took a long, swift drink before slamming it back down empty. "Is somebody gonna tell me what this is about?"

Galen and Lucian peered at one another, neither brave enough to broach the subject. "The boy, Braeden, has been taken," said Gemma wrapping Lucian's cloak closely around her.

"Taken? Where, exactly?" asked Ruarc.

"We don't know where, or by whom. His nurse, Mavis, washed up on the shore on the Isle and insisted she speak with Patrick MacCahan, Patrick O'Malley—the new Laird."

"And, how long ago did this happen?" asked Ruarc.

"Several hours," replied Lucian.

"Why am I just now being told?"

"Because the ferries were docked, the borders were closed and there were no boats available," said Gemma defensively. "The village has been on lockdown and high alert on account of the wedding this eve," she added.

"What has been done so far?" asked Ruarc.

"What do ye mean? We called for ye!" shouted Lucian. "Are ye no' the captain of the O'Malley military? What else could we have done?"

"Hold on," interjected Gemma raising her hand to silence Lucian's protests. "I sent some...uh...people...of my own to scour the shoreline, to see if they could catch sight of a boat or something. They left several hours ago. I gave them leave to go as far as just past Burke territory."

"I see, good work Gemma," replied Ruarc glaring at Lucian and Galen.

"Ruarc, this is no' the first time a boy has been taken from the village," said Gemma.

"Nay, it is no'," agreed Ruarc.

"Then pray tell me why, by the gods, is this time so different?" Gemma asked, clearly exasperated.

"Gemma, Galen," Ruarc started, looking at both of them seriously. "I invoke the Council privacy oath. What I am about to tell ye must not leave this room."

"Aye," said Gemma.

"Aye," said Galen.

"Braeden is the youngest son of Dallin O'Malley and the true Laird of O'Malley clan. He was fostered in MacCahan territory and the charge of Patrick MacCahan. I fear something is seriously amiss here. I must wake Patrick at once," he said, shaking his head in despair. Ruarc continued, "Lucian, call for Murchadh, tell him to ready me horse, prepare one for Patrick and to put the guard on high alert. Gemma, send word to Deasum the minute ye hear back from yer...people."

143

Pleased that Darina was happy with his gift, Patrick returned to the antechamber, allowing the chambermaid to assist Darina into the bath. It took three grown men to carry the large tub to the top floor of the castle, but not just any bathing tub would do. It needed to be big enough for the both of them. Patrick so enjoyed the hot springs in MacCahan territory that he wished to mimic their healing effect in his own chamber. The servants loaded buckets of boiling hot water onto the castle trolley for nearly an hour to get it filled completely and keep it warm for them. The soothing salts he added, along with the lavender oil and white rose petals, made the room smell divine.

"Me lady is resting in the bath me Lord," said the chambermaid. "Unless there is something else ye have need of, I shall excuse meself."

"Verra w-well," replied Patrick as he poured two goblets of wine. She curtsied and turned to leave. Patrick set the wine down on a side-table near the master's bed and barred the door.

A small twinge of anxiety took hold of him and he bent to sit on the bench at the end of the bed for a moment. *Contain yourself*, he thought. *This is no' yer first time. Ye are not a boy, ye are a mon and now ye are Lord of this clan.* He reached over for his wine and took a good long drink.

"Did ye say something?" asked Darina from the tub on the other side of the screen.

"N-nay," he replied. "I l-let the m-maid out and b-barred the d-door," he replied.

"Got me trapped now, have ye?" she giggled. Patrick ran his hands through his hair and smiled. *Always jesting, she's a fun one.*

"D-did I h-hear an in-in-invitation?" he asked, his voice growing louder as he got closer to the tub. "W-wine?" he asked looking down at her.

"Aye, wine sounds good," she replied and accepted the glass. She took a small drink and set the goblet on the wall shelf beside the tub, before laying her head back and closing her eyes in relaxation.

Patrick set his goblet down as well, squatted down beside the water-filled bath and inhaled the sweet aroma of lavender and bath salts. Unable to keep his hands from her long, beautiful, red tendrils, he caught a glimpse of his mother's hair comb and gently removed it from the crown of her head. The flaming red hair which was intricately weaved about her head began falling in sensual cascades as he separated the tresses with his long, lithe fingers. She moaned in delight before catching herself. How she loved having her hair washed and brushed…or simply touched. How he loved touching such silky fire.

Patrick gently patted her shoulder and motioned for her to move forward in the water. One sidelong glance out of the corner of her eye, and she was fully aware she was he was *stark naked. By the stars, he intends to bathe with me.*

Aye, I do. I intend to finish that bath we started an eve ago. He sighed with pleasure as his muscles soaked up the warmth of the wondrous water, and he settled himself against the large back wall of the structure. For a moment, Darina was unsure what to do with herself. The tub was simply too big for her. She could either float…which meant she would most likely drown if she didn't choose to steady herself by holding on to the sides…or she could turn around and sit facing her new husband, as bare as the day she was born.

Patrick solved the problem for the both of them. Grasping her gently about the waist, he pulled her backward until she was nestled tenderly with her back against his chest. He rested his chin on her right shoulder and continued stroking her head with his left hand. He dipped a small wooden cup in the water beside him and poured it gingerly down the length of her wavy hair. Pulling a bottle of oil from the nearby shelf, he opened it and lathered the scented contents in his hands. Darina straightened in the water before realizing he was washing her hair.

Relax.

Soothing and comforting, the lavender scent traveled to her nose and released her tensions, allowing her to melt into him once more. Vividly aware of his presence, she closed her eyes to fully sense the experience. His heart beat against her back and his strong legs encircled and cradled her body in shelter. She could feel his breath growing rapid and hot against her neck and shoulders, and his left arm left her hair and grasped her around ribcage; ensuring she couldn't slip away from him in the frothy waters.

Heaven, she thought. *This must be heaven.*

Patrick couldn't have waited much longer to run his fingers through the full length of Darina's golden-red hair. It was softer than he imagined and smelled simply divine lathered in the bath oils. He sought to be smothered by it, that would be a noble death indeed. To be wrapped in it, and to sleep in it as if it were a blanket. To imagine it dangling over him in their bed as it tickled his nose and chin, nearly sent him over the edge. The image of her green eyes peering at him through that hair—had an effect on him he couldn't explain. She mustn't hide it in that braid any longer; he would make sure of that. He desired it free and wild, just like her, so he could run his hands through it any time he wanted. He sighed audibly and shook his head as if to wake himself from a dream.

The magnitude of his pleasure pressed firmly against Darina's tailbone. She no longer need question whether he would desire his new bride, or whether he found her even somewhat attractive. The knowledge of his arousal caused similar passion to rise in her. The simple knowledge that she could cause such stirring in a man awakened her primal instincts and quickened her pulse against Patrick's cheek.

With one last long pour from the wooden cup, Patrick finished rinsing her hair. He separated her locks into two large sections and twisted then loosely around each other before hanging the woven loop over her left shoulder.

Darina edged closer against him. She leaned against his chest to feel his heartbeat and placed her hands on his large thighs to position herself so as not to slip away. Sitting upright in the tub, neither one could touch the other end of the vessel with their feet.

His arousal grew rigid against her backside and his breathing became deep and erratic. He blew out a frustrated sigh and whispered in her ear, "Do y-you l-like the tub, luv?"

146

She nodded her approval against his cheek and twisted her head to the left to expose her neck. *Aye,* she responded with her mind, knowing full well he would be searching there.

Unable to contain his passion, Patrick peppered her neck with his lips and tongue, leaving a trail of hot, wet bites in his wake. When he suckled her earlobe, she whimpered in delight. He tightened his grip on her hips...hoping she wouldn't move...secretly praying she would.

Darina quivered as lightning shot from her breasts to her heat. She arched her back in reflex and let a moan escape her lips. Patrick caught it with his mouth and plundered her tongue with his own.

Aye, Braeden was right, ye may be a wee bit of a hell cat.

"I heard that," she said audibly toying with him.

"I know," he said slowly and clearly in return.

She arched against him frantically and he responded in kind. His left hand drew circles across her perky wet nipple and his other glided up her thigh to her hip where it settled for a spell, seemingly hesitant. She matched his kisses with the same intensity, pleading for more as she ground against him in an almost hypnotic state.

Patrick bit her neck lightly and she let out a shrill groan, backing into his arousal with fervor. He encircled her with both his arms now, communicating possession and contentment. *Mine,* he said with his mind. *Mine.* He wrapped his left arm between her breasts crossing over her right shoulder and his right still rested on her hip, while his hand massaged her heat below the waters.

She struggled to breathe, her breaths now narrow reminders that she was very much alive. She backed into his arousal again and confirmed his intentions, moving her hips in an up and down motion that sent him into fits of pure anguish. She felt his balls tighten and rise against her backside and felt the tip of his rod lash the middle of her spine. *So. Very. Large.*

147

He was purring again, but this was not an amused chuckle. She had awakened the sleeping lion and he was eager for the kill.

Two can play this game, he said with his mind. His attention to her swollen cleft intensified, and she wriggled in pleasure, increasing the pressure her backside placed on his throbbing cock. He dipped his hand lower to find her slippery and slick, ready for him and he eased one finger, knuckle deep, into her heat. She bucked against him and increased her tempo, rising and lowering herself against his hold, and firmly pressing her backside against his tortured erection.

Their lips met again in a frenzy of lust and want, and he slipped another finger inside her velvet softness until swollen flesh met his hand. She groaned and rose up against him, and he strengthened his hold on her with his left hand, grasping her nipple and twisting it playfully.

He roared inaudibly against her back, his chest heaving in convulsion like spasms. Unable to contain himself, he grabbed both her hips to still her in the waters. She was completely immobile, unable to move and painfully aroused. She whined audibly and leaned her head backwards towards his waiting shoulder.

If you dinna stop soon, I will waste my seed in the water, my sweets. I've no wish to dishonor ye thus.

She ignored his pleas for mercy and removed his hands from her hips firmly, placing then one by one on either side of the bathing tub, before continuing her grinding assault against his manhood. He returned his fingers to her velveteen glove and stroked her mercilessly, biting her neck in retaliation. He felt her warmth clench around his digits and he rubbed her swollen nub with his thumb rhythmically.

Darina, tell me what ye want, he begged with his mind.

She groaned and intensified her pressure on his engorged cock. She felt it grow harder and longer and knew his release was nigh. She tightened her internal clasp on his fingers and began rocking back and forth against them.

"D-Darina, please," he begged in a whisper. *What do ye want?*

She mumbled something incoherent under her breath and tightened her legs in front of her. He grasped her nipple tightly to catch her attention.

"Patrick," she moaned lustfully. He broke into a cold sweat and began shuddering.

"A-aye?" he begged, unable to endure the sweet torture any longer.

"Patrick, we have al-al-alll night," she gasped, still grinding forcefully against his rock-hard cock.

Aye, but I don't. Not right now.

She slowed her movements against his manhood but increased the pressure, moving in a circular pattern with her hips.

'Twould mean me no dishonor, me Lord, she said with her mind.

What? He moaned this time—a deep guttural moan that sent ripples through the top of the water.

It would be no offense, Patrick, if ye would. "Oh." She groaned and leaned into his mouth for a kiss, still grinding and clenching her heat around his fingers.

If ye would…peak with me…me Lord… 'twould be glorious, Patrick.

He exhaled audibly and ran his left hand through his hair in frustration. Such exquisite pain he had never before experienced.

Please don't make me stop, she begged him with her mind, while her body continued its rapturous attack on his straining shaft.

"D-Darina!" Patrick moaned painfully in her ear.

"Bathe me, Patrick. Bathe me in yer seed," she groaned into his mouth as she intensified her pressure on his cock. He writhed and shuddered, shaking as he felt her spasm against his fingers, as his own release swept over him and into the water around them.

Darina collapsed against his chest and lay lifeless there for long moments. His breath finally stabilized and he released his hold on her womanhood. She jerked about, as continuing waves of ecstasy pulsed through her blood, and she settled deeper into his embrace.

Breathing in tandem, the rise and fall of their chests sent ripples into the water. Soon, the combined beating of their hearts lulled them into a pre-slumber trance. The melancholy bellow of pipes off the island and the strum of a nearby harp echoing an unfamiliar warning, became the prelude to an unwanted intrusion.

Loud banging on the chamber doors and shouting in the corridor startled Darina, and she jumped, sending water splashing everywhere. Patrick shot bolt upright out of the water, grabbed a drying cloth and a dagger from the hearth, and stepped around the privacy screen towards the barred door.

TWENTY-THREE

Burke Lands — the Shore

Orla stepped carefully and deliberately through the shallow, rocky waters of the shoreline, headed towards the wafting smoke rising from between two large rocks. Nearly certain it was their cave, Orla prayed that Shanleigh would be calm enough to permit her entry without attacking. Shanleigh was not what you would call a brave girl. More princess than pirate; she was coolly adept at manipulating the lads, and accustomed to getting what she wanted, with little to no effort. It was a toss-up as to whether she would make it through the coming days. But she would, if Orla had anything to do with it.

Scraping her knee on a flat, jutting rock, Orla cursed silently to herself before continuing her perilous scramble. It was nearly daybreak and she must find cover for herself and the group she had rescued from the dungeon. What they would do after that, she wasn't sure, shelter was her first priority. A clearing between two large rocks confirmed the entry to the cave. Picking up some loose floating coral, she tossed it into the mouth of the cave, ten counts between, just as she and Shanleigh had always done.

Two snaps of her fingers later and a light shone brightly as it grew closer to the mouth of the cave; and Shanleigh appeared, frightened and cold, but alive nonetheless. "Orla, where have ye been? What took ye so long?" she cried into the dark. "Get inside here. Mayhap you were followed?"

151

"Shanleigh wait! Wait," she called after her friend, who was already halfway down into the belly of cave again. "Did ye start a fire?"

"Aye, there is a fire in the very back. I have the baskets of food and the worn coverlets we brought before. We will be safe for what remains of the eve. That is until me da comes looking for us," she frowned.

"Shanleigh, I brought others with me. Hand me the lanthorn, I will signal to them and help them back," replied Orla.

"Others? What others?"

"From the dungeons. I released the prisoners. We killed Rufus and ran for our lives."

"Orla, what have ye done? Those were yer mam's prisoners no doubt. She will be sore at ye for sure."

"I'll not worry about that now. She has some explaining to do herself."

***

Patrick unbarred the chamber door and peeked around the edge, holding a small drying towel about his waist with his left hand and a dagger in his right. "R-Ruarc," he whispered, perching the door open with his right foot, "is th-that y-ye?" he asked.

Four shades of red, and nearly out of breath from climbing five flights of stairs, Ruarc barreled into view and nodded, bowing humbly before the half-naked clan leader. Patrick let the door swing closed quietly behind him and stood in the hallway, looking down at Ruarc in shock. "R-Ruarc?" he said.

"Aye, me Lord, I hate to bother you at this… uh… late hour," he continued, "but there is a matter requiring yer immediate…uh…attention," he finished, trying not look at Patrick directly.

"W-well?" asked Patrick, "g-go on pl-please," he said. as he straightened the drying cloth over his waist.

"Patrick, Braeden has been taken and I thought ye should know. Kyra is preparing to ride with me brathair, Rory, to search for him. and I wanted to make ye aware of the happenings."

"Have M-Moya ready me h-horse as w-well," replied Patrick. Ruarc gave him a concerned and confused glance before Patrick could clarify.

"I r-ride with them, mon," Patrick nodded. indicating there would be no further discussion. "J-just l-let me tell m-me wife," he added solemnly.

After barring the door, Patrick began to dress right away. Darina raised her sleepy head from the back of the tub. and listened to the rustling activity from the other side of the screen. She heard Patrick speaking with someone in hushed tones and couldn't begin to imagine what would warrant an interruption at this time of night. Or was it morning already?

Darina, are ye awake. luv? he asked with his mind.

"Aye," she replied audibly, rising from the tub to wrap herself in a plush robe hung near the hearth. "Patrick, what was that about?" she asked as she exited the privacy screen and tub area. Obviously startled to see him dressed and donning his chain, she covered her mouth and silenced an audible gasp.

She caught his eyes and read intensity and fear in their depths. Unable to read his thoughts, she reached to touch his cheek and smiled warmly at him. "Patrick, where are ye going?"

He sighed and responded. *Ruarc came to our chambers in haste. He requires my assistance in retrieving…uh…something, and I must go. I will return soon. Do no' worry, luv,* he reassured her. He pressed a lingering kiss to her forehead, embraced her gently and walked out the door.

CHAPTER TWENTY-FOUR

MacCahan Territory

Parkin was still awake when the sun shone through the arrow-slit window in his chamber at MacCahan castle, casting a foreboding light on the chests piled shoulder high atop one another in the corner of the room. His life was either ending today or beginning today. Of which, he wasn't sure; he just knew that major change and trial were coming, and he would never be the same. *Never. Ever.*

Winnie wriggled beside him and slapped a slobbery, sucked thumb at him before rolling onto her side and grabbing him on both sides of his face with her chubby toddler hands. "Da! Da!" she exclaimed as she sat upright on the bed.

A pungent odor battered his nose, and he leaped out of bed. "Ye wet the bed again," he said. Winnie giggled and rolled about in the wet linens, pulling at her toes. Parkin raced to the doorway and called down the hallway for Lois, their chambermaid.

Macklin left the straw mat pallet on the floor beside the bed and lifted Winnie down by her armpits. "Watch me," he told Parkin, "this is no' hard," he added, rolling his eyes at Parkin. Before Parkin could find his own plaid, Macklin managed to undress her, wash her in the soapy basin water atop the trestle table, dry her and re-dress her clean and fresh smelling—packing her rabbit-skinned over-drawers with strips of clean linen cloth. "Did ye see what I did?" he asked.

Parkin nodded his head just as the chambermaid arrived. "The bed linens are soiled," Macklin said, "as are these drawers," he added, handing her a rolled-up ball of urine-soaked linen strips and rabbit skin mini-truis. "I told ye, if ye would but lay the sheepskin run on her side of the bed, smooth side up, ye could avoid the wet linens," he added under his breath. Parkin nodded again and took Winnie from Macklin.

"I'm trying," he said apologetically to Macklin. "I promise, I am trying."

***

Cordal rose first, inching his way from the back of the hidden cave towards the sun-filled opening. Quiet as a mouse, he tiptoed past the row of slumbering bodies, and realized too late just how weak he was. Too long since he saw the sun, he was determined to feel the sand on his feet, and the salt air on his face. Stopping to lean against the cave walls, he caught his breath and persevered to keep moving forward, pressing toward the sun like a starved plant.

"Where are ye going?" whispered Braeden, grabbing Cordal about the ankle.

"Shh," he replied and placed a finger over his mouth. "Come with me boy," he said. "I need a bath."

"That ye do," Braeden replied, holding his nose in jest. Grabbing his dagger, Braeden rose to join Cordal. Sure they were alone on the shore, they both dove head first into the waves and swam until they could no longer touch bottom.

Cordal scrubbed at his beard and twisted the salt water from his hair, paddling with his arms. "Lemme' have that dagger, if ye will?" he gestured towards Braeden.

"Ye won't lose it?"

"Nay, I promise, I won't lose it," he said.

Braeden swam near to Cordal and handed him the dagger. Cautious as ever, he watched carefully to make sure Cordal didn't lose his grip on the handle. "I say, what do ye intend to…"

Before Braeden could speak another word; Cordal sliced his unusually long beard off at the chin and cut his long hair to his shoulders. Dipping his head back in the water, he placed the dagger in his teeth and then dove deep underwater to swim for shore.

Braeden took off in a flash, swimming as fast as his arms would take him; watching the shadows on the beach dance as the sun continued to rise from behind them. Thinking it a race, Braeden made it first to shore, but sat astonished when he realized Cordal was not there. He walked up and down the small area of sandy beach where they entered the water, and no Cordal.

Fearing what may have occurred; Braeden waded out several feet into the crashing waves, frantically searching for any sign of the man. From out of nowhere, Cordal rose from the crashing waters, dagger in mouth...and the biggest fish Braeden had ever seen squirming against his grip.

"Hungry?" he called to Braeden.

"Starving," said Braeden, smiling. "Let's eat."

CHAPTER TWENTY-FIVE

O'Malley Territory — Five Nights Later

"Galen, are ye able to keep up?" asked Lucian from his seated position at the triangular council table.

"Aye," responded Galen from the back of the room. "I think so."

Lucian continued, and Galen scribbled frantically on the parchment laid out in front of him on the makeshift scribe's table, "In Rory's absence, his wife, Atilde attends in his stead."

"Now, what are we to do about the bodies washed on shore and the debris that has floated up to the piers?" asked Ruarc. "I fear another slave ship has met its doom at sea, or worse yet, has crashed at one of the outlying islands past the Isle. Should we send a search vessel?"

Atilde spoke up, "I think with the situation at hand, with Patrick gone and Rory and Kyra away, we should keep to the mainland until we are sure what we are dealing with."

"I agree," added Gemma.

"I agree," added Murchadh.

"Then it is done," said Lucian. "Now for the matter of petty court. Dervilla advises that Darina refuses her duties since Patrick left?"

"Aye," Gemma said. "She wouldna leave her chamber the first two days and has only recently taken to walking around the castle grounds with that hound of hers. She doesn't eat, and she barely sleeps."

"Perhaps she is already with child," interjected Payton, Patrick's younger brother, from the other side of the room, "and feeling poorly."

Ruarc muttered, "Doubtful," under his breath and waved for Lucian to continue. Lucian stood and paced with his hands behind his back.

"Gemma, are ye amenable to continuing petty court duties until we reach some other solution?" Lucian inquired.

"Aye," she responded.

"So be it," stated the others in unison, and Galen scurried to record it in the clan registry. Lucian waved his hand toward Ruarc, who stood to speak.

"As ye know, Patrick joined Rory and Kyra five nights past to search for Braeden, who was taken by brigands in a boat just off the shore. Mavis escaped and sent word to Gemma, and she now resides in one of the newer minor cottages on the Isle. She has been given charge over Winnie, Parkin's young daughter, until such time as other arrangements can be made. Parkin arrived here yestereve with the first MacCahan ship."

Payton interjected, "Arrangements still need to be made for Macklin's care."

"Aye, it appears that Parkin has a young boy, a stepson, a foster now for Parkin—the half-brathair of his daughter, Winnie?" he half-asked, half-stated, in the direction of Payton, who nodded his agreement. "He has passed the age of twelve summers and is therefore unable to reside on the Isle."

"However," interrupted Payton again.

"However," repeated Ruarc, agitation showing in his voice, "Atilde has agreed to set him up in a privy chamber on the third floor in the Inn. It will remain his permanent residence, used only by him from here on, and the rents for the room are to be paid by Parkin."

"And, Galen will act on his behalf betwixt he and Parkin; and remain a surrogate foster when Parkin is otherwise engaged, at sea, or simply unavailable," added Lucian.

"Until he reaches sixteen summers," added Galen.

"Until he reaches sixteen summers," repeated Lucian nodding.

The sound of barking outside the High Council chamber doors alerted the group. "Darina," said Ruarc.

"Aye," replied the MacCahan guard who stood watch over the chamber. "Me lady wishes an audience with the Council this eve. She insists upon it."

"What is the nature of her request?" asked Atilde, clearly perturbed. "Can't she see we are about clan business at this late hour?" The guard nodded, bowed, and left the chamber only to return a moment later.

"Speak," said Lucian.

"She wishes to discuss the matter of an annulment."

"Bring her in," rang her uncle Ruarc's voice loud and clear through the chamber.

Darina entered the chamber, head held high, her hound Fanai closely behind and lapping at her heels.

"What is this nonsense ye speak of Darina?" Ruarc demanded angrily.

"'Tis not nonsense, dear uncle, and ye ken what I am about. I bring before the High Council me petition for an annulment, and I mean to make it happen," she responded sternly.

"On what grounds do ye bring this petition?" asked Gemma confused.

159

"On the grounds of abandonment, me lady," she sighed, now looking at Gemma, "and I have proof enough. The MacCahan has been gone nigh to six eves and has not returned, and has not sent word. I wish to dispose meself of this farce of a marriage. He left me on our wedding night and he hasna returned." Tears welled up in eyes that were met with sympathy.

"Darina, to petition for abandonment, yer spouse must be gone more than two bliadains. Ye know this," said Atilde.

"Nay, there is another way," she retorted hanging her head in embarrassment. Lucian gave her an empathetic knowing glance and rose to speak. "I should like to address the Council privately," he said. "Forthwith," he exclaimed raising his hands.

Ruarc acknowledged his request, and sent the servants and soldiers out of the council room with a tilt of his head. Darina followed them to wait outside on the bench, and the heavy wooden doors were barred from the inside once again.

She reclined on the wooden bench before realizing Fanai had not come out with her. The guards blocked her attempt to regain entry; all she could hope was that he wouldn't cause too much of a fuss. She sat alone on the bench, clenching her fists in her lap, hoping her memories wouldn't cause a flux of tears again.

A tussle against the chamber doors and raised voices indicated things were getting a might testy inside. The guard who stood on the right of the chamber door excused himself to make entry, and the remaining guard raised his shoulders and tilted his head indicating he wasn't sure what was going on. Darina sat up straight and leaned her ear to the door to listen. All she could make out was the muffled sounds of loud argument.

Inside the chamber, things were indeed unruly. After hiding in the shadows, Payton resumed his seat next to Atilde, representing his brother the Laird who was not present. Patrick named Payton his Second-in-Command during his absence and the Council had no choice but to honor his request.

160

"Payton, what have ye to say of yer brathair?" asked Ruarc staring angrily at him.

"I don't get yer meaning?" Payton replied, confused.

Gemma spoke up, "Payton, the only alternative method for gaining an annulment for abandonment…" her words halted, and she faltered for a moment before looking to Lucian to continue.

Payton sat forward in his chair laying his arms across the table and stared directly at Lucian who didn't speak. "Well, Lucian, is somebody going to tell me what is going on here?" he asked.

Lucian grunted and pulled at his beard. He stared at Gemma and spoke. "Payton, there are only two ways to obtain an annulment by abandonment."

"And?" asked Payton.

"And the first is for the spouse to be missing more than two bliadains; with no word or missives about their whereabouts, safety, life or death. This is essential in times of war and travel—life, and our clan, must go on."

Payton leaned back in his chair, nodded in response and made a circular motion with his right hand in the air for him to continue.

"If one is missing two years Payton, with no word, they are presumed dead or having abandoned their clan. They are pronounced banished and their spouse is released from the bonds of the marriage," interjected Gemma.

"I ken," said Payton. "But what has this to do with me brathair?"

"There is another way," said Ruarc, slightly embarrassed.

"And what is that?" he retorted impatiently.

Atilde interrupted and laid her hand on Payton's forearm, "If the marriage is not consummated in ten night's time, the bond can be annulled by petition of either party on the grounds of abandonment."

161

Payton choked and leaned forward in his chair. Ruarc rose to pace the chamber and Atilde grew red with embarrassment.

"What have ye to say of yer brathair, Payton?" Ruarc asked angrily, pointing a worn right index finger at him.

"What have I got to say about this?" he asked sarcastically. "I have nothing to say about this."

"Did ye know that Patrick was im-im-imp...oh by the gods...unable to perform the duties of a husband?" questioned Murchadh under his breath, toying with his goblet.

"Patrick has no such issues to me knowledge and I don't believe her," he shouted, and stood pointing an arm right back at Ruarc. "I invoke me right to question her in my brathair's stead."

The Council members gasped and chaos stole order from the room. Murchadh was pounding his fist on the table and Ruarc's face turned three shades of purple from holding his breath—his temper threatening to get the better of him.

"Silence!" commanded Lucian. "I've heard enough. Payton, 'tis yer right to question the lass. I would caution ye to be noble and honorable. She is the Next-in-Commandof the O'Malley clan and should this marriage be annulled, 'twould cost the MacCahan's a great deal...especially yer brathair."

Payton nodded his acknowledgement and gestured for the sentry to send her back in. Fanai met Darina at the door and lapped at her ankles sending waves of calm throughout her body. Her shoulders relaxed and she took a deep breath before entering the chambers again.

Here it comes, she thought.

Lucian motioned for her to take his seat next to Murchadh and it was then she noticed Payton sitting aside her aunt Atilde. "What is he doing here?" she asked pointing an accusing finger at Payton.

"Darina, Patrick placed him as Second-in-Command before he left. He has invoked his right to question ye concerning yer petition for annulment and the Council has agreed to let him do so."

She nodded at Payton, casting a warning glance his way and said, "Then by all means let's get this over with," and sighed heavily, melting into her chair.

"Darina, I'll not waste any time with pleasantries. I'll ask ye but one question," said Payton.

"Alright then, please do so."

"Darina, was my brathair Patrick unable or was he unwilling to consummate the marriage on yer wedding night?"

Gemma stood straight up and pushed her chair back with her legs in one loud, swift movement. Her hands landed on the table in front of her with a thud and she groaned audibly. "This is unnecessary," she bellowed and turned to walk towards the hearth.

"Nay, he is being as courteous as he can, considering the matter," said Lucian, rubbing Darina's shoulders in comfort.

Darina was unable to contain the flood of tears that were walled up behind her lashes. They spilled forth as if a dam had broken, and they drenched her face. Ruarc handed her a cloth which she used to wipe her face and blow her nose. Every attempt she made to speak was met with another wave of tears that made communication nearly impossible.

"Oh! What difference does it make, Payton," demanded Atilde angry at this point. "Can't ye see she speaks the truth? She has been dishonored and no mon will want her now."

Payton replied, "It makes a great bit of difference here. Ten nights have not passed, only six. There are four more nights that the marriage can still be consummated. My brathair may return any moment now and here we all sit contemplating the annulment of this marriage. Her petition is four days premature and I intend to find out why."

He stared at Darina who continued to weep quietly.

"I'll give ye each notice right now, that before this day is over, I intend to tell Darina everything she needs to know. This annulment will not happen and ye all know why! Ye have hidden a delicate matter from her and as the Lord's wife, she has a right to be informed."

Darina raised her eyes to meet Payton's. She saw the same fire and ice in him as she did in Patrick. He was coming to her defense. *But…whatever for?*

"Darina, wait outside!" commanded Lucian. "We will call ye back in just a moment, we've some things to discuss with yer husband's brathair."

Once again, Darina took up residence on the bench outside the council chamber. This time, Fanai sat beside her with his head in her lap. The tears continued, but her heart turned, there was promise of some answers…finally. Mayhap now she will know what took him from her so abruptly in the middle of the night. Why he abandoned her.

"Darina, did he make any attempt at all to consummate yer union?"

"Darina?"

She was back in the chamber and being questioned again. Someone interrupted her memories, her train of thought. *What did she ask?*

"Darina," continued Gemma. "Did Patrick make any attempt whatsoever to consummate yer union? I ken this is difficult, but we must have the answers," she said apologetically.

Payton interrupted, "Darina, I will ask ye again. Was my brathair unable or unwilling to consummate the marriage?"

She bowed her head in thought and answered sheepishly, "Well…he was not…unable, if that is what ye wish to know. He was mostly…unwilling…I would say."

"Unwilling!" hollered Ruarc over the sounds of the Council. "Unwilling! A dishonor I tell ye, he has brought grave dishonor to this clan!"

"Hold on a minute," interrupted Lucian.

Darina began to cry uncontrollably again and Payton's face grew white as snow. "I don't believe it!" he shouted back to Ruarc. "I don't believe it," he repeated. "Tell us *exactly* what happened," he demanded to Darina, who had now grown angry as well as humiliated.

She rose in defiance to pace the room, both fists on her hips and she strode towards Payton. She held out an accusing finger and retaliated. "Nobody calls me a liar, ye imbecile!"

"Then tell me the truth!" he shouted back to her face. *That did it.*

Ruarc lurched towards them, but not in time to prevent Darina from landing a solid punch to the left of Payton's jaw that sent him reeling backwards to the floor. He cringed in pain and held the side of his face.

"What sort of ladies are ye raising here, Ruarc?" Payton asked sarcastically.

"The kind that ken how to defend themselves, and their honor Payton," he replied.

Lucian grabbed Darina by the shoulders and led her back to her seat. He motioned for a servant, who brought a large goblet of wine and set it before her. She quickly returned with a flask of whiskey as well and set it before her.

She grabbed the whiskey.

"Darina, I realize this subject matter much cause ye great embarrassment," said her Aunt Atilde.

"And what of me brathair?" interjected Payton impatiently. "We speak of matters he is in no way able to address not being here."

165

"Ye," she said pointing at Payton who was holding up the stone wall, still grasping the side of his mouth, "will hold yer tongue and stay right there."

"Ye," she said pointing at Darina who just downed the last of the whiskey, "Will think long and hard and speak carefully...for ye tread on thin ice," she warned.

Darina closed her eyes and let the rest of the burn settle into her stomach. The whiskey would help her. She could speak her mind without faltering. This wouldn't be so bad.

"Darina, answer the question. Darina," said Atilde. "Are ye alright dear?" she asked wiping the tears from Darina's face. "Can ye answer his question?"

"Darina, was it his choice not to consummate the marriage?" asked Payton again, slowly and methodically this time.

"I... I don't know...how to answer that."

"Does the blame belong with ye or with him?" asked Ruarc abruptly tired of the questioning.

Darina untied and retied the belt covering her tunic and truis and petted Fanai who lay at the ground beside her. "I would have to say, that the blame lies with ye, Uncle Ruarc," she answered stoically, looking him right in the face.

Payton coughed and Ruarc rose from his chair to address her directly. "How on earth would the consummation of yer marriage in any way be me responsibility lass?" he asked angrily.

"Ye took him Uncle. Ye took him from our chambers and he has never returned."

A hush rose over the Council and Lucian shook his head back and forth, an apparent fear rising in him. Pain and anguish festooned Ruarc's face and he sat to collect his thoughts. His niece's accusation met him with force. *She was right. I did take him from her on their wedding night. I had no other choice. He had to know.*

Payton interrupted, "That's it…I've had enough of this charade. It's time she knew, and since none of ye other pussy willows have the bollocks to tell her…I will!"

Payton strode towards Darina and bent to kneel down beside her. Fanai got up and moved to her other side, sensing it was needed. "Promise ye won't punch me again, me lady?" he asked sheepishly, grinning up at her.

"Don't Payton, let me," said Lucian.

"Nay, I won't. Ye've had eleven years to get to the right of it, and I'll not give ye the opportunity now."

Darina shook her head in confusion and looked up at Payton. "Payton will tell me. I trust him."

"Good," he said as he rose and walked towards the stony wall. "Darina, Ruarc came to get Patrick that night in yer chamber, did he not'?"

"Aye, he did. We were um, in the bath. I mean…I was in the bath and we were wet, and a fierce banging came on the chamber door and Patrick rose to open it," she said from behind flushed cheeks.

"He did, and who was there, Darina?"

"From behind the privacy screen, I could hear Uncle Ruarc and Patrick discussing something that seemed to be of importance."

"And then what happened?" he asked as he waived his hands across his chest animatedly, as if making a point to the Council.

"Then Patrick returned to the room, shut the door, adorned hisself with his chain and armor, and told me that he was needed to retrieve something and he would be right back."

"And ye haven't seen or heard from him since?"

"Nay, I haven't. Payton, what is going on?"

167

"Ruarc, would ye please tell Darina why Patrick left at yer request."

Ruarc flinched at the mention of his name and his face grew red with shame. "We were told by Mavis that the boy, Braeden, was abducted at the piers and taken off in a boat. Mavis managed to escape by leaping from the vessel, and she swam for hours until she reached the shore of the Isle; just past midnight."

"And?" bade Payton motioning for him to continue.

"And I sent for Rory and Kyra to accompany Patrick to retrieve the boy."

"Ye sent Patrick?" asked Darina not believing it. "Ye sent my husband after his bastard child on me wedding night, on the advice of his mistress?" Tears threatened to spill themselves down her cheeks again.

Payton interrupted and spoke directly to Darina this time, "Braeden is no' Patrick's bastard child and Mavis is no' his mistress."

"I've heard tell of yer brathair and his many illegitimate bairns. His reputation precedes him unfortunately," retorted Darina angrily.

Payton's voice rose in anger. "Ye don't know what ye are talking about, ye snotty wench," he said behind clenched teeth.

Fanai rose from the floor beside Darina and growled loudly and deliberately, clearly showing Payton his teeth. He scampered until he had placed himself between Payton and Darina and sat, teeth raised, inviting him to continue.

"Payton, ye would do well to lower yer voice," Darina mused. "Explain yerself."

"I've no doubt ye have heard tell of my brathair, Darina. And, he does have a reputation as that of a lady's mon, a lecher some might say."

"See," Darina responded, nodding her head and gesturing to the Council members.

"But that brathair, Darina, would be Parkin—not Patrick. Parkin is the one with illegitimate children and a handful of heartbroken women following him about. Patrick is the most honorable mon I have ever known. Patrick is more honorable than me own da even…though it would shame him to hear it."

"Then why by the goddess, would he leave his wife on their wedding night to chase after a no-account bastard child?" she spat at him, the indignation rising in her voice.

"Shall I tell her then?" asked Payton to Lucian who stood stone-faced and pale against the hearth. Lucian nodded.

"Because Darina, that no-account bastard child is yer brathair."

***

It only took moments for Darina to return to her chamber and don her armor and cloak. She called for Riann to be readied and for Moya to prepare her steed. She was situating her helmet when Payton burst through the door.

"Where do ye think ye are going?" Payton asked accusingly. She ignored him, and jumped into her boots as she tied Fanai to the bed post and instructed Minea to care for him in her absence.

"I asked ye a question, seesta," he jabbed sarcastically at her.

"I'd like to ken the same thing," interrupted Ruarc, who was out of breath after having followed her up nearly seven flights of stairs.

"I am the best hunter in the clan and no one else has me tracking abilities," she said as she gestured towards the window where Riann was seen circling the keep. "I intend to bring me brathair *and* me husband home."

"I will deal with ye later," she pointed at Ruarc. "Ye've sent yer brathair, a ship builder, with Kyra and me husband, who does not know our lands, to retrieve the true Lord of O'Malley clan."

"And ye, I would thrash ye within an inch of yer life if ye hadn't been the only mon brave enough to tell me the truth," she directed at Payton.

"Well?" she gestured towards Payton impatiently. "Aren't ye coming with me? He is yer brathair, an honorable mon ye say? Don ye armor and ride with me," she insisted.

"Nay," said Ruarc from the other side of the bed. "Patrick has named him in-charge in his stead."

"And I am leaving ye in charge in me stead. I trust ye won't muck this up?" she shouted angrily, loud enough for the rafter to shake.

Ruarc nodded and Darina and Payton headed through the corridor and down the stairs to meet the night.

TWENTY-SIX

Burke Shores

Orla met Cordal and Braeden at the cave opening, a look of disgruntled satisfaction about her, "I told ye they left to find sustenance," she spat at the priest, pointing to the two hares dangling across Braeden's neck. "They wouldna' leave us here alone." Placing a long arm about Shanleigh's shoulders, they retreated into the safety of their cavernous shelter and watched as the priest added wood to an already loudly crackling fire.

"Hand that pot o'er here, child," Father MacArtrey implored. "I'll tend to the hares and ye two wash up." Acknowledging the priest's judicious permission to leave her own cave, Orla kicked sand into the fire and over his robe as they made their way back to the cave entrance.

"What do ye make of them drawings there, priest?" asked Naelyn, pointing to the rear of the cave which went back, it seemed, nearly ten yards or so into dank obscurity. Naelyn bent her head and carefully examined the cave drawings, inching further down into the cave's depths, and bending her head further and further down as she went, until finally she had no choice but to scoot on her knees. Tracing the outline of the drawings and symbols on the wall, she noted mentally that they appeared to be several decades, if not, several centuries old.

"I noticed them when we first arrived, but I was too tired, ye ken, to examine them further," he murmured. "Appear to be nothing more than ancient pagan scratching to me. With some pictures, mind ye, that look as if they were placed there by a wee child," he added.

Naelyn mumbled something under her breath as she continued to follow the storyline on the cave walls. It was written in vivid color, initially, she surmised symbols of a dead language. It was the figures of the people, a clan or tribe of some kind that interested her most. They were fisher peoples, she assumed, based on the vast amount of ships set out just from the shore, of this very location she believed. Apparently, there was wreckage of some kind washed ashore—and visitors came and met with the inhabitants. The land dwellers welcomed the visitors, but were unhappy to find that the visitors were not well-meaning and intended instead to take their land. There was some kind of battle and another ship came, except it didn't come up on the shore, it appeared to have arrived from out of nowhere, from the sky perhaps. *What on earth?* she thought to herself.

"I wouldna' waste my time trying to decipher that bit of nonsense if I were ye," the priest interrupted. ""Tis likely the work of some ole' sorceress or what not, doubtless it's meant to scare the likes of ye," he chuckled.

"I'm no' so sure," Naelyn whispered in reply. "It all looks strangely familiar to me, almost as if I've seen it before."

"Ye were the scribe, were ye no'?"

"Aye, I s'pose I was the closest thing to a scribe here."

"Do ye recognize the language then?" he asked.

"Nay, some of it resembles ancient Gaelic scripting, but then it goes on, and I can't make it out it all. I've never seen anything like it."

172

"'Tis Vedic," interjected Braeden, reaching down to turn the hares with a piney stick. "Vedic Sanskrit, I believe, ye ken?" he asked looking up at Naelyn who was staring astonishingly at Cordal.

"Ye have seen this scripting before?" she asked.

"Aye."

"And ye can read it? Ye can make out what it means?"

"I think so, mayhap not exactly, but I can gather the gist of it."

***

Gemma sat at the large table in the main dining hall on the Isle of Women. Most of the ladies had left after their noon meal and she and Kyra were planning their duties for the remainder of the week, and the festivities for the Lunar Bacchanal, later that evening.

"And yer sure ye did no' tell him?" asked Gemma.

"Positive," replied Kyra. "I've no good idea how Patrick divined my condition, but he did. He told me flatly that there was no way he would take me into Burke lands in my condition, and that ye would know how best to use me services here, on the island," she added laughing. "Thank ye for putting me up in the new round cottage with Mavis, that should help me much in ferreting out the spy amongst us. Rory believes still that we have a Burke spy amongst the women, and I am to identify her."

"Well, I hope ye are successful. I'd like to believe I ken these lasses, but ye never can tell about some people. They seem to have a gift for deception. How is Mavis doing?" asked Gemma.

"She seems a warm and friendly type, has been through I lot I gather, from what I can tell. Misses that boy something terrible, but I will tell ye that Winnie is keeping her busy. Us really, keeping us busy I should say. Good practice for me though," she said rubbing her belly with animation. "I've never cared for a bairn before, much more work than messaging."

"Well," said Gemma. "I'm certainly glad ye are here. I have need of yer…uh…special abilities with one of the men."

"One of the men?"

"Aye, only a few more hours until the Bacchanal and we already have a mon sneaking about without a formal invite, mind ye. Caught up near, well, near the cottage where ye and Mavis stay. Peeking in the window slit. Shadrae brought him back down here last night, to the main keep and he's in the storage cellar. Wouldn't speak, wouldn't identify himself and acted like he had no idea what the Bacchanal was," Gemma laughed.

"What has been done about it?" asked Kyra.

"Nothing really. Ordinarily we would send him onto the mainland, but with the sentries posted everywhere and the ferry docked, we've no way to get him back down there now without causing a big ruckus with yer father. I'm in no mood for yer father today, lass," she added.

"I ken ye aren't", said Kyra. "Me neither, if ye want to know the truth of it. I still haven't told him about the babe, he just kens I've set up for spying here and I'm going by Kara instead of Kyra. With Patrick and Darina both gone, how long did the council say that we would remain on high alert?"

Gemma reached across the table and handed a mug of water to Kyra, "I guess until one of them returns. We have another council meeting tomorrow eve and I have petty court duties all day tomorrow on the mainland. Ye know, it will be the first time I've been back on the mainland in quite a while, mayhap six days I s'pose."

Gemma rose and stretched her long arms high up into the air. "I've much work to do in preparations for the Bacchanal celebrations. It will be a small one, only men from our clan can attend this eve and they have to be approved by Ruarc before coming over on the ferry. "'Tis why the one we have in the cellar is a poor suspect. His story doesn't add up."

"He wouldn't tell ye anything?"

"Not a word, acted surprised to be here. Shadrae has done her best to interrogate the captive, but ye know how Shadrae is. He's probably a little roughed up, but no worse for the wear. Take a look a' him and let us know what ye think can be done. Follow me," she motioned.

Gemma gestured for Kyra to follow her down the long, winding corridor at the back of the kitchens, This led to the doors which opened into the underground storage cellars. The ale and salted meats were stored underground, as were other supplies like grain and special herbs. The chandler had an antechamber just offset from the bottlery and adjacent to that was the storage cellar where the prisoner was detained.

Kyra slowly shoved the door open and caught a glance of Shadrae standing a few feet in front of the prisoner. He was seated on a three-legged stool, back to the door with his arms tied behind his back and his head hung low against his chest as if he were sleeping. There wasn't much light in the room, save for the large candelabrum in the right corner and the lanthorn setting atop a small wooden chest to the left of the man.

She could tell he had been whipped with something, but only small welts rose on his backs and shoulders and not a drop of blood was in sight. He was sweating, or he was wet, perhaps Shadrae has dunked him in the water bucket, she wasn't sure. She motioned for Shadrae to join them in the corridor and she obliged, shutting the door behind her.

"What ye got there, Shadrae?" she asked glibly.

"A very uncooperative mon, I'd say. Won't tell me who he is or where's he from, or why he was so interested in that wee babe."

"Wee babe?" Kyra asked.

"Aye. He nearly scared the life outta Mavis and reached his hands through the window slit as if to take that babe. Ye know we've had some problems of late with stolen chillens."

175

"Aye—I know," gasped Kyra placing a hand over her mouth.

"Mavis hadn't outfitted the babe proper yet, ye ken? She wasna' exactly dressed, still toddling about in her wee rabbit-skin breeches she was. So he may'a thunk her to be a lad, rather than a lass."

"Oh my," said Gemma. "I hope he is not one of them child thieves, Patrick will kill him."

TWENTY-SEVEN

O'Malley Lands

Darina rose from the cold, flowing river and squished the water down the length of her red hair until she expelled the most of it. "Do no' turnaround," she repeated for what seemed the hundredth time to a very impatient Payton. Grabbing her extra pair of truis and a tunic from her saddle bag, she jumped into the clean linens soaking wet. After she fastened her belt and secured her dagger and broadsword she punched Payton in the back, "Yer turn."

Grabbing her horse by the lead, she made her way up the sloping hillside and beckoned, "I'll wait up here. When ye are done, we are going to the plateau whether ye like it or not."

The noonday sun was high in the sky and although she wasn't certain she could make an audience with Covar, she knew it was her only hope of finding her husband. After all, hadn't they both told her that Covar could find Patrick anywhere, if he was wearing his ring? *This has to be the way,* she thought. For the last six days, she and Payton scoured the Burke lands, and save for a close scrape with some vagrants on the main road to the castle, had found nothing. Nothing, that was, except an eerily empty monastery, an unguarded castle and no sight whatsoever of any Burke soldiers. Even the market was empty; it was as if all the people had vanished into thin air. Payton managed even to examine the armory, and there was no one at all. There were plenty of weapons, but not a soul in sight.

Darina spread out her cloak on the fresh green clover and removed the pouch of nuts, fruit and dried meats. Eating was a welcome break from the monotonous and unyielding search of Burke lands. Happy to be back in her own territory, she sent word on ahead that they were returned but had one more task to settle before they would arrive at the keep.

She hadn't let herself cry yet, that was a part of herself she wouldn't share with her husband's brother. She saved those tears for her husband, to be unleashed along with her wrath at a later date. For now, her heart beat mostly for the brother she never knew. The true Lord of O'Malley lands, as young as he was, was her own flesh and blood, and she dearly hoped to find him before something horrible happened. She wasn't able to tell her four sisters yet that they had a brother; and she wasn't sure she could do so without bringing him with her. *No, it couldn't end this way. Better to never tell them they had a brathair than to tell them and then mourn his death.*

It was simply unfathomable that her mother was not told the child lived. How could her father have been so insensitive—letting the entire family, the entire clan, mourn the death of a child without a word? She would take that up with him in the afterlife, she swore to herself under her breath.

"What are ye mumbling about now, Darina?" Payton asked throwing himself down on the ground beside her and grabbing the last bit of cheese, shaking his wet hair about sending splashes of water all around them.

"I just don't understand what me da was thinking sending Braeden off from the clan and his family. Look where it's gotten us," she sighed.

"I ken yer father was a wise man, Darina. I believe he knew what he was doing and I think that whoever has Braeden, doesn't know who he really is and has no idea what they are dealing with."

"What do ye mean?"

"Braeden is a warrior in his own right, Darina. Been trained with the best of them, he has," he said, taking a big bite out of an apple.

"Trained, how?"

"Yer trained, are ye no'?"

"Of course I am, I had to be, there are so many women in O'Malley land, we all serve in the forces at some time or another. 'Tis a requirement prior to marriage. Why?"

"Well because, I am no' at all sure if ye know this or not, but Lucian from your clan is the brother of Airard from my clan," he said.

"And?" she asked.

"And—it appears that Gemma kens my father somehow."

"How do ye ken that?"

"I can't rightly tell ye, but I ken it's the truth. I believe that there was some planning going on between our clans with regard to Braeden's…uh…learning. Me da insisted from the time he could walk straight that he be trained in self-defense and archery and sword use and the such. He is a very skilled combatant."

"Well, that's good then," said Darina.

"So, that's why I say—if he was taken, whoever has him has no idea what he is about. I wouldna be surprised if he's already escaped and just can't find his way back to us.

"I hope yer right, Payton. But for the life of me, I can't figure out why we haven't heard back from Patrick yet. That bothers me immensely."

Payton stood up and readied his horse. "Don't let that bother ye either, lass. Patrick is a smart mon. No doubt he has a plan and we'll know the right of it soon enough."

***

Odetta sealed the missive with the candlewax and handed it to Reni. "Make sure that Dougal takes this straight to O'Malley lands. He is to speak with no one and to only return when he has a response. He is not to return without a response. Do you ken?"

"Yes, me lady. I understand," replied Reni, wiping tears from her cheeks and bowing before her mistress.

"Now stop that weeping, it does us no good. Send him in now, and come back here at once, when ye are finished."

Odetta rose from the table and fumbled with the fire in the hearth. The abandoned wharf was a good enough place as any to meet Dirk to discuss their predicament and she knew that Easal, who was now Eaton in reality, would never find them here. She had taken to spending her afternoon "naps" at the wharf and along with Reni, was making some considerable headway in undermining much of Easal's destructive behavior.

The sound of footsteps broke her attention and she turned to Dirk, "Dirk, thank ye so much for meeting me here. Ye were not followed?" she asked.

"Nay, me lady. I was no' followed," responded the armory overseer. "Any word on our girls?" he asked forlornly.

"Nay. I've sent out me own sentries to search for then. Easal has refused to assist in the matter."

"I see. What need have ye of me services?" he asked, absentmindedly running an index finger along the edge of the trestle table.

"I need to speak with ye privately, of a matter of most importance, and I need ye to do yer absolute best to believe what I tell ye. I say this because it may be verra difficult for ye to do so. Do ye understand what I'm saying?" she asked.

"Aye. I think I do."

180

"Easal is no' himself," she started, and turned to pace with her hands behind her back across the rickety floor of the abandoned wharf.

Dirk nodded his agreement in confusion.

"I believe, and I'm not sure whether or not ye believe, but…oh well," she sighed. "Dirk, do ye believe in spirits and such?" she asked tentatively.

"Aye. I do me lady, verra much so."

"Well, Dirk, there is no kind way to say this, especially about me own husband, but I may as well share this w' ye as it appears it affects us both."

"Go on," he bade.

"Dirk, I believe Easal, my husband, the mon I love, has been overtaken by an evil and malevolent spirit."

Dirk gasped, grasped his sword by the hilt and swinging it away from his body still entombed in its belt casing, sat himself down upon a three-legged stool that nearly toppled under his weight.

"Ye don't mean?" he asked, his face as pale as a ghost.

"I do, and I have no idea what can be done. Naelyn and I have tried everything, we even consulted with the priest from O'Malley lands and he confirmed our greatest fears. Easal is possessed."

"Me lady, what can be done about this?"

"Dirk, I don't know but what I do know is that we have to be verra careful. He doesn't know I'm here, I am hiding from him and if he knew I was speaking with you, it would not be good."

"Ye do no' think he has anything to do with our daughters missing, now do ye?" he asked.

"Of course I do. There is no other explanation," she replied.

"I'll kill him!" Dirk shouted, causing the unsturdy stool and rafters on the wharf house to shake, pitching him to the floor.

"Calm down a bit. Ye won't be able to kill the likes of him, at least not by yerself. Let me tell ye what I've done about it. Here, have a seat," she bade, motioning for him to attempt the stool once more.

"I've had Reni, my maidservant, contact all of the Burke clans' members with family in McTierney territory, and they have all gone for a little visit. Took our biggest sailing vessels with them, gets them there faster. I've asked that none return for two fortnights. Those with contacts with the McDermott's to the east are doing the same, they are travelling on foot. There are only a few remaining in our territory then and what few are left, are not necessary to take up arms, I'll be sending to the O'Malley lands for refuge."

"O'Malley lands?" he gasped. "Ye think they will heed our request for sanctuary? They are our enemies, are they no'?".

"Well, yes they are, they have been, I've no idea what they think of us now. Ye ken they have a new laird?"

"I had heard the O'Malley passed, but I didna' know there was a son?"

"There wasn't—at least to me knowledge. The eldest daughter has married the son of a Lord from up north and he is the new O'Malley. Took their name and all, swore an oath, he did."

"Ye really think they will offer us refuge?"

"I think they will. I have sent Dougal on ahead with a missive and request. I have explained that me daughter and your daughter is missing, and we believe that Easal has been behind the childnapping's all this time, and we intend to deal with him swiftly and severely from within our own clan. But, our people will need refuge until such time as that is accomplished."

"Verra clever, me lady," he said as he bowed.

182

"Now, what I need from ye is this," she began.

TWENTY-EIGHT

Isle of Women

Kyra rattled off a list of items she would need for her interrogation of the prisoner. Gorman, the elderly butler, and one of only a handful of males permitted to live on the isle, nodded his aging head and scampered off at the last of her requests.

"Ye sure ye know what yer doing?" asked Gemma with a look of confusion.

"Whatever ye do," added Shadrae, "do no' look him in the eye."

"What do ye mean?" asked Kyra.

"Do no' look him in the eye, lass. Trust me," said Shadrae and took off down the corridor towards the stairs. "Call me if ye need me."

Gemma and Kyra looked at each other and laughed. "She always was a very dramatic one, wasn't she?" Gemma chuckled.

"That she is," added Kyra. "Now, ye can station a guard outside the door, but tell them they are not to enter. Under no circumstances, no matter what they hear or don't hear, they are no' to enter unless I bid them to, ye ken?"

"Aye," said Gemma.

"Ye gonna be alright, Kyra?" Gemma asked, as she watched Kyra remove all of her clothing, except her thin yellow chemise. She twisted her shoulder-length hair into an almost-bun and secured it atop her head with a hair comb. Removing her leather slip-on boots, she began wiping her body down with a damp cloth and then applied lavender and sandalwood body oils up and down the length of her long, muscular legs. She opened one of the decanters Gorman left her and plopped a rose petal soaked laurel leaf into her mouth, chewing ferociously before spitting it out and rinsing with water.

"Uh…Kyra, what are ye about?" asked Gemma.

"I mean to *torture* the mon," Kyra smiled.

"I don't understand…" Gemma began.

"Ye want information, do ye no'?" she asked

"Aye, we must have information Kyra, but what do ye…"

Kyra interrupted again, "Shadrae has no idea how to get a mon to talk, let alone wield any power of him. I will simply give him an…uh…incentive," she smiled wickedly. "Now, wish me success."

Gorman led the way into the storage room and lit two additional candles, which he secured atop the long table to the left of the doorway. The prisoner grunted and fumbled about, obviously in and out of some type of deep slumber or suffering from a small concussion, she wasn't sure.

Kyra spoke softly and slowly, unseen behind the prisoner's back. "Gorman, would ye please assist the *gentleman* in relieving himself and washing up? I will return shortly to attend to his…uh…other needs," she said as she handed a chamberpot to the elderly butler. "There is no need for him to remain tied up at this point, there are plenty of guards around, he'll no' get far," she added. "Oh…and see he has a bit o' that fish and some oatcakes."

185

Some twenty minutes later or so, Gorman exited the chamber and nodded to Kyra that the prisoner was well-fed, had attended to his privileges and was more alert, therefore ready for whatever she had in mind.

With one last visit with the lavender oil, Kyra stepped through the doorway and barred the door behind her. The man was still seated on the stool facing the furthest wall, his back to her. She stood still, less than three feet from the man and waited. She twisted her body about causing her chemise to swing back and forth sending the scent of lavender and sandalwood flowing through the room.

He grew rigid on the stool and sat bolt upright, senses reeling. She stepped towards him and repeated her sinuous moves, the muscles in his neck and shoulders clenched and she could make out what a truly fine specimen he was. *Pity I'll have to torture ye,* she thought.

She laid a warm hand on the back of his neck and shoulder blade and he jumped, nearly toppling over as he did so.

"Do no' be afraid of me," she said. "I am here to attend to yer needs," she added, placing the other hand on his other shoulder. His breathing grew ragged and he stiffened further under her touch.

"I do no' intend to hurt ye. That is, unless ye should force me to. There are guards about, prepared to handle ye in a manner which is not as pleasant as mine. Ye would do well to cooperate," she added as she began massaging his neck and shoulders gently, after having thoroughly drenched her hands in the lavender and sandalwood oil. Up and down she kneaded his neck and shoulders, and she reached over ever so lightly to draw her hands across his cheeks to feel the day-old stubble.

From behind, she could tell he was a brawny man indeed; chiseled, high cheekbones, prominent nose, strong chin, long elegant neck that housed a thunderous pulse—that grew more thunderous the more she rubbed his neck. He clasped his hands together in his lap so hard that she sensed they were losing feeling, as he was forced to release them and shake them, mayhap they had gone to sleep?

186

He grunted and leaned forward on the stool and she gave her attentions to his long brown hair, wavy and sun-kissed, it touched nearly to the middle of his back.

"I've only need of some information from ye, ye ken?" she asked, knowing he would not respond. "As soon as I have me information, dear sir," she added, "I will be on me way and this *torture*, will stop." He struggled to sit upright and she let him, backing away for a moment before the sound of ripping linen caught his attention.

Taking a piece of her thin yellow chemise, she raised it to her neck and wrapped it languidly about her, ensuring her scent and that of the lavender was ingrained in the fabric. She rubbed it between her breasts one last time before securing it about his eyes and fastening it behind his head in a crooked bow.

"I realize that yer hands are no' tied, my fine sir, but I would request that ye honor me by not seeing my…uh …person. Ye will agree that most inquisitors maintain a bit o' privacy by covering their faces?" she asked. "Ye see, it makes it hard for me to do my…uh…work, if *me* face is covered. Therefore, it only makes sense that should I wish to go unseen, ye would oblige me by not watching me and wearing this blindfold?"

He nodded in apparent understanding or submission or other some such acknowledgement, and grunted and sighed at the same time, frustration rising again through his body, sending him bolt upright and rigid on the stool. She walked towards the front of him and spoke in soft tones.

"As I said, I have no intention of hurting ye, although I am more than capable. It will be therefore, up to ye, sir, to trust me as we get through this unpleasant torture—together," she added as she placed both of her hands on his shoulders again, this time from the front side.

"I am going to touch ye now, I do not want ye to jump, or be startled. I am going to take ye by both of yer hands," she said grabbing his large strong hands in her own small delicate ones and turning them palm up by the wrist so she could look at them.

"I very truly hate to see what becomes of a mon's hands when they are tied. It pains me so, the unnecessary force one must take when others will no' simply cooperate."

Still holding his hands by the wrist, she turned them and placed both of them on her hip bones, one on either side. "Now…let us get to know one another. Since ye canna' see me, I think mayhap ye would like to know…at least…who ye are being tortured by."

She inched towards him, standing between his knees, placing both of his hands on her hips and grew even closer. Her breasts were mere inches from his face, and he inhaled sharply at her scent. She raised his hands from her hips, up her sides towards her shoulders and resting them atop her shoulders, she let go.

"Now, see," she said. "This is more fair, wouldya' no' agree?' Ye know me size and where I am and I can see yer…uh…size from here, as well." By this time, the man was turning white from holding his breath, and she reached down to touch his cheek with her right hand. He gasped and let out the long-held breath, causing himself to choke and go into a coughing fit.

"I dare say, me sir, that ye must breathe if ye hope to survive me torture," she giggled, and placing both her hands at the nape of his neck, forced his blindfold covered face upwards. Grasping him by the hair, she nuzzled his neck with her check and whispered in his ear, "Is this becoming too much for ye now?"

He vehemently nodded otherwise and she relinquished her rein on his neck.

"Now then, I've need to make ye presentable to the council. That is should ye survive me inquest," she added. Leaving the boundaries of his legs, she stepped to the side and began rattling about with the items on the table, her flowing shift rubbing his bare legs as she went by. Adorned only in his kilt, bare feet and all, she could see the hairs on his legs stand straight-on-end. *'Tis working,* she thought to herself.

The muscles in his chest striated and heaved up and down with his every labored breath, growing more determined each second. As if the spell had been broken now, he unlocked the tight grip he had on his own fists and placed his hands on either side of his enormous thighs, unsure what to do with them.

Before long, the sound of dripping liquid across the floor revealed that she was coming back up behind him. He straightened his back and flexed his heels which were no doubt falling asleep, considering the position he had sat in for so long. Placing his feet flat on the ground, he crossed his arms across his chest and waited. For what, he didn't know, but he waited nonetheless. More relaxed now, he took a deep breath.

"Do no' move," she whispered into his right ear, as she placed her left hand around his neck as if she would strangle him. He jumped at the familiarity and gulped.

"Do no' move, sir," she added, "else I will cut ye."

With her left hand she began washing what part of his face was not covered by the blindfold. Thinking better to herself, she warned, "I'm going to remove this tie for a bit, do no' turnaround."

Tucking the blindfold around his neck, she washed his face from behind with a cleaning linen and warm soapy water. After rinsing, she gripped his jaw and turned it to the left exposing his neck. He flinched and she gently nipped his ear this time, "I said do no' move."

He stopped breathing when he felt the cold blade of the knife at his neck. She fisted his hair in her left hand and held it tightly, then ran the blade up and under his neck in one quick moment. She dipped the knife in a watery vessel then ran the blade up and under his neck on the other side, continuing this pattern on both sides of his ruddy cheeks until he was clean shaven.

"Ye are a brawny one, me good sir," she said as she cleansed the remnants of her handiwork from his face and replaced the blindfold. He jumped under her touch when she returned with a large fabric and draped it about his shoulders. Grabbing his hair in both hands she insisted, "Now lean yer head back a bit for me."

He did as instructed and muscle rippled into more muscle as his back arched like a jungle cat and his shoulders tipped into her breasts. He shifted abruptly and sat back straight up.

"I told ye to lean yer head back," she whispered into his ear. Easing his back to lean his head against her pillows, she grazed her hands over his head and pulled his hair back and away from his face. With her right hand, she drizzled water from a pitcher down the length of his golden-brown locks and began to untangle the tresses. Reaching for a bottle on the table she poured a musky-scented concoction into her hands, lathered it and massaged it into his hair.

She grabbed his right hand and brought it up to his forehead, "Here," she said, "hold yer head this way, so this willna' get into yer eyes." He complied, now holding himself atop the stool with his left hand splayed under the base of it and his right hand holding his head against his arching shoulders.

Continuing her assault on the length of his hair past his shoulders, she rubbed the tendrils together and against each other as the aroma filled the chamber. "I must apologize, I am sure this is most uncomfortable for ye," she said as she reached his head to grab at the loose ends of some wayward hair. Rubbing her protruding nipples against his shoulders, she was sure her shift was completely wet at this point, and she knew that he knew it as well.

"I'm going to do something completely awful now, but I beg yer forgiveness me kind sir," she added. "I must needs to rub on yer...uh...scalp."

He blew out a long sigh and began to breathe deliberately. "Now ye can sit up if ye like, no need to strain yer shoulders. But if I am to make sure ye are good and clean—then I must get the top of yer head as well, ye ken?

He nodded and she warned, "I'm a going to leave yer blindfold off and I need yer assurance that ye willna' look? Else, I may have to get rough with ye."

He nodded again and clenched his thighs together as tightly as he could. To his shock, she walked around to his front. Unable to contain himself, he peeked through his eyelids just enough to make out the outline of a wet chemise hanging seductively off the peaks of round, bountiful breasts.

Clenching his eyes tightly, he made the sign of the cross in front of him and put both hands on either side of the stool, holding on as if for dear life. With her knee, she pressed his legs gently apart and stood in front of him to do her worst.

Long, lithe fingers glided mercilessly through his hair. Lathering the musky-scented oil through his hair and over his scalp she grew closer, closer, so much closer that he could almost bite her neck when she reached back to gather the length up on top with the rest.

"Here," she said, "ye will fall off that stool if ye are no' careful." Prying his tense hands from either side of the stool, she raised them once again to rest on her hips. "That's better. Just ye hold on to me and I won't let ye fall," she said.

Like a blind man searching for structure, he gripped her hips and relaxed, then gripped harder with each motion she made washing his hair. Unsure whether it was better to hold tight or loosely, he wavered between the two, sending chills up and down her spine.

She stepped back a bit and he loosened his grip on her hips. "Now, don't let go, me prisoner," she said, confirming her intention with a squeeze to his hands on her waist. "I must needs rinse yer hair now, and ye will need to hold on verra good, let's ye tip over backwards and take me with ye."

She brushed the left side of his cheek lightly and cupped his temple and forehead, giving him a good long look. Beautiful was not the right word for the creature she was holding in her hands. Beautiful didn't begin to describe him. Doubtless, there were no words. Thankful she had told him to close his eyes, she secretly wished she could get a look at them anyway. Shadrae be damned, she had to see. She imagined what color they might be. Green probably, but no—not on this man. Dark, wild and powerful…they had to be blue …and she knew she couldn't take it if they were.

She sighed audibly and reached over to grab the rinsing pitcher from the table. Rising up on her tiptoes, she stretched up and over his torso, tipped his head ever so slightly backward and poured the warm water through the length of his hair. With her breast pressed gently into the curve of his neck she repeated the motions over and over and over again, feeling the heat rise in his face. So hot it nearly scorched her.

He tightened his grip on her hips, not so much because he thought he would topple backward, more so that he thought he might be overtaken by a wave of passion he would be unable to control. He moaned audibly and let out a breath.

"I see me torture is working," she whispered playfully into his ear. "Are ye no' ready to talk yet?" she asked.

He shook his head from side-to-side sending water splashing everywhere, drenching her in the process. "I shall punish ye for that," she said as she bit into his neck causing him to jump, startled.

She finished wiping his wet face with a cloth and spread his legs apart with her own as she stepped back. The top of his kilt fell from his lap leaving rigid evidence of his reaction to her torture in its wake. He blushed and relinquished his hold on her hips. Deliberately forgetting to replace his blindfold, she worked her way behind him and began combing the tangles from his freshly washed hair.

"If ye shallna' talk, I must persist in mine endeavors to break ye," she said sardonically.

"Will ye no' talk?" she asked.

He shook his head again, pulling it from her clutches and sending the brush flying to the other end of the room. "Now keep yer eyes closed," she said, "while I get that brush, ye ken?" He nodded.

Stepping in front of him slowly and sensually, she sashayed towards the lighted candelabrum allowing the illumination to cast shadows on her form as she did. He peeked through his eyelids as she walked in front of him to stoop for the comb. Near to soaking wet, with her shift clinging to her wet form, she smelled of lavender and sandalwood. Reaching with her right hand to remove the comb from her hair, she used her left to retrieve the brush. Her chestnut tresses fell to her shoulders and framed her lithe neck in the candlelight. The contrast of dry hair and wet form tickled his innards and he groaned in delight.

"Yer no' looking are ye?" she asked with her back turned toward him.

"Uh uh," he grunted. *An audible reply*, she thought. *Won't be long, now.*

192

"Now, close them tight," she demanded. "Here comes the worst part," she said. "Are ye sure we canna make an agreement?"

He shook his head again in silence. He was not to be broken apparently. At least *that's what he thinks*.

TWENTY-NINE

O'Malley Territory

Darina sat in the warm afternoon sun, twiddling her dagger between her fingers. Payton was not happy with her decision he should remain behind under the first ridge of the plateau, but he relented when she threatened to separate him from his head. The fact she was wielding her broadsword when she said so, drove home the point.

Uncertain she could accurately retrace the steps she had taken with Patrick in the dark, her fears were eliminated when she found the level spans of green clover between the rocky formations—which were set about in a circular pattern. The ridge looked much different in the daylight. *How does one go about calling an otherworldly being?* she thought to herself, fear and trepidation rising to the surface.

"Oh—what am I doing?" she shouted out loud as she threw a rock between the rocky arches. "I am such a fool."

Staggering to get up, she lost her footing and the ground began to jiggle around her. An ominous humming noise assaulted her ears and she collapsed back down to the soft, green ground and held her head with both hands. A bright light shone in front of her and a familiar chatter greeted her. Tiny orbs of light swarmed her neck and shoulders and she sat, face to shin, in front of a very amused Covar.

"Covar," she said startled. "How did ye know to come?" she asked.

The striking, tawny god-like creature reached down a hand to assist her up, slapping her with his long golden tresses in the process. Stable and on her feet, she became lost in his eyes for what seemed minutes and just stared.

What need have ye, Darina? he asked her with his mind.

She stood still, dumbfounded and unable to speak or think. He reached down and touched her on the shoulder, and a sudden surge of electric-like power jogged through her body. From the base of her spine to the nape of her neck, fire shot through her being and froze her blood. Every element of her being was on alert and she felt *alive. So. Alive.*

Unable to take her eyes from Covar's, she simply asked, *Where is Patrick?*

Patrickme husband, Patrick. He has been gone six days hence and has not returned. I and his brathair have searched and have found nothing. I fear for his safety. I believe ye are the one…person…who can help me locate him," she said audibly.

Why have ye not searched with yer mind? he asked.

"I have, but he has blocked me somehow. I canna sense him any longer," she said as she began to cry. "And…I fear that…something horrible may…"

"Stop," Covar said as the ground shook around him. He held up the palm of his hand to her in demand. It was the loudest, deepest, most authoritative voice she had ever heard. It was as if the heavens opened up and God himself spoke to her.

"Fear is not a useful tool, Darina," he said. "Fear is not for ye my child. Fear comes from a very deep, dark place, so negative is its form, it leads only to destruction."

Darina bowed her head and wept loudly, "Can't ye please help me, Covar," she begged.

The magnificent giant reached a hand down and laid it upon her shoulder. A soothing wave of calm, warmth and peace surged through her and she looked up into his eyes, pleading, begging for resolution.

Taking his hand back, he stepped away and turned around, heading in the direction of the stone circles. Disillusioned, Darina took off after him, anger rising in her. *Are you just going to leave me...*

Wait! he responded, still heading away from her. She stopped dead in her tracks and watched in astonishment as Covar rose off the ground, levitating, about four feet above the rocky ledge, with arms outstretched to his sides and fingers pointed upwards. Soon, a mighty wind arose and he began spinning as if he were a tornado, turning in increasingly advanced speed, taking the flowers, clover, grass and anything close to him with him in the funnel.

Darina stepped backwards, never turning, leading herself away from the twister, so as not to get caught up in it. The earth shook again and she was sure this time it would be felt at the castle. Water spouts littered the coast and she could the see the waves growing high and crashing towards the shoreline. The wind was so loud and her hair thrashed about her face in an almost painful fashion, as if she were literally being whipped.

Finally, she edged herself back down on the ground, grabbing hold of a nearby jutting rock and praying she wouldn't break loose. As quickly as the funnel had appeared, it disappeared. In a magnificent implosion of light and melody, Covar's form disappeared in midair leaving only glittering dust particles floating about.

Silence. Unbearable silence broke the ridge and she was alone. She straightened to a sitting position to survey the empty plateau. Save for herself and the rocky formation, there was nothing. Covar was gone and she had no better idea how to find her husband. Tears turned into burning wrath and she screamed, a bloodcurdling, rage-induced scream that sent a gaggle of grouse reeling into the sky.

Afraid she may have scared Payton, she quickly stood up, wiped off her truis and turned in the direction of the castle. Meeting her at the top of the ridge was a white-faced, obviously traumatized Payton who appeared to be paralyzed. He looked straight at her, or straight through her, but straight past her in any regards—towards the stonehenge.

"Payton," she said, "are ye alright?"

Unable to speak, he nodded his head up and down.

"Did ye hear me scream?"

He nodded his head again and raised his arm to point towards the circular ornament of stones.

"I have no idea where to find Patrick," she said forlornly.

"I do," he said, not taking his eyes from the henge.

"How's that?" she asked taking him by the arms now, still unable to get him to remove his eyes from their target.

"He told me," he said. "He told me."

***

Dirk half-ran, half-walked towards the armory, hoping to avoid Easal's clutches. He sent his best boy on in front to gather his best fighting men, and his eldest son to take his wife and family to McDermott territory. Satisfied he had not been followed, he opened the outer door to the armory and gulped in shock. *Empty*.

"Looking for something?"

A curious spine tingle overtook him and he shuddered visibly.

"Easal," he said turning around, "how are ye?"

Not two steps behind him and gaining at that, Easal strode determinedly towards the armory himself, fire and mischief in his eyes.

"Dirk, can ye tell me where the weapons have gone?" he asked.

"Weapons?"

"Yes, Dirk. The weapons —they are all gone," he echoed. It was a sound that made Dirk's skin crawl and caused him to stumble backwards, miss his footing and topple head first down the shallow stairwell into the armory itself.

Easal loomed over Dirk's crumpled body, as he lay twisted and mangled on the floor. His left hip was shattered and the long bone of his right shin protruded through the skin. Too terrified to move, and in more pain than he could fathom, Dirk was certain he was hallucinating. Easal's image was hazy, out of focus, moving and twisting, and at times—he didn't resemble Easal at all. He envisioned that his hands were no longer human but were dark-skinned, sinewy daggers which arched like a meat hanging hook and were coming to slice into him. Easal exhaled a black noxious smoke from his nostrils and bent down to his ear.

"Where is me wife?" he asked.

Dirk rose on his elbows, now painfully aware that his right wrist was twisted and out-of-socket. He inched backwards, perhaps a foot or two, before Easal dropped a boot on his chest, preventing his further movement.

"I'll ask ye one more time. Where is me wife?"

Dirk shook his head silently from side-to-side and Easal calmly removed his boot. Starting back up the narrow stairwell, Easal turned to gaze down on Dirk one last time. In a sadistic show of spirit, Easal transformed to Eaton…the dark visitor…before Dirk's very eyes, sending his heart clenching and spasming in his chest.

Easal raised his gnarled claws upward and towards Dirk and the back of the armory, and spheres of molten fire shot through the tips of his claws, lighting the wooden shelving and rushed flooring in its path. The armory became engulfed in flames and lapped about Dirk's legs and feet, catching his truis on fire. He writhed about in pain unable to move with his broken hip and shattered leg. His hair was aflame now and the smell of burning flesh permeated the chamber. Suddenly realizing the hideous screams of pain were his own, Dirk crossed himself with his left hand and began to pray audibly for mercy.

"Enjoy hell," Eaton said, transforming into Easal in the process. "I hope to see ye there soon."

THIRTY

Burke Lands

Naelyn crouched down beside Braeden on the cave floor and grabbed him by the jaw. Jerking it just slightly enough to bring them eye to eye, she repeated herself, "I said, ye can read it boy?" she asked.

Pulling his jaw back and placing his dagger at her jugular, Braeden responded, "If ye are fond o' that hand there lassie, ye will no' grab me such ever again."

In one short flash, Cordal unarmed the boy and stood steadfast between he and Naelyn, "What's all this?" he asked.

"She grabbed me," snorted Braeden.

"He pulled a dagger on me," Naelyn said.

"Sit! The both of ye!" Cordal shouted and the cave echoed.

"I canna be sure about where ye came from there, Cordal, but I will tell ye that when I was a boy, my elders were not liking to me storytelling," said the priest nodding in the direction of Braeden.

"And where I come from, *fathair*," said Braeden sarcastically, "we don't take kindly to being called liars; it's akin to bearing false witness—is it no'?"

Having had enough of the drama, Orla pushed her way through the tangled group of weary travelers and stomping her foot, shouted, "What the devil is the matter here?"

Naelyn reached towards her and placing a hand on her shoulder, quietly said, "The boy is addled, ye ken?"

"Is that so?" asked Orla, "and how do ye ken?"

"He claims he can decipher the cave drawings and I ken the better of it."

"Ye ken this how, Naelyn?"

"Well…for one…he is but a cotter's son…"

"Ye don't ken me, ye snotty wench!" he shouted, inching towards Naelyn.

Orla raised her hand up chest level to Braeden and he stopped immediately in his tracks. "I see but one way to remedy this," she stated matter-of-factly. Turning towards Braeden, she said, "Read it then."

"Ye want me to read it?" he asked, surprised.

"Aye, prove yerself, read the blewdy drawings and be done with it," Orla responded.

"Ye must understand, I canna decipher it, ye ken?"

"What do ye mean, boy?" asked Cordal.

"Well, I can tell ye what it says, but I canna' tell ye what it means," he said tilting his head to one side and looking at Cordal.

"How so?" asked Cordal.

"Well, if ye are at all familiar with religious texts, ye will understand that I can tell ye what it says, but it's up to the individual person to gather what it actually means, ye ken?" he added.

"I think we are smart enough to figure that out," interrupted Father MacArtrey. "Now. Out with it boy!"

"Verra well," said Braeden, motioning with his arms for the others to back away. Lighting a small torch, he started at the front of the cavernous alcove. Tracing the symbols and pictographs with his fingers, he began, "A verra long time ago, the people of this land had a sore time with their crops and harvests and what nots." He searched the faces of the group and continued, "Well, there was a holy man, a shaman from the clan and he held a ceremony and called up the spirits and asked for help."

"Fairly soon after that, a shipping vessel had an accident at sea and many lives were lost, but some were saved," he said, excited. "It seems that there were bodies washed to shore and some lived, and took up residence here in Burke lands. Others lived, but they didna' stay here, they went to an island just to the south of here, I think it's in another territory now, but that doesn't matter."

"Go on," said Orla, crossing her arms in disbelief.

"Well, at first they thought this was the help the shaman had prayed for from the spirits, but things didn't get better, so they held another service. This time the shaman broke the laws of the land, and they sacrificed a young boy, the Lord's boy! Oh no, the people kidnapped the clan leader's boy and they drained his blood and they all drank it and he died later, from the blood-letting."

Naelyn froze in her tracks. Chills ran up and down her spine and she collapsed onto the cold stone floor, unconscious. The priest went over to attend to her and waved for Braeden to continue.

"Well, it seems that shortly after this service, a shipping vessel came with visitors, but it was no' exactly a ship."

"What do ye mean?" asked Shanleigh, "not exactly a shipping vessel?

"Well, it didna' sail on the sea, ye ken?" he asked to a cave filled with astonished onlookers. "Look here, won't ye? See that the vessel here does no' come from the waters, but instead, from the clouds?" he asked pointing to the drawing. "It sails on the sky," he added.

"That's nonsense," the priest interjected, "he is playing us for fools."

"Remember what I told ye a'fore, ye old goat?" responded Braeden. "I can only tell ye what it says, not what it means. Ye can clearly see the image here on the rock. I did no' draw it! And this crooked symbol here, this one that raises up on the edge, that is the symbol for sky!"

"Let him continue," said Orla, patting Braeden on the shoulder, "What happens next?"

"Well, the sky people take up with the land dwellers and they make their home with them. It seems the shaman believes that the sky people are the helpers sent by the gods to the clan."

"But?" asked Cordal.

"But," continued Braeden, "they are no'."

"How do ye ken?" asked Shanleigh.

"Come over here," said Braeden, leading the others further down the cavern with the torch lighting the way. "I canna' read that part," he motioned to a three-to-four foot space to his left, "the drawings have worn and I canna' make out the symbols."

"So," added Orla.

"So, it appears from this section down here, that the land dwellers and the sky people go to war against each other. The sky people want to take the land dweller's lands and they want the land dwellers to leave or be killed. They need the shore...no the shoreline, no...they need the beach. For some reason the sky people want the shoreline as their own, so that they can bring more vessels here. The land dwellers will no' agree to give up their land to the sky people."

"What happens next, after they go to war," asked Cordal.

"Well, many people die; the lord and his family, the shaman, most of the land dwellers flee to other clans. The sky people, what's left of them, they get in their vessel, and they leave. Except that, they don't travel in the clouds, their vessel goes under the water somewhere, just off the shore."

"Under the sea, ye are pulling our legs, ye are," laughed Shanleigh.

"Nay, look right here, I am just showing ye what it says," said Braeden. "Then some time later, many moons, mind ye, a new group of people arrive on their boats to take over the lands, all but a few of the previous land dwellers are gone, and there is a new lord and his family, and they build a new castle and the such, and the land is prosperous and there is trade."

"What happened to the sky people?" asked Naelyn, fully alert and now fully engaged.

"Well, one day there is a terrible storm. The land dwellers do their worst to secure their shipping vessels at the piers and the clan's people, well the most of them, hole up in the main castle keep for safety. The land dweller's leader, he has a dream. In his dream, the sky people leave their place at the bottom of the sea. They set about on the shoreline, looking about, digging at the rocks and such and then as they are getting ready to leave, there is a tussle between the sky people. The leader of the sky people, he makes that two of them canna' leave with them. He leaves two of the sky people behind, on the shoreline."

"And they just leave them?" asked Orla.

"Aye, leaves them right behind. Two strong males of the sky people, they are left behind."

"And what happens next?" asks Cordal.

Braeden grew very silent and placed an index finger over his mouth, motioning for the others to be silent. He cupped his right hand over his ear and held up the torch with the other.

"There is someone out there," he whispered almost inaudibly to Cordal.

Gesturing for the girls to move to the back of the cave, Cordal took Braeden's dagger and handed him a handmade spear he had used for fishing. The two made their way slowly to the cave opening, leaving the priest and women behind.

***

Kyra finished combing the prisoner's hair and fastened it with a leather thong at the nape of his neck. For the most part, she had managed in garnering a semblance of submission from the man; although he still refused to speak. Grunts, groans and grumbles were common though, so he wasn't adverse to audible communication. Not in the least. He moaned loudly when she resumed her massage of his tight shoulders.

They released gently though as she continued to stroke his back, but quickly re-tensed at the brush of a nipple against his shoulder.

"Ye should be verra glad that it was me they chose, to do your…uh…torture," she whispered into his ear. "I have gentle hands, or so I hear." She left his back for the moment and worked at something at the table for a bit before coming back up behind him. "Do no' let this startle ye none," she said. "'Twil be wet, but warm," she breathed.

He lurched forward at the touch of the wet cloth between his shoulders but quickly relaxed when she placed a knowing hand on his cheek. Before he knew what to do with his hands, she had one raised to the sky, and she bathed him languorously with the linen rags which smelled sweetly of citrus and lavender. Back and forth, and up and down, she moved the smooth soft cloth across his muscled back and shoulders; dipping ever so lightly,only occasionally to re-wet and then squeeze the warm liquid over his form again. Confident she had covered every available square inch of his back side; she placed the bucket of sudsy water on the table and retrieved a new one.

"Now, open yer mouth," she said. He shrugged his shoulders and moved his head to the side, unsure of what she meant. "Open yer mouth, *please*," she added. Opening his mouth, she caught sight of his near perfect teeth, gleaming white and inviting. His pouty lips framed his wet tongue, swollen and pink. Placing

205

a laurel leaf in his mouth, she instructed him to chew, then rinse with the water in the cup she held to his mouth, and then to chew and rinse again. He obliged, ever the obedient prisoner.

"Now, me prisoner, won't ye tell me yer name? Please?" she added as she stood in front of him again and nestled his taut thighs apart.

He grinned and shook his head back and forth again, reaching up to find her hips to station himself.

"Aye, I ken ye think this is a game?" she asked.

He nodded his headed in agreement, up and down, and a smile broke across her mouth.

"Well, I ken I must make ye believe me then," she said. "Do I need to blindfold ye again or can I trust ye not to open them eyes?" she asked.

He shook his head from side-to-side indicating he would not look and she scooted far from him for a moment, situating some items on the table and something on the floor beside his feet.

"Alright then, if yer sure," she asked.

He nodded again and she removed his hands from her hips and placed them back on either side of the stool. "Hold here lest ye fall now."

She began at his bare chest; squeezing lathered suds of warm, soapy water over him like it were a waterfall. His head moved in tandem to her motions, from side-to-side, never able to anticipate from where it would come. From the tops of his shoulders to his waist, he was now covered in soapy, sudsy water and his kilt was soaked. After he was thoroughly drenched, she took the cleaning cloth and rubbed circles around his upper torso. Easing closer into him, she noticed he gripped the sides of the stool so fiercely his knuckles were white.

She stopped for a moment and stood back looking at her victim. He was *helpless*. His chest heaving violently in wracked breaths you would expect from a dying man, he struggled to sit upright and his thighs were now shaking violently against her legs. *He has much resolve*, she laughed to herself.

"Have ye had enough?" she asked.

He gasped and let out a long-held breath and ultimately, shook his head otherwise.

"Verra well then," she continued, grabbing the cleaning cloth and starting at the top of his shoulder, she made her way down to his well-defined arms. Using her fingers, rather than the cloth, she stroked the back of his arms and massaged his bulging biceps with her thumbs, making them quiver.

"I can do this all night," she whispered in his ear. His hands shot up to her waist and he gripped her hips, bidding her not to move. Not an inch, not a breath. *He was hers*.

"I just have need to reach this one little spot," she breathed. Stepping backward she closed his legs, dropping his hands back to his lap. She sat at his feet on the floor in front of him. "Don't be alarmed," she said, "I'm working down here now."

What seemed like an eternity passed between them and the silence became unbearable. He careened his neck upward and grunted as if asking her whereabouts and she answered with a cleaning cloth on his right ankle. "Now put yer hands on the stool, lest ye fall over."

He grasped each side of the stool with his hands and held on as if for dear life. Before he could anticipate her next move, she had inched her way up his long legs and over his kneecaps, drawing wet circles on his skin with her hands. Lathering the curly hairs of his legs, she added more pressure until she was full-on massaging his thighs on both sides, breasts rested on his knees.

His face grew red, then pale, then purple before she finally shouted, "Breathe mon!" and he gasped and choked for air.

"Ye must be presentable to the council for yer trial, I presume," she said. "Seeing as how ye are a childnapper."

He grunted and his disposition changed visibly. Now tense, and what she thought may have been offended, he stiffened in his seat and sat indignant before her.

"Put yer legs together, me prisoner," she said and raised from her position on the floor. "I am almost done with this. Have ye a name?"

Silence.

"Won't ye at least tell me yer name, mon?"

He shook his head back and forth, but no smile adorned his beautiful mouth this time.

"Verra well, ye leave me no choice," she said and she climbed atop him to sit on his thighs with her legs wrapped around his waist on the three-legged stool. He inhaled and clenched, tightening his legs and sending his now jutting member against the soft pallet of what he presumed was her belly. Both soaking wet and dripping, she reached her arms around his shoulders in a kind of erotic bear hug that sent his pulse racing.

"Now, I have only a few places yet that need to be cleaned," she breathed into his ear as she drew her wet tongue over the lobe giving him chills. With her right hand, she displayed her intention and pushed a sopping wet cleaning cloth up the length of his thigh torturously slowly.

Grabbing the back of his head with her left hand, she intertwined her fingers in his hair and it broke free of its leather thong shackle. She pressed her nose into his neck and bit him gently and he jumped, sending the cleaning cloth higher up his leg still.

He was shaking now, nearly unable to keep her in his lap as his thighs vibrated uncontrollably under her body. She moved her lips up and over his neck towards his cheek, whispering an unnamed warning to him. Pulling his hair further back with her left hand she moved his head to meet her forehead and searched his face.

"Will I have that name, sir?" she asked.

Silence.

His chest heaved up and down and met the distinct sensation of pert nipple with each exhalation. She kissed his cheek and cupped his face with her hands now, bidding his cooperation.

"I will have that name, sir," she said before placing a tender kiss on his swollen lips and rubbing her own cheek against his freshly-shaved face.

"Must I go on torturing ye so?" she asked. "Or shall I end this now, the pain must be exquisite," she whispered.

He grunted in acknowledgement and she pressed her lips firmly to his, an invitation to submit. He grew rigid, body and soul, and his hands shot up and grabbed her about the hips as before, attempting to stabilize them on the wobbly stool.

She bit his neck, he groaned loudly this time and his legs gave way beneath him as she slipped down almost in a fall; before he hoisted her back up atop his big thighs and settled her there with his large hands encircling her belly. His was a tall man that much was certain. With his knees high in the air from his position on the short stool, she couldn't avoid slipping closer to him, to it, to his throbbing wet need pressed firmly against her stomach.

She cupped his face in her hands again and rubbed her cheek feverishly against his. Returning to his mouth, she licked her lips and asked, "Yer name, sir?"

Before she could continue her brazen assault, his eyes flew open and met hers with restrained force. *Sea blue, by the gods*, she thought to herself, drowning in their fevered depths. His hands left their familiar perch on her hips and pulled her into him further. His left hand swept behind her neck toying with her hair, his right hand splayed across her back and he brought her in for the kill.

He kissed her. It was an angry, violent warning of a kiss where swollen tongues fight for dominance in a warm crowded space, unsure of their goal. He won, of that she was certain, by the way he had her spread out over his big lap and half way on the floor, his left hand holding her up with the slightest bit of effort.

"Yer name, madam," he grunted restlessly against her neck.

"Kyra," she returned, staring up into the devilish eyes Shadrae had tried to warn her about.

"I'm Kyra," she repeated, now lying like a rag doll in his arms.

"Yer name, sir," she begged in a whisper.

He smiled a triumphant, arrogant smile that lit the room, and pulled her up to reposition her on his lap. Never taking his eyes from hers, he rubbed the back of her shoulders with his strong hands and whispered, "Parkin. Parkin MacCahan, maám."

THIRTY – ONE

O'Malley Council Chamber

"By the gods, Gemma! Ye mean to tell me ye had the Lord's brathair tied up like a common prisoner?" shouted Ruarc. He slammed his thick, red-haired fist on the council table and shook the mugs of ale that were placed there by Galen.

"Da, it was but a mistake," interjected Kyra from the entry way. Making her way to one of the empty chairs, she briefly touched Lucian on the shoulder and nodded at Galen who was busy making entries in the council records. Gemma, Ruarc, Atilde, Galen and now Minea stared disbelievingly at the door, as if they saw a ghost.

"Good eve'n," it said.

Ruarc nearly fell over rising to greet the newest council chamber occupant. Standing only in his damp kilt, bare-footed and all, Parkin MacCahan made quite a picture. Nearly as tall as his elder brother, but with long hair to his mid-back, which was now neatly tied back with a leather thong, and crystal blue eyes that could mesmerize any fae, Parkin strode assertively into the room. He stopped to grab a tray of fruit and dried meats from a maidservant, accepted a mug of ale graciously and sat down between Atilde and Minea who promptly turned beet red at his presence.

Lucian offered him a cloak, but he waved it off with his right hand, before sucking the sticky grape juice off his fingers one at a time, locking eyes with Kyra.

"Ruarc, I must say it is nice to finally make yer acquaintance."

Ruarc choked and stood upright at the council table and began, "Lord MacCahan…"

"Parkin," he interrupted, correcting Ruarc, before waving his right hand again and then licking an invisible line of wayward fruit juice down the length of his wrist.

"Parkin," Ruarc nodded. "I must offer ye our sincerest of apologies. We simply did not ken ye were coming so soon, we had no idea who ye were and the ladies of the isle were under strict orders to allow no asylum to strangers. With yer brathair, I mean, with the Lord off in search of Braeden, we placed our lands on high alert and unfortunately, it appears when Mavis saw ye at the window…"

"Never mind that," Parkin responded. "Mavis kens who I am well enough, however I was wearing a cloak and I disguised myself," he explained with his hands, raising them above his head as if he were covering his face with the cloak.

"I meant to find what became of my daughter, Winnie."

Kyra gasped and leaned forward in her chair. "Winnie is yer daughter?" she asked.

"Aye, Winnie is mine. She came with me and me charge, Macklin. When our boat arrived, verra late I might add in the night; I bid that Macklin see to her while I and me men cared to the ship and our stowage. When we finished our work, there was naught hide nor hair of either one. Atilde here saw to our tents, and me men set us up for the night but I could na' make out what became of me Winnie."

Gemma motioned for the servant girls to bring the whiskey bottle, and she poured herself and Parkin a stout drink. Parkin raised his glass in deference, took a shot, and set it down loudly on the table.

"So, I heard tell of this 'island of women' as is customary I believe, to be heard from the men leaving the tavern of the inn?" he asked raising his shoulders. Minea agreed.

Lucian nodded as well and waved for him to continue.

"Well, yer mon Odhran came along—quite a nice gentlemon I might add, and a good storyteller—anyway he explained that only the women and some children live on the Isle and that orphaned or otherwise parentless bairns are sent there to foster. I naturally presumed that Winnie was somewhere in the midst of the other women and children."

Galen coughed from beside the hearth and Parkin stood upright, "I did no' see ye over there, fathair," he stated. Grinning widely from ear to ear and red-faced from the whiskey, he visibly surveyed the others at the table and continued, "Ye have ye own wee little fathair, have ye?" he asked giggling.

"Ye must excuse me, me...me behavior please," he said, "as ye will note, I've had more of the spirits than I have had food, and therefore I am prone to some silliness, as me brathair Patrick would put it."

Grabbing a mug of ale, he sat back down at the table and toyed with a bit of cheese before him.

"Where was I?" he asked, looking around, the world obviously spinning before him. "Oh...so last night, I paid a young boy near the docks to row me out to the island, in the dark mind ye, he said we can have no light. So seeing as how I couldna' get anyone to assist me in finding me daughter Winnie, at that late hour, I surmised mayhap I would have to do it meself."

Gemma covered her head with her hands and rested her elbows on the table in front of her.

"Where is Winnie now?" asked Ruarc.

Atilde spoke up, "We sent her back to the mainland. She is with Macklin at the inn. I have a servant girl looking in on her from time to time."

Ruarc interjected, "Parkin, I am most positively remorseful that such has befallen such an honorable and noble…"

"Stop right there," Parkin said, raising his right hand palm forward to Ruarc. "There is no need to ap, apo, apology…" he hiccupped. "Pardon me," he continued. "I think it best we remove the whiskey, no?" he gestured towards Gemma who was smiling in spite of herself.

"Ye have some of the finest, some of the best, ye have the best soldiers I've ever laid me eyes on," he spat staring directly at Kyra. "That first guard ye had me with, she was a blewdy shrew!"

Gemma and Lucian both leaned forward in laughter and Lucian, asked, "Shadrae?" to which Gemma replied, "Aye."

"It was the next one that roiled me. She had me fearing for me life. She-devil she was, I tell ye."

Kyra straightened her back and clasped her hands in her lap so tight she thought they would lose feeling. Ruarc looked at her strangely.

"There was no' a square inch of me body that lass did na' manage to torment. I thought at one point, I might rightfully burst!"

Kyra coughed and Parkin stifled a smile.

"Why did ye no' tell us who ye were?" asked Atilde.

"I tried. I told the guards at the shore I was needing to speak to whomever was in charge and they said that the Bacchanal wasn't to start 'til the next eve, and that I was in a heap load of trouble for trespassing. I managed to get away though and when I heard Winnie's laughter, I followed it to the cottage where I saw her through the slit. With me cloak over me head, Mavis did no' ken who I was."

"So the guards came and got ye?" Lucian asked.

"Yes, I think there was four of them. I fought real good for awhile until that Shadrae, did ye say, until she stuck a dagger at my neck and I figured as much as I did no' wish to die that day, I may as well go along with it."

"I see," added Ruarc.

"Why did ye no' tell them who ye were?" asked Galen from the corner.

"Well, fathair," Parkin started, "I did no' ken much about this 'island of women' and so I saw the makings of a festival and such, and was worried that mayhap these women were witches or some such other and mayhap they meant to harm or even sacrifice me Winnie. And, I ken I needed to devise meself a plan to rescue the babe a'fore night fell."

Lucian groaned and wrinkled his nose. "Parkin, I hope by now, that ye understand that no one was planning to hurt yer Winnie."

"I got the right of it now," he said leaning his face in close across the table to get Kyra's attention.

Kyra sat back in her chair and her face grew pale.

"I have only one request, if it please the council," he added gallantly.

"Go on," said Ruarc.

"I would be most grateful if ye would ensure that no other mon, prisoner, vagrant, thief or otherwise be subjected to the anguish I suffered at the hands of her!" he said as he pointed at Kyra. "'Twas enough to kill a mon. Me heart almost burst," he added.

Ruarc turned and looked at Kyra strangely, confused. "Kyra, ye questioned the mon?"

"Aye," she responded.

"I think under the circumstances, sir," said Parkin, "I should be allowed the privilege of meting out some just punishment of my own against this fiend ye call a lass." Parkin stood on wobbly legs and

215

attempted to dramatize his point before the council. "Aye, I should have leave to question her…in private as well ye ken…in the same manner in which she questioned me! Tis only just!"

Kyra stood and clenched her fists against the council table, looking Parkin in the eye. *Ye handsome bastard!* she thought, before breaking out in a smile that left the others in the room thoroughly disjointed.

Lucian spoke, "Ye wish to invoke the reciprocity doctrine?"

"Aye. I do."

"What is the reciprocity doctrine?" Minea asked, leaning over and whispering in Gemma's ear.

"What is he talking about?" asked Ruarc.

"He knows what I'm talking about," said Parkin, pointing at Lucian.

Lucian stood and motioned for the others to quiet as he spoke. "Lord MacCahan here is indeed correct. He knows the law." He began to pace back and forth before the hearth and struggled to speak on several occasions before stopping mid-way between the two pillars in front of the council table and stroked his long beard.

"Verra well," he started, "Ruarc, the reciprocity doctrine says that if an ally is treated as an enemy or spy, and bodily…uh…harm is used against said ally, that said ally…once cleared of all charges…may reciprocate said bodily…uh…harm against the perpetrator of such bodily harm."

"Ye mean to harm *me* daughter?" shouted Ruarc pointing a thick finger in Parkin's chest, sending him toppling backwards onto the stone floor of the chamber.

"Yer daughter?" asked Parkin astonished. "She is yer daughter?"

"Ye won't touch a hair on her head, do you ken?" shouted Ruarc.

Kyra stood and the room silenced. "We are a just and honorable people. I have taken my vows to protect our people *and* our laws," she began.

216

"But Kyra, he intends to harm ye," said Atilde, tears welling in her eyes.

"He only intends to mete out what was mete to him as is provided by law," she said forcing herself not to look at Parkin, heat rising in her face. "I am a well-trained soldier, having served our clan for many years," she continued.

"I will not permit this!" commanded Ruarc, physically shaken by his rage.

Lucian laid a worn hand on Ruarc's shoulder. "Look at him," said Ruarc. "He is our Laird's own brathair. I hardly think we can refuse his lawful request to abide by the law. I ken he won't permanently harm yer daughter, he only intends to take what is rightfully his."

Ruarc grunted and shook Lucian's hand off his shoulder.

"Ruarc," whispered Lucian in his friend's ear, "look a' him, he is utterly blotted. I doubt he is any match for Kyra, should he corner the lass, she will rip him to shreds like a barn cat."

"When do ye intend to take yer rights of reciprocity?" asked Ruarc.

"Right now," retorted Parkin, grabbing Kyra by the forearm and heading towards the chamber door with her in tow.

"How long will this go on?" asked Ruarc helplessly.

"All night," replied Kyra. "That is how long he was prisoner on the Isle, I expect he means to take all night about it?" she stated looking at Parkin, who nodded in agreement.

"And—where will ye be, we must know yer whereabouts," begged Minea.

"In me chamber," replied Kyra, "with the door barred."

THIRTY-TWO

Burke Lands — The Cave

Cordal returned to the cave as abruptly as he left, albeit with a shiny blade thrust to his quivering Adam's apple. Orla gasped and moved forward, rather than backward, toward the cave's mouth. Shanleigh tugged at her tunic in an effort to prevent her forward motion, but was unsuccessful. *Too brave for her own good,* Reni would say. That much was true of Orla. She was the type that grew bolder in crisis, rather than shrinking.

"What is the meaning of this?" shouted Orla, raising the black kettle pot she grabbed from the fire with her skirts, intent on burning someone.

Cordal raised both his hands in apparent submission and the voice behind him started, "Hold on there, lassie, we aren't here to harm anyone."

"Show yerself," she demanded.

"'Tis alright," shouted Braeden, now standing at the cave's opening, furiously tugging at the truis of a giant of a man with broadsword and dagger splayed before him. The first man who spoke released Cordal and Braeden began yapping so quickly and so loudly that Orla just knew her head would rupture.

The large man replaced his dagger and sword and knelt down to accept the incessant affections of Braeden and the other man watched in dismay, as if he were a new pup greeting his master after a long time away.

"What the devil is going on?" screamed Orla, this time sending her vocal tirade echoing through the chamber.

Braeden turned around to address Orla, "Calm down ye fiery devil," he said nonchalantly. Orla's face grew white, obviously unaccustomed to being spoken of in that manner. She drew her arms to her chest and tapped her foot, inhaling sharply.

"B-Braeden, c-can ye n-not see, that is n-no way to sp-speak to such a f-fine lady as sh-she?" said Patrick, kneeling before Orla as he took her hand and placed a delicate kiss on her palm.

Shanleigh huffed and rolled her eyes. In two seconds flat, a man had succeeded in controlling Orla Burke's wild temper. Making a mental note in her head, she saved the information for a later date, when it could be used against her friend, to her own advantage, of course.

"And who is this angelic being?" asked Rory, following Patrick's suit, much to the chagrin of Shanleigh.

"Shanleigh," she replied hastily, unwilling to succumb to the charade.

"This is Naelyn, this is Shanleigh, and that is the priest," said Orla flippantly pointing at the dark figure hiding in the furthest recesses of the cave mumbling to his self. "Who in the world, are ye?"

***

"I'm leaving ye here now," Payton whispered into the darkness.

"Leaving me here? By me self?" replied Darina. "Why are ye leaving me here, what is this place?" she asked.

Having tirelessly trekked by horseback for several hours; Payton steered them off the main road through Burke lands, secured their horses and they journeyed on foot a'ways through steep terrain, over rocky outcrops and through a hay field, until they arrived at a broken down remnant of a structure set alongside a bubbling stream between foothills.

"Payton, what are ye talking about?" she asked. "Ye can't leave me here, where is…here…?" she begged.

"He told me to bring ye here, ye ken?" he said, still not meeting her eyes. "Ye will be safe here, and Patrick will return shortly. Wait for him here," he commanded.

She watched in shock as Payton started a fire between two walls, no doubt which were the remnants of an antechamber in the crumbled building. With pieces of thatched roofing missing overhead, she could see the light of the rising moon and the twinkling stars. It began to sprinkle and she pulled her cloak over her head.

"Payton, what is this place?" she asked again in barely a whisper.

"Patrick was here, ye ken?" he said, pointing at what was left of the stony wall. He ripped a portion of his tartan and wrapped it around a piece of wood to fashion a torch, and he pointed again—this time with the fiery scepter.

Along the small section of knobby rock wall, Darina could make out the outline of a symbol, or an image, she wasn't sure. Grabbing the torch forcefully from Payton, she bent low at her knees to examine the image further. It was red. Tracing it with her fingers, she slowly moved her hand up and over to the right, back down and finally back to the starting point.

"It's a dragon," she gasped, clasping her hand over her mouth. "A red dragon, but how did he…?"

Payton placed his hand on her shoulder. "It's his blood, Darina. He left ye a message in his blood. He means to find ye, lass, and bids ye to remain here in wait."

"And what are ye to do?" she asked.

"Aye, I am to return to the piers and get me brathair's ship."

"Patrick has a ship?"

"Nay, lass, Parkin does," he said as he walked away.

***

Odetta recognized the stench of burning human flesh instantly. How she became trapped in the burning armory, she wasn't sure but of one thing she was. Eaton was to blame.

There was nothing more she could do for Dirk. He had prayed for death and she became his death angel. One swift grip on his neck, a forceful turn, and he was in agony no longer. The fact that she did not burn alongside him perhaps frightened him more than his own distress, she could not be sure as he was unable to speak.

The flames died and she stood, completely unscathed in the center of the armory, awaiting her fate. She would not cry, she would not beg for death, as she was certain that was as impossible as killing the Visitor. She would wait, and she would devise a plan. Her only interest at this time had to be the safety of Orla, a child she raised as her own, the only reason she breathed, the future of her clan, if there ever would be one.

It was dark now, and she could make out the faint footsteps overhead, and see between the wood planks as passersby crossed above. No doubt they smelled the smoke, as it wafted upwards into the night. They went about their business, intent on leaving due to the impending war she had proclaimed. Dutiful always, she was secure in her decision—to send them away—should have done it years before. Eaton, now Easal, would show no mercy, and she would permit few victims. A formidable match, she would make his plans difficult and she would die, if only she could. *Immortal,* she sighed. *How do ye kill yerself when ye are immortal?*

It was too soon to think of that. Even suicide wasn't a valid option, at least not until Orla was safe and as far away from Burke lands as possible.

Her head rattled and she screamed. The earth shook around her and her blood boiled in her veins, as if on fire, or frozen, or both she wasn't sure.

Odetta.

It was him.

Odetta, darling.

Her skin prickled and she shook violently as if she were to implode.

Odetta, I found yer manuscripts, at the monastery. I ken what ye are about.

Her manuscripts! She forgot about the ancient texts. All of the writings, the spells, the curses, all of it—he had it and he knew.

Odetta, I am not amused. Witchcraft? Ye think to use witchcraft—against me?

"Where are they?", she screamed into the darkness, balancing herself on her knee, still grasping her head.

Here me dear, he said, and from nowhere, a near to three foot stack of manuscripts, scrolls and other writings appeared on the ground before her.

Odetta reached forward to touch the priceless artifacts when they suddenly burst into flames. Her right hand blistered and boiled, the skin peeled and fell off and she screamed in agony.

She could hear him laughing. A sinister swell of devilish triumph echoed through the armory. And then, the roof caved in.

THIRTY-THREE

O'Malley Territory

Payton shrugged his shoulders and turned to Murchadh, "I dare say they may have left."

"Nonsense," grumbled Murchadh.

"Are ye *sure* they came up here?" Payton asked for the third time.

"Aye, I'm sure. Seems yer brathair intended to invoke the doctrine of reciprocity and Kyra chose her chamber for the…uh…ministrations."

"Reciprocity? Did Kyra harm me brathair?" asked Payton in astonishment.

"It seems as much. He was taken prisoner on the Isle and she was the last to question him," replied Murchadh. "And they've been up here ever since, with the door barred."

Payton chuckled and turned his head so that Murchadh would not see his reaction. "The sun will be out in a few hours, we need to get that ship on course straight away. Just ye let me handle this, will ya?" he asked as he waved Murchadh on, indicating he should leave the corridor. "I know me brathair, and I've a way to get him up and about."

Not twenty minutes later, Macklin met Payton outside the doorway to Kyra's chamber, carrying a very sleepy-headed Winnie.

"Thank ye ever so much, Macklin. Now ye can be gone back to yer slumber. I'll make sure to get Winnie back to Atilde a'fore the sun raises."

Payton whispered softly into Winnie's ears and straightened her nightshirt. Setting her down on the stony floor before the chamber door, he patted her on the butt for encouragement, and made motion to knock on the wood.

As expected, Winnie let loose, "Da! Da! Dada!" she yelped in her toddler voice, pounding the door with all the force she could muster. Sucking her left thumb, she sat down before the formidable barricade and reached her chubby fingers under the opening at the bottom. Payton turned and concealed himself to the side of the doorway, sufficiently out of view of the soon to be opening door.

"Blewdy Christ," he heard from inside the chamber. "'Tis me bairn." It was Parkin's voice. Muffled grumbling and innumerable swear words pervaded the chamber and the roust and tumble of someone attempting to hastily exit the bed, but falling instead in tangled linens, tickled his ribs.

There was a brief silence before the chamber door flung open and Winnie began her joyous screaming of, "Da, Da, Da."

Not one to miss an opportunity, Payton clambered around the shutting chamber door and appeared inside, at the foot of the bed, before Parkin could blink twice.

"Hello Brathair," Payton said, scaring the life out of Parkin and causing him to nearly drop Winnie. Eyeing the remnants of clothing strewn about the floor and an empty trencher of food left waning on the side table, his eyes quickly moved to the bed.

Winnie had the same notion and scampered to the large four-post bed, intent on climbing atop, when a whimper sounded from the same general direction. Payton eyed Parkin, who blushed and then straightened, giving his brother a warning glance.

Winnie was not as easily convinced Instantly, she was at the foot of the bed, promptly peeling back layer upon layer of linens and pulling them down towards the foot of the bed, an inch at a time.

The whimper became an audible, high-pitched squeal, and Payton raced Parkin to the head of the bed, where misplaced linen soon revealed a delicate wrist tied loosely to the bedpost with a long strip of plaid.

"What have we here?" asked Payton, pulling the bedclothes away from the other side, revealing a similarly tied wrist.

"Help," yelped Kyra, her face now clearly visible and the bedclothing inching their way down her neck and shoulders, dangerously close to her heaving, bare breasts.

Parkin gathered Winnie in his arms, pulled a heavy quilt up over Kyra's form and gently released the ties that bound her. Utterly self-conscious, Kyra raised her eyes to meet Payton's look of surprise and shrugged her shoulders as she pulled the quilt all the way up to her neck.

"Reciprocity," said Parkin, grinning satirically at Payton. "Reciprocity," repeated Kyra from under the quilt.

***

Kyra assisted the portly priest aboard the ship docked not far from where the group's cave had been; gratefully cognizant that his stay in Burke lands resulted in some weight loss. Shanleigh was all but asleep, lying against the side of the ship's galley. Orla, ever vigilant, now stood at the helm, listening intently to three ship hands explain the intricacies of sailing to a mildly accommodating priest.

Naelyn sat off to the side by herself, painfully aware that there would be much explaining to do, knowing she was too mentally exhausted to sleep.

Rory interjected, "How long until we dock at O'Malley port?" he asked again.

Parkin spoke up, "By my observation, based on the waves and the tide, no more than an hour or two. We should arrive just after sunup."

"Good, good," he retorted. "Patrick said not to expect him for at least another day. Made mention, he did, of some business he intended to take care of or the what-not."

Parkin burst out laughing and Payton jabbed him in the side.

"Reciprocity," said Payton.

"Reciprocity," repeated Parkin.

THIRTY-FOUR

The border between Burke Lands and O'Malley Territory

Darina tossed and turned in the darkness, waking in short intervals to survey her surroundings, check the height of the moon and confirm that the stars were in fact, still twinkling. It was quiet there in the broken down ruins she had since determined to be an abandoned abbey. *An appropriate sanctuary* she surmised, and made note to thank her husband at some future date for his choice.

No need to thank me.

Darina sat bolt upright in the dimly lit ruins. Groggily rubbing her tired eyes together, she peeked out into the darkness, and save for a scampering field mouse, saw nothing of import.

"Patrick?" she spoke softly.

Aye.

"Where are ye?" she asked.

Not far, a good ways, but not far. I'll be there soon. I've missed ye.

She sighed heavily and tears sprang to her eyes. Before she could contain herself she was weeping loudly into the bottom of her nightshirt and she sat back with force against the stony wall, nearly knocking the breath out of herself.

Do no' cry, luv.

Patrick, I was so worried and angry and upset and I though ye had abandoned me and I asked the council for an annulment, and I'm so verra verra sorry, she sobbed. *Oh Patrick, did ye find me brathair?*

"Aye," he said audibly, standing before her now in the crowded dimly lit corner of the abbey.

"D-do no' b-be an-angry with m-me, D'rina," he began, falling to his knees in front of the fire. "I h-had to g-get Br-Braeden, and I d-did no' want y-ye c-coming after me. He is s-safe n-now and on h-his way b-back to th-the castle."

"Patrick, I could have helped, I could have helped, I swear it," she pleaded as she ran to him and wrapped her arms around his shoulders, cradling his head against her chest. They sat there like that, for what seemed long moments, before he raised his head and pressed his forehead to hers, searching, longing for something.

Covar.

"Aye," she replied. "I didn't know where else to go, and he did no' speak to me, but he told Payton what to do. And Payton brought me here and then he left, but I couldn't understand why until he showed me the sign, the dragon ye left on the stone," she said pointing to the image.

"Patrick, did ye hurt yerself to do that?" she asked turning his wrists and his hands, not finding anything.

He let out a long breath before standing to remove his sword and his belt. He pulled a blanket from his satchel and laid it out in front of the fire as he motioned for her to lie down. Sitting down next to her, near the fire, he placed one hand on each side of her face and placed the gentlest of kisses on her lips.

Ye are my heart, Darina, he spoke to her mind as he gasped. Pulling off his linen shirt, and returning to the fire, she saw it. Crudely etched between his breasts, above his heart, was carved a triquetra. It had broken his skin and was still pink and weeping, tainted with crimson remnants, threatening to finally scar over.

"Patrick" she gasped, lightly touching the skin around the three-cornered knot. "Patrick, by the gods, what have ye done?" she asked softly.

Ye are me heart, luv. Like the triquetra to our people. Like the earth, the sky and the ocean, I exist only for ye. This symbol will remind me always, that ye are my heart. When ye see it, ye will know it is true…

Patrick, why are we here? Why did ye choose this place? It is an abbey, isn't it?

Aye, Darina. It was. I knew I wanted, nay, I needed to be alone with ye. I ken that if we returned together, we would not have that luxury with the excitement of the return, the questioning, the council meetings, the celebrations. I had to have ye all to myself.

Why this place, Patrick? she asked.

There was no priest to bless our bed. The priest was gone, and Galen was otherwise occupied. I intended to take ye, luv. But, not without a blessing. I ken ye wanted a blessing.

Darina nodded her head and tears poured down her cheeks. Patrick pulled her into his arms and stroked the back of her neck with his right hand.

Darina, as best as I can gather, this is a holy and sacred place, at least it once was.

She nodded against his bare chest, and he flinched at the motion of movement across his wounded skin. She pulled away and his eyes met hers, *Do not pull away Darina. I need ye, I need ye like the birds need the wind, like the fish need the sea and like the trees need the sun. Ye'll no' hurt me lass, each stroke will only remind me where me heart belongs.*

He dipped his head down to meet hers and tongue met tongue in a fevered frenzy which threatened to overtake them. Slowly, he pulled away and gestured to speak.

Darina, this place is sacred. It is because it once was, and it is because I prayed it so, and it is because we are about to perform the most sacred of rituals, here, this night, in front of these witnesses, he said as he pointed to the heavens above and glided his hand down the length of her long arm, tracing the moonlight in his path.

Darina, I bless this bed, he spoke to her heart and he rolled her over onto her back. Lightly outlining the contour of her check with his left hand, he looked her in the eye, "If ye will h-have me as y-yer p-priest," he spoke slowly.

She quivered and buckled under him, arching her back against his now rigid member. Moaning audibly, she said breathlessly, "I will, Patrick. I will."

Needing no further encouragement, Patrick raised himself from the tartan. A golden god, that's what he was, standing bare-chested in the moonlight, with the outline of the red triquetra glittering off his burly chest.

Mine, she thought, before she thought better of it.

"Mine," he repeated audibly, looking down at her as if she were prey. Never taking his eyes off of his wife, Patrick removed the last of his clothing, and stood unmoving for a moment, under the amber moon, graciously conscious that he was exposed, completely, and strangely vulnerable in her presence.

"Patrick," she breathed, raising the quilt and exposing her own silken flesh to his eyes. Clad only in a nightshift, her creamy legs beckoned to him and he relented, joining her under the stars.

You couldn't call it a kiss. That wouldn't do. It was more like a conquest. He lead his tongue into battle, and she waved a white flag of surrender, ripping her shift from her own body. Such sweet affliction, the wanting of him, it would be her death, and *such a sweet death it would be,* she thought.

Darina, stay with me.

She wept against his chest and he rose to face her, tenderly turning his mouth to her ear and uttered a strange and erotic tune. It wasn't Gaelic, but it was something ancient, of that she was certain, and it was meant to entice her.

The heat between her thighs rose and she felt as if she were on fire. Moisture pooled beneath her as Patrick traced the tip of his pulsating member over and around her throbbing mound. Finding her tiny bud, he lingered for a moment, overtaking her mouth again with his own. She gasped and clawed at his back, pleading for more, more.

He placed his forehead on hers again and froze.

Please, she said with her mind.

His eyes darkened and he grunted, tortuously positioning the tip of his cock at her entrance. She rose to meet his hips, but found she was completely immobilized, paralyzed under his weight.

She whimpered and turned her head to the side, exposing her neck. He began his verbal assault again, uttering words that had no meaning. His large hands now cradled her head and his words turned into fire as he swept his hot tongue down the length of her neck, over her pulsating arteries and back up to her ear, repeating the ritual over and over again. He began rocking back and forth again and rubbing her nub mercilessly.

She felt his sack tighten and his cock throbbed, rising above and then thudding back down against her wet petals.

Please, God, she begged inaudibly.

He grasped her by the shoulders, raised himself on his elbows and peered into her eyes.

Lowering himself back down to her neck, he suckled the lavender smelling flesh and bit her playfully. Sensation sprang from her womanhood and she at once realized he was inside her. Only an inch or two, but enough to know he was there. Startled, she clenched her legs and straightened her back. He was enormous. There is no possible way that he could…

He bit her again and he clamped down hard this time, teeth unyielding. She was completely impaled, she thought, but evident by the fact she didn't feel his bullocks, she was almost certain there was more. *Saint Brigid,* she swore to herself.

Darina, relax.

He released his teeth from her neck, and rose higher on his elbows, gripping her head tenderly. Uttering the now familiar otherworldly lyrics, he soothed her with his canter and reached down with his right hand to stroke her breast tenderly.

He bade her to meet his eyes and she relented, as he rested his forehead on hers. Gently, he pushed forward, just a smidgeon and her body involuntarily reacted. Her feminine walls retracted and then contracted against his lengthy rod and then squeezed tightly.

He groaned and pulled out before pushing back in, all the way in this time with a slow, solid movement. Sliding effortless into her depths and then resting himself, buried to the hilt, he stopped to examine her face.

Tears spilled over their damn and she quivered beneath him.

Have I hurt ye, lass?

Darina shook her head from side-to-side and reached up to cradle his chin with her hand. "Patrick," she said softly, "take me, please."

As if in a trance, Patrick's fluid motions overtook them both. Rocking in unison, their passion spiraled until the night sky exploded above them, spilling silver-lighted fireworks to grace their sanctuary.

Convulsing with aftershocks of ecstasy, Darina lay her head on his chest, tenderly tracing the outline of the triquetra on Patrick's sweat drenched chest.

"Mine," she whispered into the night.

"Mine," he replied. "Mine."

About the Author

Of Irish and English descent, Romance Author Delaney Rhodes is a native Texan from birth. She is a Graduate with double Majors from The University of Houston, in Law and Writing. She has two teenage daughters, and is married to an entrepreneurial husband. Three of her favorite people are her three rescued Russian Blue cats; Sebastian, Sasha, and Sissy. The family would not be complete without "13", an adopted Bearded Dragon.

Together they live life at a fast pace, enjoying each other and striving to help the world become a better place. Besides her writing and family, Ms. Rhodes is active in many charitable organizations that benefit animals and children, both through volunteering and fundraising.

Ms. Rhodes' writing was prompted and inspired by many hours of research and study into her Irish and Celtic family lineage and heritage. Many of the stories you will find in the chapters of her writings were birthed while striving to connect with those that had walked these paths and lived before her.

Celtic Steel Series

Book 1: Celtic Storms, February 2012

Book 2: Celtic Shores, May 2012

Book 3: Celtic Skies, June 2012

Book 4: Celtic Stars, August 2012

Book 5: Celtic Sun, October 2012

Celtic Skies
Celtic Steel, Book 3

Flynn Montgomery has just taken a new commission as the chieftan of the O'Malley clan troops in Western Ireland. His cousin, Patrick MacCahan-O'Malley, is the new Laird of the O'Malley clan; and they are expanding their shipping enterprise across the seas. Flynn is needed in O'Malley territory to lead the clan's defense and military operations.

O'Malley lands are far from his home in the Shiant Islands of Scotland. A highlander by descent, Flynn is well respected among his people but unknown to the Irish clan he is bid to serve. Will the O'Malley clan grow to accept him as one their own?

Is someone stealing the MacCahan and O'Malley clan ships? The O'Malley Laird, his brother Payton, and Ruarc O'Connell, the former chieftan, must investigate the strange disappearance of three vessels and ensure the clan's safety during their absence. Are there pirates on the sea, or could this be the work of a much darker force?

Dervilla O'Malley has watched as her sister and friends have found love. Are the goddesses ignoring her? Is she destined to remain alone as most of the women of O'Malley territory; or will her knowledge of clan maps and nautical charts introduce her to a life she never imagined?

Warning: This book contains adult subject matter and adult material not suitable for children. It may contain any or all of the following: explicit sexual contact, graphic language, occult references, and violence and adult subjects.

Any similarities contained herein between fictional characters and actual events are merely coincidental and represent the imagination of the writer and are used for entertainment purposes only.